Praise for Suzanne Hayes & Loretta Nyhan and *I'll Be Seeing You*

"I devoured this story in one greedy, glorious gulp.
Oh, the women! I love them. I love their families
and their voices and their stories. I bet you'll love them, too."
—Marisa de los Santos, bestselling author of *Love Walked In*

"Timeless and universal…a deeply satisfying tale."
—*Booklist*

"A delight! *I'll Be Seeing You* made me want to get out a pen
and paper and write a friend a good old-fashioned letter."
—Sarah Jio, bestselling author of *The Violets of March*

"As beautifully written as it is captivating.
An absolutely terrific debut."
—Sarah Pekkanen, author of *The Opposite of Me*

"A moving portrayal of women waiting and enduring and
re-inventing their lives in wartime, and a wonderful affirmation
of the life-enhancing potential of female friendship."
—Margaret Leroy, author of *The Soldier's Wife*

"Vivid and well-crafted….
Readers will laugh, cry and be inspired."
—Pam Jenoff, bestselling author of *The Kommandant's Girl*

"I read this sweet, compassionate novel
with my heart in my throat."
—Kelly O'Connor McNees,
author of *The Lost Summer of Louisa May Alcott*

"An all-around beautiful tale of the power of love
and friendship."
—*RT Book Reviews*

Also by Suzanne Hayes & Loretta Nyhan

I'LL BE SEEING YOU

EMPIRE GIRLS

SUZANNE HAYES
& LORETTA NYHAN

HARLEQUIN® MIRA®

Recycling programs
for this product may
not exist in your area.

ISBN-13: 978-0-7783-1629-9

EMPIRE GIRLS

For questions and comments about the quality of this book, please contact us at
CustomerService@Harlequin.com.

Printed in U.S.A.

First printing: June 2014
10 9 8 7 6 5 4 3 2 1

www.Harlequin.com

To my daughters, Rosy, Tess and Grace.
Sisters who save secret smiles for one another. I adore you.
—Suzanne

To New York, city of my dreams.
—Loretta

EMPIRE GIRLS

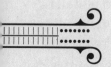 # CHAPTER I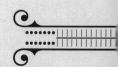

Rose

THE EVENING MY father died, I was stirring the stew in our big comfortable kitchen as I read another chapter of *Bleak House*. The pages, already wrinkled from breakfast and lunch, now had a big smear where I'd laid the spoon down. Most of my books wore the same battle wounds. But I didn't really mind because I thought that the smudges and stains added character to their pages. A story within a story. It was careless, and I meant it to be so. Most nights, when all the work was done for the day, I could sit and look at those messy pages, remembering the young girl I was before becoming the only responsible person in our little family of three.

As the grandfather clock in the foyer struck six, I'd already placed our dinner on the table. Six had always been our dinner hour. Our mother was the one who'd chosen that time, and I worked hard to maintain the tradition. We lost her in 1918, when the flu swept through the world, cleaning out the dusty corners and finding everyone... even those of us who lived quiet lives in small towns like Forest Grove, New York.

I turned fifteen that year, and Ivy, fourteen. Our parents always babied and favored her, so she seemed younger then. Even though our mother was far too ill to pull me aside and give me a dramatic talk about passing the torch, I still believed she'd want me to be the one to look after our household. I was her best helper, and I took that role seriously. It was my job to watch over Ivy, my father and our home, Adams House, as well.

None of that seemed to matter to Ivy and Father when I had to coax them in from their garden every night. It was our evening ritual of cat and mouse. I cooked and then had to chase them, and by the time we were seated around the dining room table, the meal I'd prepared would be cold.

Mother and Father had traveled the world before they found out I was "on the way." That's when they gave up their vagabond ways and returned to Father's ancestral home. I always believed that Adams House belonged to me. It became a living breathing part of my soul. Every clapboard of it, each column, all the curved arches. Mine. From its spires to the precarious-looking turrets, to the wide, wraparound porch. All mine. None of them loved it as much as I did. I considered Adams House to be a full member of the family, and as the years went by after Mother died, I took solace in the fact that I'd traded in the last bit of my childhood for full ownership. Adams House would be my legacy, payment in full for the years I spent in charge.

"Are you coming in or aren't you?" I shouted out the top of the cottage door in the kitchen. "I prepared your favorite, Papa. Beef stew and biscuits. If you don't come inside now, it will be a pasty mess."

That evening was damp and raw. There'd been a lot of rain, and I watched the two of them come up from the ground, each with mud on their knees and flushed with the raw spring winds. Ivy began to yell something back at me, but father hushed her, placed his arm around her shoulders and guided her toward the house. It was good to see some pink in his cheeks. He'd gotten a pale, gray look over the winter months. I'd started to worry over him.

"Make sure you clean up before you take your seats," I said.

"Make up your mind, Rose. Do you want us eating cold food or not?" said Ivy.

Father interjected before the two of us could begin a real argument. We always seemed to begin to argue if there was less than ten feet between us.

"Don't fret, Rosemary. We'll wash our hands at least."

"There's soapy water in a basin in the sink already. I know how long it takes to wash hands, so make sure you don't dally. The both of you," I said and returned to the dining room to arrange the silver.

Though we were twenty-two and twenty-one respectively, Ivy'd held on to her childish ways, and our Father never discouraged her. Ivy, at dinner, absolutely had to sit next to the French doors closest to the foyer so she could bolt from the room as soon as the meal was over. She despised being still and any sort of hard work, and was always running off here or there, dropping everything at the first opportunity to go on trips with Father, or swim and frolic in the small lake next to our house.

My wild little sister, Ivy, made the promise I'd given my

mother—to watch over her—difficult to keep. She was different from the rest of us in both demeanor and appearance.

I'd always wondered if the physical contrasts between Ivy and myself were a manifestation of our distinctive personalities and constant disagreement. I had light hair, where hers was dark. I carried more of our father's looks, though my hair was not quite blond enough, and my face had more angles. When I was a little girl, still free to daydream about things, I liked to imagine that our parents picked up bits and pieces of the distant lands they'd explored, and Ivy and I were born with those traits, as well.

As I got older, I began to believe Ivy was born of their more exciting adventures, while I was born of more bland destinations. I did have one feature that could be construed as mysterious, though. My eyes. They were a bright, icy blue. Ivy's eyes were light green, calm like a tropical sea. I swear, I often thought that some terrible mistake was made. Ivy had an aloof streak that would go along with *my* eyes, not hers. And for whatever reason, Father and Mother—when she had been with us—could never see it.

"She has the soul of an Egyptian Goddess!" Father would say when she'd do something absurd. When we were little scraps, those statements would make me cringe, slam doors and run to my room. After Mother died, I had no time for tantrums, so I grew used to Father's adoration of Ivy. Just as I grew used to Ivy's way of curling around Father's feet like a cat, or waking him up early in the morning when he'd shout, "Aces high in the ever-lovin' sky!" to greet the new day, and the two would erupt in rollicking laughter. I'd listen from my own tidy room and pray they wouldn't bring any neighbors over. Or stray cats.

But I envied her beauty and simply adored her thick,

exotic hair. I almost went mad when she came home from town with her hair bobbed the previous autumn. I was weeding in the garden, planting tulip bulbs at the precise time of the season our mother would have been doing the same.

"Ivy! Your hair!" I said, getting up and pulling off my gloves so I could touch the ends that angled in toward her face.

Father, who'd taken her and approved of the drastic cut, smiled. "I think it's marvelous. All the modern women are doing it, Rosemary. You should, too. I'll take you next week, if you'd like."

"I'd rather die," I said, and went back to my chore. Ivy and I didn't speak for days. She glared at me with those eyes of hers, and I glared right back.

Father and Ivy finally sat down at the dinner table. I looked through the doorway to the grandfather clock and noted the time.

"It is almost seven, you two. I simply cannot keep chasing you around. Soon you'll have to make your own dinners," I said, giving them both a good stare as I ladled the stew out into their bowls.

"Your eyes are a peculiar color for a practical girl, Rosemary," Father said, reaching for a biscuit. "People might get the wrong impression of you."

"Her posture will erase any sort of misunderstanding about our Rose's disposition, Papa. She stands straight like a board. No flexibility whatsoever," said Ivy.

"I'm going to agree with you, sister. I *am* vain about my perfect posture. You should try it, you know. Mother always told us..."

Ivy shot me a look across the table. She was right to stop

me. Father didn't like it when we talked about Mother. It made him sad, and that was one place where we agreed. We both loved our papa very much…even if it was for different reasons.

"Ivy," said Father. "Be a love and pour your old papa a drink. And Rosemary is right, you know. You should stand up straighter. It's a skill that comes with practice, not birth. You do slouch, my darling."

"Papa, you shouldn't! It's not good for you. And you've barely touched your food. I made your favorite on purpose."

He'd been picking at his meals for weeks, and I couldn't tell if it was worry, or if it was his health or if it was a simple matter of our father beginning a new project in his mind. He was a botanist and illustrator, and he frequently lost himself in new ideas for drawings, books and experiments.

"Oh, Rose. Don't be such a stick. I wonder, do you ever get tired of worry? It must be exhausting." Ivy went to the cupboard under the china cabinet and brought out a bottle of Scotch. Father had bought cases of it before prohibition became law.

She poured father his drink.

"Thank you, Ivy," he said, pushing himself back from the table a bit and taking a long sip.

"And you can have another if you'd like. I'll keep the bottle right here," said Ivy, looking straight at me as she said it, holding the neck of the bottle protectively.

"If that bottle makes a ring on my lace tablecloth, I'll have to soak it for a week. You could be careful with my handiwork, even if you don't want to be careful with our father's health," I said. It was a mean thing to say.

One would think my sister and I would be closer. We even shared a bedroom when we were small. It was a sweet, lovely space with whitewashed walls. Mother and Father knew that I liked things clean and crisp. Not Ivy, though…. As soon as Ivy turned seven, she demanded her own room, stating, "I hate all that white. May I have a bedroom that is painted blue?"

Our distance doesn't come solely from our separate rooms; it comes from differing priorities and versions of the world. Ivy always saw things in a way that I could not. The world, it seemed, was made for her. Every tree, every idea, every bit of love was created for her, and she was determined to take it all. I didn't understand her "the world is my oyster" view of life. Hard work has always been the thing that makes me proud. In the time since our mother's death, I'd become the provider for our household, as well, making lace and sewing clothing for the dress shops in Downtown Forest Grove.

As Father picked at his meal and drank his Scotch, I looked at the three of us closely. Memory seems to understand important moments before our consciousness has a chance to catch up. I suppose a part of me knew that everything would be different in the morning.

I looked at my sister, who was trying to hide her boredom, looking over her shoulder at the clock. She was eager to leave the table and didn't like to wait until everyone was finished.

And then I looked at Papa, ready with a smile or an approving nod for each of us, sitting at the head of the table, holding court. With Ivy and I on either side. His companions.

I was about to clear the table when a visitor came calling. Father rose quickly and had to steady himself before he walked slowly into our foyer to answer the door.

"Who do you think that is?" Ivy asked.

"I don't know," I said.

There were murmurs, and Ivy started to get up, as well, but I motioned for her to stay put.

"Yes, I am aware," I heard Father say, and then the hushed dialogue continued.

"Join me as I smoke a pipe, won't you, Lawrence? This is a lot for me to take standing up," said Father as both men walked into our line of vision. Father looked into the dining room as our visitor took off his fedora. We'd known Lawrence—we all called him that, because Father did—for two years. He'd become our solicitor. He was a tall, thin man who reminded me a bit of a willow tree.

I stood up with as much grace as I could muster and walked to the two of them.

"Lawrence, how nice of you to stop by. Are you hungry? I have plenty of dinner left over. You remember Ivy, of course."

"Of course," said Lawrence. "Talented Ivy, who we are sure will be famous one day."

Ivy got up and gave a large, exaggerated bow.

"And Rose, it's been only a few months since I saw you, but you seem so grown-up now."

"She is grown," said Ivy. "She's twenty-two, and that makes her a spinster."

She was at my side, and she nudged me with her shoulder. I had to look deep into her eyes to make sure she was teasing me. Ivy likes to tease when she's unsure of herself.

Mr. Lawrence cleared his throat. "As ever, it's lovely to see all of you." He looked a bit nervous.

"And you, Lawrence, though I wish it could have waited until tomorrow. My daughters and I do cherish our evenings together," said Father, and then turned to me. "Rose," he said, trying to keep his voice calm. I could hear the tension, though. I knew it because I shared that trait with him. A tightening of the voice when you want to remain calm. "Mr. Lawrence and I need to discuss business. Might you stay away from the drawing room this evening?"

"But Father, my monologue. I've been working on it for days," whined Ivy.

"Hush, Ivy," I said.

She rolled her eyes at me.

Lawrence was the one to save the moment. "There's no reason for us to rush our talk, Everett. Why don't we all go into the drawing room, I'd love to see Ivy's monologue. It's been an age since I've been to the theater. I do enjoy a good play."

"Why, Lawrence, I never took you for a man of the arts!" said Ivy.

"There is much you don't know about me, Ms. Adams," he said, taking her arm and escorting her to the drawing room.

"I have always found it odd that you are a young man with an old man's profession. Solicitors are sneaky characters in novels and films. Are you a criminal, Lawrence?"

"I don't think so, Ivy," he replied, and they laughed.

Ivy was always a flirt. She couldn't help it, really. Her whole body flirted. Her swinging short hair was as good as a wink. Her painted lips were practically a kiss. Her short dress, an invitation. I was both jealous and fascinated by her. And that night, she fascinated Lawrence, as well.

As our father took Lawrence away toward his cigar box and phonograph, Ivy stuck her tongue out at our guest's back. One thing I do love about my sister is that she can always make me laugh, and at that moment I had trouble suppressing my giggles.

Gathering there together, as was our usual evening ritual, was strange with a guest. My parents used to have parties when Ivy and I were little girls. But as the money grew tighter, there were fewer and fewer gatherings. I'll admit, that night was exciting because of his presence, even though we all sensed the gathering storm.

Our rituals were sacred to me. Every night, after dinner, we'd gather as a family in the drawing room and end the day with entertainment and comfort. This was the best time of the evening for all of us, even restless Ivy. Though old and well used, the furniture in the drawing room was beautiful, and I always made sure to place fresh flowers in the most curious and delightful places, as our mother used to do. In the fall I replaced the flowers with colorful leaves, and in the winter, pussy willows from the marshland by the lake.

Usually, I'd commence walking up and down the room with books piled on my head, while father smoked his cigar.

Then I'd take out my sewing, and we'd watch Ivy perform.

Ivy, whose lifelong dream was to become a famous actress, would write terribly melodramatic stage plays, and then act them out for us on a platform Father had built especially for her. She was quite good, even if her heroines were overwrought and usually died at the end of her plays, at which time Father and I were obliged to act quite sad.

With Lawrence as our guest, I did not practice my posture. I sat down and took out my sewing so Ivy could begin her dramaturgy. I knew Father and Lawrence had things to discuss, and I was curious about them. But I didn't want to take any time away from Ivy, because I knew how she looked forward to her own practice. Though I made fun of her acting sometimes, I wanted to support her.

Ivy preformed her monologue that night—this time, from *Romeo and Juliet*:

"…and, when I shall die,
Take him and cut him out in little stars,
And he will make the face of heaven so fine
That all the world will be in love with night
And pay no worship to the garish sun…."

I noticed the way Mr. Lawrence could not take his eyes off my sister.

I took a better look at him myself. His hair was light, and his features were soft yet strong. It was his laughter at the end of the evening that made me begin to feel I knew him. That perhaps he could be a friend.

As the evening drew to a close, Mr. Lawrence made pleasant conversation. The Scotch Father had served brought a blush to his complexion.

"Are you working on anything new, Everett?" he asked.

"He's working on a glorious botany book, you know. Drawings and such of plant life. You should see it," said Ivy, interrupting.

"I'll make sure to take a look," he said, looking at Ivy. It was then that he turned his attention back toward my father. "Everett, thank you for this delightful evening, but as the time grows late, I fear we must get down to business."

"Yes, yes, of course," said my father, who guided Mr. Lawrence into his study.

I went about cleaning the kitchen and making sure Ivy was settled and not staying up all night reading *Photoplay* magazine until her eyes popped out of her head. I was looking forward to getting back to my novel, *Bleak House,* which was waiting patiently on my nightstand with other books. Books are my only passion. Father and Ivy used to go off on their excursions, never knowing that I was relieved when they were gone. That I'd wear my nightgowns all day and read from dawn till dusk.

It was very late when Father ascended the stairs and went to his rooms. I hurried out of bed, flew down the stairs and then brought his bedtime tea back up.

"Here you are, Papa. See, I will always bring your tea. No matter how late I must stay awake," I said, placing the cup by his lamp and pulling the quilt up tight around him as I fluffed his pillows. He didn't complain or tell me not to fuss over him like usual.

"Is something wrong, Papa?" I asked.

He settled back against the pillows and took his tea. The cup clattered in the saucer. I held his hands steady as he took a sip, and then guided them back to place it safely on the nightstand once again.

"I suppose I could tell you that everything is fine. But you are Rosemary Lillian Adams. Not Ivy. And you deserve the truth."

"You are scaring me, Papa. What did Lawrence say?"

"Just a bit of trouble with money. But don't worry too much, Rose. I'll sell the new book any day now."

"I can sew more dresses, Papa. And I should be charging more for the lace collars anyway," I said, sitting on the bed next to him.

"Well, to be honest, Rosemary, we may need far more than my book of plants and your sewing skills. But I must tell you that now may not be the best time to speak about it, because I am very tired. Perhaps the sun will shine on us tomorrow and our financial future will be less bleak. Let's look at it from a new perspective in the morning... what do you say?"

"I believe it will all work out. And I don't want you to worry about anything," I said.

He reached up and placed his hand on my cheek.

"You've taken such good care of us. Promise me you'll keep looking out for Ivy. No matter what. She needs you. Things may get... Well... If I'm busy. Promise me?"

"Of course I will," I said and kissed his cheek.

"Rose?" he said, stopping me as I went to leave...and stopping my heart because he'd called me Rose and not Rosemary.

"Yes, Papa?"

"I love you."

Hot, unbidden tears came to my eyes. Father was always lavish with his love for Ivy. It was not the same with me.

"I love you, too, Papa," I said.

I read my book late into the night and thought about ways to make money. I'd convinced myself that I'd go work at a mill or even become a housemaid. Something that would keep us afloat until our father sold his books.

I woke feeling unworried, and stretched in the silvery morning light.

I heard Ivy's laughter as she entered our father's room,

and smiled. Though I was sometimes jealous of their close-ness, I was happy that morning because I knew Ivy could cheer our father like no other.

But then her voice broke off, and a deep wail began. It grew into a hollow sound that broke my heart before I knew it could be broken. I ran to her, my sister. I ran to her and tried to make sense of what she said to me through her choking sobs.

"He's dead. Rose. He's dead!"

She hid her head against my chest. My knees must have gone weak, because I stumbled backward, and we both fell against the wall. We slid down it, together, grasping at one another, staying entangled there until the sun rose too high for us to ignore our reality.

 # CHAPTER 2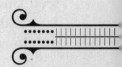

Ivy

I DIDN'T KNOW how to grieve.

While the undertaker began discussing finalities with Rose, I sneaked out the back door. The weather was pleasant, and I imagined my father throwing up his arms as he always did on the warm days of late spring, shouting, "aces-high in the ever-loving sky!" to the blinding sun. The garden he'd recently turned ran wide and deep, leading to a freshly planted field of barley. Beyond that, the road beckoned, the one leading to Albany, and beyond even that, New York City. After squelching the urge to hitchhike, I stretched out across the damp grass and tried not to think about the sound of the casket being transferred to the waiting hearse. The ground held the trace of a chill, and I shivered, closing my eyes as the cold seeped into my dress. What would it feel like to sink into the endless earth? To never feel it under my feet again?

"It's time to leave, Ivy."

I blinked up at my sister. She wore a dress she'd sewn the night before, a prim, black buttoned-up number that covered everything but her face and hands. Rose's eyes were puffy and raw, and her soft blond hair was twisted into a tight, unforgiving knot behind her head. I wished she'd let it loose, unfurled like Rapunzel's rope. I could climb it up to the bright blue sky, leaving this awful day behind.

"Do we have to go now?"

She frowned. "I'm going to pretend I didn't hear that."

The sun's rays kissed the top of Rose's head. I didn't want to do anything but watch it shimmer. "You should let your hair down," I said. "You'd feel the breeze if you did."

Rose grasped my shoulders and pulled me to my feet. "I'm not sure where your mind is at, but the undertaker is ready for the procession to the cemetery."

Procession? The few mourners from town—some clients of father's and the odd academic or two—had departed once they'd satisfied their morbid curiosity. Our neighbors, respectful of our privacy, left sandwiches and canned asparagus at the back door, along with a prayer card. I preferred their method.

Rose brushed the dirt from my dress and guided me toward the hearse parked on our cobblestone portico. Dressed in black suits, the undertaker and his men rushed about like a flock of Poe's ravens, flittering in and out of the house, opening and closing doors, ushering us into the hot cocoon of the hearse's inner cabin. I immediately opened a window and stuck my head into the spring air. Rose kept her window closed and turned her back to the glass.

The car moved slowly through downtown Forest Grove. We passed the grocery, where Mr. Madden was sweeping the entryway. He stopped and saluted as our sedan passed.

"Does he know father wasn't in the armed forces?" Rose asked. I nearly jumped a foot when she said it. I hadn't noticed she'd moved so close to me.

"I don't think he knows what else to do." I saluted him back.

We passed the butcher, the watchmaker, the cobbler—the three men standing in front of their establishments, heads bowed as we lumbered by.

Rose leaned forward to get a better look. "Are they praying?"

"I think so." A lump formed quickly in my throat. Father had been an eccentric presence in town, but never failed to offer a smile and a tip of the hat to every soul he encountered. They remembered him, and their tribute touched my heart. I twitched with the unexpected desire to embrace the entire town.

We turned down Plum Street, just blocks from the graveyard. Mrs. O'Neill herself stepped out of O'Neill's Coiffures. Father brought me to her salon the previous fall, where I sat perched at the edge of a lavender stool while the old lady bobbed my hair with a ruler. I'd asked her to make me look like Clara Bow and she didn't bat an eyelash, humming "Ain't We Got Fun" the whole time she had the scissors at my neck. I waved and called to her.

"This isn't a parade," Rose muttered. She retreated to her dark corner of the cabin.

"But it is," I said. "Open your window and have a look behind us."

Mrs. O'Neill joined a group following the hearse on foot. I spotted Mr. Madden, white starched apron still tied tightly around his waist, and Mr. Lawrence, father's solicitor. He seemed to have come out of nowhere. Mrs. O'Neill offered him a quick smile, and he took her arm.

"Do you think they'll come back to the house afterward?" Rose asked, worrying at her lower lip. "I don't have enough to feed everyone. If I'd known we were hosting a reception, I would have made a casserole."

"Why can't you just take it for what it is?" I gently chided her. "Don't you understand? They're part of father's legacy."

The driver rounded the entrance to the small cemetery and parked in full view of the dogwood tree we'd planted next to mother's grave. It had just begun to bloom, the flowers bursting pink and white as newly hatched chicks. The air smelled fresh, and the bright green grass seemed painted onto the rolling hills by an impressionist's hand.

The beauty was an insult, an affront.

Rose took a deep breath. "It's so pretty today."

"Then why does it hurt my eyes so much?"

Before she could respond, the townspeople caught up with us, and we all walked over to where the men were finishing up their digging. I could hardly look at the upended earth.

We had no minister, but no one seemed to mind. The undertaker said a few words, and townspeople formed a line to pay their respects. They patted our arms and shared quick remembrances. And then they were gone.

It was time to lower our father into the ground. Rose stepped forward, but then she whipped her head around, her expression panicked. "I forgot the flowers to toss. We have nothing to send him off, Ivy." She began to cry. "How could I have done that?"

"It doesn't matter," I said. "Please, let's just go."

Rose wiped under her eyes with trembling hands. "It's tradition. We did it for Mother, and we'll do it for him. Don't you want to say goodbye properly?"

No, I wanted to scream. *I don't.* Instead, I snapped a few branches from the dogwood tree, careful to keep the blossoms intact. "Here," I said, handing them to her. "Now you won't break with tradition." I turned, unable to watch, and walked back to the hearse.

A tall, lanky man leaned against the hood, deep in conversation with the undertaker. When I approached, I realized it was Mr. Lawrence. He noticed me and straightened up, removing his fedora. In the sunshine his hair was the color of burned oatmeal, and the smattering of freckles on his nose made me want to hand him a tin can and send him down the road to kick it.

"My condolences, Miss Adams," he said, dipping his head.

"You said that already." I liked that both men looked away, my sharp words making them uncomfortable. An anger had flared inside me, hot and destructive, burning away the last of my courtesy. I glared at them.

The undertaker excused himself and escaped into the car. Mr. Lawrence and I leaned back against the sedan, watching Rose as she bent to place the flowers on my father's casket.

"So what it is?" I asked. "Is it money? Gambling?" I paused, my heart lifting ever so slightly. "Did he sell a book?"

"It concerns your father's estate," Mr. Lawrence said, staring at the damp ground. "I'd like to speak with you and Rose privately. We could go to my office, or I could accompany you home."

"From the look on your face, it ain't good news. Why not spit it out right here?"

"Your sister should be with you. Your father expressed concern that you two aren't very...close." He stepped in front of me, blocking my view of Rose as she began to tidy up mother's grave. "Today, it's necessary to bridge that chasm. I don't mean to frighten you—"

"You're doing a pretty good job."

"But these things are never easy, and your father was an unusual man."

"He was a good man."

"I know," he said. "I didn't mean to imply otherwise."

"Just so we're copacetic." I felt something on my cheek and swatted at it. It was a tear.

Mr. Lawrence reached into his pocket, pulled out a clean handkerchief and handed it over. "I have a poor memory for quotations, but there are a few that stick with me. I've got one I think you might know. Do you want to hear it?"

"I'm going to anyway, right?"

He reddened and cleared his throat. "'For in that sleep of death, what dreams may come.'"

"*Hamlet,*" I said quickly. I knew Shakespeare's plays inside out and upside down.

"It always appealed to me because of its optimism," Mr. Lawrence explained. "It doesn't have to be the end, Ivy," he added gently. "Not entirely. I believe those who've passed on still have a stake in our affairs from the other side."

I nodded, unsure of how to respond to his kindness. The thought did provide some comfort, but it wasn't until we were riding home, the three of us silent in the shadowy cave of the hearse's cabin, that I realized he'd misinterpreted Hamlet's words. The dreams of the dead were not of the living, they were of regret for the sins of life, the unfinished deeds, the mistakes that could never be fixed.

We convened in father's study. The afternoon had grown chilly, and Rose started a fire and fixed some tea. I should have helped her, but once I'd settled into father's comfortable leather chair, I didn't want to move. I could still smell the last cigar he smoked.

Mr. Lawrence drained his teacup and placed it on the mantel. He refused our offers to sit and began to pace, file folder in hand. "Your father lived a colorful life before marrying your mother. I suppose I should start there."

Though I didn't like the idea of father telling Mr. Lawrence his secrets, the care with which he chose his words bothered me more—he knew what was to come next would be distressing. I glanced over at Rose. Her pale face and wide, fearful eyes meant she'd come to the same conclusion.

"Go on," I urged.

Mr. Lawrence stopped moving, took a breath and looked at me directly. "Your mother was your father's second wife. His first marriage produced a son, and your father has left the management of his estate to this man."

"That can't be true," Rose said after his words sank in. Her voice sounded weak and faraway.

"I don't understand," I added. "Why would he have kept something like this hidden?"

Mr. Lawrence placed the folder on my lap. "I'm not certain. I've only just learned of it. Perhaps you should read this, and then we'll proceed."

Rose got up and sat next to me, and I placed the document between us. I read through it a few times, but the repetition wasn't necessary—for something that would change our lives so irrevocably, it was remarkably straightforward.

In his beautiful handwriting, all measured slopes and perfect loops, our father had clearly communicated his wishes. He'd left the management of his estate to this man, a son he'd sired six years before marrying our mother. Asher John Adams. It was an untouchable name, mysterious with a dash of history, and so naturally one my father would choose. To my surprise I felt a stab of affection for this lost half brother, the unending possibility of him stretching my imagination. I pictured him dark and mysterious, with a certain Valentino exoticism. I'd studied the great actor in the theaters of downtown Albany, memorizing the way he crushed his eyebrows and widened his eyes at the same time, the magnificent strength as he folded his arms, muscles rippling. My brother would look like that.

Asher. Was he a gift from the grave? "When can we meet him?"

Rose gasped. "Ivy, please take this seriously. This is our house. Ours. Father's mind must have been compromised." She sat forward, appealing to Mr. Lawrence. "Can you provide proof? How do we know some swindler didn't concoct this scheme? Where is this first wife? How do we know this man is father's son?"

"If you'll sift through the file, you'll find the necessary documents," Mr. Lawrence said. "I looked them over closely this morning. I think they'll settle any question of legitimacy." He touched the open file with his finger. "Please remember that seeing things in black and white can be a shock," he added, his voice a touch softer. I knew he wasn't warning me. It was Rose who'd gone still.

I began sifting through the memos from the bank, threatening letters from the state assessor's office and countless hastily scribbled notes in my father's handwriting. Asher's name appeared periodically, with no other information than his birth date. April 29. Mine was May 1. Had father thought about him when I came into the world? He must have. I felt a constricting of my chest. Was it a pang of loss or anger or sadness? I shook it off.

"And Asher's mother?" I asked as I continued rummaging through the paperwork. "What of her?"

"Deceased," Mr. Lawrence said, frowning. "There are no other known relatives."

I'd almost exhausted the file when I spotted our brother. As large as a letter, it took a minute to register as a photograph. "It's him, Rose."

The photograph had been enlarged and cropped, and I stared into his extraordinarily light eyes. They were Rose's eyes. In fact, he was the male embodiment of Rose—aquiline nose, lean frame, full mouth. He was in shirtsleeves, arms crossed, the thickness of his forearms hinting at manual labor. The half smile cocking his mouth was a brash challenge hidden under a thin layer of civility. A metal plate lay tucked behind his left shoulder. It was stamped with two words: EMPIRE HOUSE.

"He could be your twin," I said, trying not to sound as disappointed as I felt. I'd sat across from Rose at thousands of family meals. Though good-looking, Asher's features were as exotic as a jar of strawberry jam. I thought at the very least he'd look like an outsider, different, like me. "He is definitely an Adams," I admitted. "No one can deny it."

"He's still a stranger," Rose said in a choked voice. "If he wasn't, he would be here, wouldn't he?"

Mr. Lawrence sighed. "There lies the problem. Asher John Adams seems to have vanished from the face of the earth. It appears your father had very little contact with his son over the years, no more than a handful of terse phone calls. When your father wished to finally speak to his son in person, he learned Asher Adams has no known address in New York City or the whole Eastern seaboard, for that matter."

I didn't like that. Was Rose right? Had my father been swindled? No. He could be flighty, but he was too intelligent for that, too sharp-minded. "Yet, something in those conversations convinced my father to make Asher manager of his estate," I said. "He could have given it to Rose or me, or even you."

"I'm not the eldest anymore," Rose said. "But I am here, and he isn't." Her posture regained its straight line. "Could the problem be solved that easily? If we can't find him, everything stays as it is?"

Mr. Lawrence looked pained, indecision clouding his hazel eyes. I stared at him, mercilessly, as he waged debate within himself. How he must tip his hand in the courtroom! I began to wonder why father picked this man. Then it hit me, his fee was probably right next door to nothing. I glanced down at the bank notices. "There are further financial complications," I said evenly. "Could you explain what those are?"

He nodded. "The mortgage and property taxes are in severe arrears. If the heir does not make claim on the house and bring the tax bill to date, the home will be sold and the bank and state will see its money."

"Did my father leave any funds in his accounts?" Rose asked, though we both knew the answer to that one.

Mr. Lawrence paused. "I'm sorry, but not very much at all."

My mind reeled, the implications of this development still unclear. "What if Mr. Asher John Adams can't be found? What happens then?"

"If he doesn't come forward within a year, the house will revert to the bank," Mr. Lawrence explained, his tone regaining a professional aloofness. "The bank will pay the property taxes and sell the home as soon as they can get the stake in the ground."

We were silent a moment as we considered that image.

"What if we could raise the funds?" Rose said, growing desperate. "Could we pay the bank in installments?

Mr. Lawrence looked away. "I'm afraid you'd need Mr. Asher to approve that route, Miss Adams." He pitied us. I hated pity. It was a thin veil hiding the firm belief that a similar fate could not possibly happen to him. "Your father was in the process of finding Mr. Adams when he passed on. He'd begun searching in New York City, but hadn't gotten any further."

"Could we hire one of those private detectives?" Rose asked. "That seems the logical route."

"Of course," Mr. Lawrence agreed. "However, there is the matter of the fee. Pinkerton charges a thirty-dollar per diem, expenses not included. New York is not an inexpensive town."

Rose slumped in her chair. "I see."

"I'll go," I volunteered.

Mr. Lawrence cleared his throat. "I don't think it wise

to go alone, but if you went together, you might find Mr. Adams quickly and we can get this sorted out."

Rose stood and tugged at her shirtwaist irritably, displacing her black silk belt. "We're supposed to pick up and go to that awful city and allow a stranger to make decisions about our future?" she said, shaking her head. "I can't, Ivy."

"Can't what?"

"Allow any of this," she said, rising. "I know you're not accustomed to it, but listen to me for a minute. If we continue to let our life fall away, piece by piece, we'll be left with nothing." Her eyes filled and brimmed over, but she didn't brush at her cheeks. Tears had already replaced our home as Rose's most constant companion. "There must be something we can do to keep the house. I can get a job, two even. We have a year, don't we?" Rose asserted, her voice gaining authority. "You just said it."

"Most men don't make that sum in a year's time," Mr. Lawrence said gently.

"But we're women, Mr. Lawrence," I interrupted. "Unless you hadn't noticed."

He reddened, and I decided to take advantage of his discomfort. "I can't shake the feeling we're not getting the whole story," I said. "Is that true, Your Honor?"

He looked away. "I'm not a judge."

"You're sure acting like one. Why not tell us everything?"

"*Ivy.*" Mr. Lawrence met my eyes. All the wavering had disappeared from his, and now they bored into me, direct and clear as a midsummer's sky. "I don't enjoy bringing bad news. I hope you understand that. Any decent person would be concerned about the sheer number of revelations it's become my responsibility to impart."

"Revelations aren't meant to be experienced piecemeal. I assure you very little shocks me. Please continue."

The corner of his mouth twitched, and he glanced quickly at Rose. "Bankers are not patient men. Eviction proceedings have begun. I paid a visit the other night to tell your father of the bank's decision. I'll never forgive myself for adding to his misery."

"It's not your fault," Rose said automatically, but something tore inside her, a messy, ragged break. She covered her face with her hands and really let go.

Mr. Lawrence looked as helpless as I felt. I knew I should comfort her, but I hesitated. And as I crouched down, she lifted her head, and I knew I was too late. There was something new in her eyes, a coldness that frightened me a little. "I'm going with you to New York."

"You haven't been past Albany," I said to my sister, but not unkindly.

"Neither have you." She sniffed.

"I've been to the city a thousand times *in my mind*. That counts for something." I was meant for Manhattan; Rose was not. The city would find a thousand ways to hurt her, one sucker punch at a time. I picked up the photograph of Asher. "Look at how he's standing, like the devil himself. Let me go first and see what we're getting mixed up with."

Rose snatched the photo and held it at eye level, as though she was speaking directly to him. "This man is my brother," she said, her voice steely. "It can't be denied. He won't take the house, not after seeing me."

"Is it that important to you, to keep the house?" It was a roof over our heads, nothing more. A prison, even. Rose was already too old to be living at home, and I was determined not to follow in her footsteps.

"Yes," Rose said. "I've built my entire life around this house. It's all I have, and we both know it."

I couldn't argue with that. Rose needed something tangible to prove her worth in the world; I had what was in my head. My father had given that to me, and only me. Guilt wasn't something I experienced often, but I could recognize it. "We'll find Asher," I promised, taking the photograph from her hands. I held it up to Mr. Lawrence. "Where did you get this?"

"According to your father, the photograph was sent to your house approximately eighteen months ago," he explained, obviously relieved I'd asked a question he could answer. "No return address. Empire House is a boarding hotel for women, so either he knew someone who lived there or the spot was chosen at random."

"It's a start," I said, growing excited at the prospect of traveling to the city. Empire House sounded grand. I pictured ladies in their finery, sipping gin rickeys on the sly and admiring each other's diamonds. "We'll send a telegram to let them know we're on our way."

Mr. Lawrence reached into his suit coat pocket and extracted a white card. "My address. Please write to let me know you've arrived safely and keep me apprised of whatever you find. I'll see what I can do from here."

We both knew that was nothing much. I added his card to the folder and tucked it under my arm. "We'll keep in touch," I said as he took my hand. "Thank you." When it was Rose's chance to say goodbye, Mr. Lawrence returned to his valise. He lifted a small framed drawing from it, an India ink rendition of a single rose. "Your father admired this when he visited my office, Miss Adams," he said, handing it to my sister. "I'd like you to have it."

"That's very kind of you," Rose said in a small voice.

Perhaps I'd misjudged Mr. Lawrence, I thought as I watched Rose hug the frame to her bosom. Given his closing argument, he was probably quite good in the courtroom.

"I suppose we can't blame him," Rose said after he left. "He does seem a decent sort of person."

"For a solicitor," I muttered. We stood there in silence, neither of us moving. I had no idea what Rose was thinking, but I had only one thought: *let's get started.* I gestured toward the drawing. "Should we put his gift on our wall, even if we only own it for another few hours?"

She smiled bitterly at my choice of words. "All right."

Father frequently changed the paintings on the walls in his study, leaving a hodgepodge of bare nails and crooked frames as a result. Though I admired his work, the sheer volume made careful scrutiny impossible. As I scanned his makeshift collage, looking for the perfect spot to hang Mr. Lawrence's drawing, my eye fell on a small painting I was certain had been gathering dust for years. It featured a woman holding a wiggling toddler. Blonde and pretty, she stood on a stoop in front of an imposing brownstone, a copper plaque half-hidden by the child's flailing arms.

"Rose, bring that photograph of Asher over here."

She did, and I held it next to the painting. The door, the plaque—it was Empire House.

Rose squinted at the two. "I suppose I should send that telegram right away."

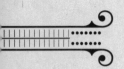 # CHAPTER 3

Rose

WE RECEIVED AN answer from Empire House two days after Ivy sent the telegram. She'd come running up the driveway and into the kitchen, bringing the spring morning behind her like a trail of hope. I was pressing her dresses in the kitchen, where I'd set up an orderly "Packing Station" so that we wouldn't bring too much or too little. We could only bring the most necessary items, and the rest of our things would be sold lock, stock and barrel with the house if I did not succeed in New York City. Choosing what to take and what to leave behind was more of a chore than I'd anticipated, and soon I wanted to bring nothing at all.

"You haven't had your toast, Ivy."

"Who cares about toast! We've gotten our rooms, Rose! Listen…

"'Dear Ms. Adams,'" began Ivy, reading me the letter and pacing back and forth with excitement.

"Did you want tea, Ivy?"

"No…I don't want tea. Would you listen?"

I nodded.

"'Dear Ms. Adams,'" she began again.

"'Though it is not our usual rule to lease space to young women we have not already met and interviewed, it seems you are in luck. We've had a recent vacancy here at Empire House, making room for you and your sister. Please be advised that the accommodations are modest at best. If you do not arrive within the week, we cannot assure the room will be available. Please send a telegram on the day of your arrival, so we may prepare. Note, as well, that if we deem you unsuitable, you will be denied occupancy. Please send us your arrival date, and we will have a driver waiting for you at the station.

Nell Horatio Neville (Proprietor of Empire House)'"

"Not very warm, is it?" I said, misting a cotton night-dress with water.

"It *is* the city, Rose. I swear, you are so…so…"

"What?" I asked.

"Pedestrian…"

Then she ran off again. She'd been spinning in circles since Father's funeral. I had, too, only my circles were in my head, while Ivy seemed to be walking on a cloud.

I was worried.

I put the hot iron back onto the stove and sat at my kitchen table folding father's shirts. I was going to give them to Mr. Lawrence, but I wanted them to be tidy. It was the proper thing to do.

I knew Ivy was devastated by our father's death. We both were. But when Lawrence gave us the news...the unspeakable news about Asher, Ivy seemed to forget all her sorrow. Part of me was glad that she had a diversion. Glad that her dreams of living in The City were coming true. I knew that eventually she'd fall back into grieving, but her excitement set me free to take care of my own sorrows.

I'd lost my father, my house and my future. It was a quiet loss, one that no one seemed to notice.

I wasn't going to New York City to throw myself into Asher's arms. I was going to New York City to find a stranger, make a great deal of money and get him to sign my house back over to me.

I knew the resemblance could make the difference in allowing him to accept us. Ivy didn't seem to be at all worried that, once found, Asher might not want to have anything to do with us. I feared her romantic, theatrical view of life was clouding her view of reality. Our father had raised us...not him. Was it not fair to assume he might want to avoid being found at all? That he might resent us? I didn't mention this to my sister. In truth, as Ivy hid from our father's death inside a bubble of expectation and hope, I hid from it by convincing myself I'd slipped into a new narrative. I couldn't help but think we'd been thrust into a Dickens or Austen novel almost overnight. It kept me separate...it kept me curious instead of dead inside. When we found him—if we found him—he would not be able to turn his back on me. No good character can walk away from another who could be their very twin. It's the denouement of all great mysteries.

Father always said that "Everyone has an inner narcissist...." I would be his conscience, and Asher would sign my house over to me. If you understand a bit of human nature, and don't overestimate people, getting what you want is simple enough. I knew I could get the house back if we found him. The question was, how would we find him?

I picked up one of father's shirts and held it against my face.

"I don't want to believe you did any of this on purpose. I want to believe you thought you were protecting us somehow. But from what? Oh, Papa!"

I wanted him so badly at that moment. I wanted him to come into the garden and have tea and toast. I wanted to tell him of the horrible dream I'd had. Nothing seemed real.

It occurred to me that grief is like a tunnel. You enter it without a choice because you must get to the other side. The darkness of it plays tricks on you, and sometimes you can even forget where you are or what your purpose is. I believe that people, now and again, get lost or stuck in that tunnel and never find their way out.

I had no intention of doing that. I'd leave myself notes in my pockets saying, "Father is dead," if I had to.

I got up from the table quickly, held back my tears and packed the rest of Ivy's dresses.

Later, I was sitting on our front porch, reading, when Ivy came and sat at my feet.

"It's like he left us a present, Rose. Papa gave us one last adventure. I can't tell you how that comforts me," she said, a dreamy look in her eye.

"Did you know about him?" I asked.

"Know about who?"

"Did you know about Asher? Did father tell you on one

of your trips? I know you two had your own language. Be honest, Ivy. I need to know."

She stood up, her face red and angry. "No. I didn't know. Do you think I could have sustained this whole charade? Do you think so little of me that I would have kept so large a secret from you? Honestly, Rose...sometimes I think you don't know me at all."

Then she stormed back in the house.

I followed her inside. My whole world was bobbed, like Ivy's hair, at bold angles. Very little was making sense, so I did the proper thing. I made supper.

A few foggy days full of packing and planning passed. Ivy flitted around, but I wasn't surprised. I saw her at breakfast and at dinner. She must have been wandering by the lake, because she'd come home disheveled and muddy. If she'd chosen to grieve alone, it would have been nice to let me know. As it was, I thought she was simply running away again.

I was surprised at how easy it was to empty the house of our personal belongings. Life is much more fleeting and changeable than I'd thought.

I was the one who sheeted the furniture and put the better china in the secret attic space. I was the one who got the locksmith to put dead bolts on the doors. I was the one who rang Mr. Lawrence when we knew the date we were to leave. And it's a good thing I did, or we would have had to drag our trunks to the station.

The morning Ivy and I left for New York City, Mr. Lawrence came to fetch us.

"How very gallant of you, Lawrence...but I'll walk. I feel as if the air would do me good," said Ivy. "Besides,

I've always had this vision of myself walking down the road without turning back. I'm no Lot's Wife. Not me."

"Would you like to make sure you have everything you need, Ivy?" I asked.

"You are the most organized person I've ever met, sister. I'm sure I'll be all set." Then, with a quick nod to Lawrence, and a "See you on the platform, Rose!" to me, Ivy left for the train station where she would send the telegram to Empire House letting them know what time we'd be arriving, and purchase two one-way tickets to New York City.

"Father babied her, and now I'm going to have to make sure she doesn't get ruined by New York. She really is impossible," I said.

"I know it isn't my place, Rose. But do you think you could learn to trust one another, you and Ivy?"

"Trust her? You must be joking. Have you sat too long in the sun?"

"Would it make a difference if I told you that your father mentioned he wished the two of you were closer?"

"Are you hiding something, Lawrence? Because if you are…."

"Let's go, Rose. I'd hate for you to miss your train," he said, saving me from trying to conjure up an empty threat.

As he started his motorcar, I walked through the house one more time. Saying goodbye to it. "I'll come back to you," I said. But it didn't answer me, the house. It felt hollow, and its hollowness hurt my soul.

I found Ivy sitting on a bench at the very end of the platform.

"Hiya!" she said, getting up to greet me.

"You didn't even say goodbye to Mr. Lawrence. You can be a very self-centered girl," I said.

"I don't like anything drawn out—you know that," she said, melting back onto the bench, slouched over. I sat next to her as tall as I possibly could.

"I'm afraid your dress may make the wrong impression when we finally meet Nell Neville," I said. She was wearing a purple satin drop-waist dress with a beaded fringe. The back fell into a deep V and the front exposed more neck than I wanted to look at. Her stockings were showing, and her shoes were black heels with a small strap, showing the top of her foot as well as her ankles. She was as good as naked.

"No, Rose. *You* are the one who will make a poor impression. I told you to leave those clothes behind. You look like a servant or an old lady. Either way, it's not good. Plus, you're going to sweat to death in The City. No lake breeze there, honey."

She threw one of her legs over the iron arm of the bench and leaned into me.

A train far off in the distance sang its song. Ivy bit her nails. "When we were little you loved that sound," she said. "Did you know that? We used to lie in bed together and play that game 'Where is it going?' and then we'd make up fantastic adventures."

"Don't bite your nails, Ivy. It's a childish, unclean habit." I said, not acknowledging her memory, even though I did, in fact, recall it.

She looked at me and smiled. A true, infectious smile, one that always softened any roughness I felt toward her. Ivy has that affect on people, causing whiplash of affection. "Darling, of course I remember," I said. "I'm just not in the mood for memories right now. Tunnel of grief and all that." She nodded her head and sat back up.

On that platform, with my high-laced boots crossed at the ankle, and Ivy slinking lower down on the bench every second, all I could do was read my copy of Edna St. Vincent Millay's *A Few Figs From Thistles*. I especially liked the poem entitled "MacDougal Street," though it made me cry.

"He laid his darling hand upon her little black head,
(I wish I were a ragged child with ear-rings in my ears!)
And he said she was a baggage to have said what she had said;
(Truly I shall be ill unless I stop these tears!)"

I clutched the book to my breast and hoped against hope that Empire House wasn't anywhere near MacDougal Street.

Ivy settled in by the window on the train. She had father's leather rucksack on her lap and kept buckling and unbuckling the straps. She was quite talkative, which was different than usual.

I was hoping she'd sleep on the train and I could read. Ivy slept when she was excited about something she had to wait for—she was always the first to bed on Christmas Eve. But as she spoke, I began to understand that she was as nervous as I was about the trip. I found myself worrying about what the city would do to her. It never once occurred to me to worry about myself. My objective was clear: find Asher, convince him to sign the house over to me and get a job to acquire the money to pay the back taxes on our home. And I told her as much when she asked me.

"Aren't you the least bit curious?" she asked, frustrated.

"I wouldn't be human if I wasn't, Ivy. But please remember, I don't intend to get involved in any sort of life once we get there. I plan on finding work, finding Asher and then finding my way home. What you do after all is said and done is your prerogative."

"So you'd just give up whatever life we make for ourselves, and return to that desolate place?"

Desolate?

I leaned across the narrow space between us and took her chin too sharply in my hand. "Have you ever even considered that as you made your life plans, that I was making plans of my own? Or did you think I was an empty-headed fool who lived to serve you and Papa?"

She yanked her face away and leaned her forehead against the window.

"I suppose I thought you'd... I don't know. Did you? Did you have plans?"

"Of course I did. My plan was to live quietly at Adams house until I died. That sounds terrible to you, doesn't it? A wretched sort of existence. But let me tell you something, Ms. Ivy Adams. As we grew older, the fact that I would not marry was not lost on me. How could I? Who was I to meet? I thought you would finally get up the courage to leave Forest Grove, and I would look after Father until he was an old, old man. I would be the keeper of our traditions...I would be a safe harbor for you, if you ever needed anything. And I would always have the house. And just look at the both of us now. Our father died too soon. He left us with lies, secrets and no money. I no longer have the peaceful future I set out for myself. And yet? Here we are! On our way to YOUR future. So, to answer your question…YES. I would return to that desolate place. Because that was my dream."

Ivy took a moment to respond. I could almost see the thoughts brewing behind those lovely eyes of hers. I could see her deciding whether to be mean, or sarcastic or simply honest. In the end, she chose humor.

"Well, now, Rose. That was quite a monologue. I should note that down. Really. I'm not kidding…you'd be a good writer I think. You read enough. Have you ever thought of that instead?"

"And you, Ivy, would make a good politician," I said. I had to smile at her. She could have lashed out at me, but she chose not to.

"I think I'll read my book now, if it's not too rude," I said.

But I never got the chance, because we'd already arrived at Grand Central Station.

"Come, let's get the trunks," I said as we disembarked.

"No, you get them. I'll go find the driver they sent from Empire House."

She ran away from me quickly and was swallowed by the crowd.

"Ivy!" I yelled, climbing back up the steep steps of the transom, trying, in vain, to catch a glimpse of her, and holding my hat against the hot, smelly air that came flying at me like the breath of a beastly giant.

I was pouring sweat already, and my lace collar—the one Ivy'd begged me not to wear—was sticking tightly to my neck. I was choking, probably to death, and I'd already lost my sister.

"Here you go, ma'am," said a young man who'd taken my trunks from the luggage car.

"I say, are you planning on helping me get these trunks through the station and out…side?" I had no idea where I was going.

He held out his hand, and when I went to shake it, a man pushed passed me, laughing. "He wants a tip, not a handshake… Country girls, I swear, you're all knee-slappers."

Our money was so limited that I wasn't going to waste it on handouts. Chivalry should be free, anyhow. So I looked at the trunks and convinced myself I could do it on my own.

I shook my head at him and tried to politely explain why I was not filling his hands with coins. Only no one could hear anything over the din of voices, the steam and chaos. I reached down and placed my gloved hands on the straps of each trunk, stooped over and began to drag what remained of us through the station. I can only imagine what I looked like. Finally, I saw the glass doors ahead of me, and I saw Ivy in her purple satin dress with the beads at the bottom shining in the sun. I wasn't upset she'd worn it anymore. I'd be able to find her anywhere.

I lurched outside banging the trunks against people and bricks and anything that got in my way.

She was leaning against a black sedan, but it was the driver who saw me first. There was a sign taped to the passenger window that read EMPIRE HOUSE.

For some reason, it was that sign…affixed haphazardly to that dirty window that brought the whole ordeal into focus. No longer was this some foggy, dark dream. This was my life, and I was suddenly very present in it. Nothing was going to fit neatly into the pages of a book. Life, it seemed, was busy, and messy and loud. *Everything* about this city was so loud.

Ivy turned to look at me, following the driver's gaze, and put her hand over her mouth. She laughed so hard I thought she'd lose her breath.

"Thank you ever so much for the help," I said, trying to push my hair back from my sticky forehead.

"I know how much you like hard work," she said as she came to me and took the trunks a whole three steps to the waiting automobile. "But I never considered you would try to become a mule. Why didn't you let the porter take these?"

"Because he wanted money."

The driver took the trunks from Ivy and opened the door for me.

"Thank goodness, a gentleman," I said as he held out his hand, I thought, to escort me into the cabin of the car.

I started to place my hand on his palm, but he pulled it away. "Sorry to disappoint, miss, but I was sorta askin' for a tip," he said.

"Are you going to embarrass me every single day of my life, Rose?" asked Ivy as she reached into the outside pocket of Father's bag and pulled out a few coins. She dropped them in his hand, slid into the sedan next to me. Then she batted her eyelashes, which made him smile at her. The whole flirtation happened practically in my lap, forcing me to lean back so that their hands didn't touch me by accident.

"What's your name, fella?" asked Ivy.

"Jimmy, doll," he said cocking his hat to one side. He was darker, this Jimmy. "Black Irish" Mother used to say, when we were impressionable young girls. She'd say it with a bit of disdain when we'd see them in town. Wrong side of the track kind of people. We Adamses didn't belong on the track at all, so we could always identify people on, off, on the right side or the wrong side of any situation. Father said it made us well rounded.

"Do you have a name?" he asked my sister.

"Ivy," she said. "I'm Ivy and this is my sister..."

Jimmy cut her off. "Ivy, huh? You don't look like something stuck to the side of a house. I'll have to come up with another name that'll suit ya better."

As if he'd see her again. Not to mention he hadn't wanted to know my name, which is when I realized that if anyone could become invisible in a city full of people, it would be me. That thought brought me back around to thinking about Asher. If it was true, and we were similar people, then perhaps he was invisible, too. I shivered at that thought. It would be too hard to find someone who could not be seen.

Ivy, however, didn't seem to notice Jimmy's dismissal of my presence. Or if she did, she didn't care. He sat behind the wheel again, and Ivy scooted up to sit with her arms crossed on the back of the front seat. I could see their exchanges in the rearview mirror.

"So, Jimmy...which way are we headed? Uptown, downtown? Where is this Empire House?"

"Where do you want it to be?" he asked.

"I don't care if it's smack in the middle of the East River. I've been waiting for this moment for my entire life," said Ivy.

The truth that I felt in her statement hurt me. I always knew she wanted more from life…but could she have been that unhappy in Forest Grove? And for how long?

She leaned back her head and winked at me. And before I could stop myself, I reached out and tugged hard at the fine edges of her bob that just grazed her exposed back. It pulled her neck in an unnatural direction and she snapped her head away from me yelling "Ow!"

"You all right?" asked Jimmy, even though he was glaring at me in that infernal rearview mirror.

His blue eyes met mine, only I decided to give him my best glare, and it made him turn away.

"Yes, I'm fine," answered Ivy. "My hair got caught on my sister's broach. Who even wears high necks anymore?" They were laughing at me, but I knew Ivy was hurt because she kept rubbing the back of her neck. *Good,* I thought. *My shoulders won't be the same after that trip through the station with our trunks….*

"So, you never answered me. Where is this place? Uptown, downtown?" she asked.

"The best part of town. Only the best for you, uh…two. It's in The Village, right off MacDougal."

That did it. I put my head into my white-gloved hands, already gray with the filth of the city, and I cried.

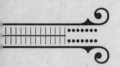 # CHAPTER 4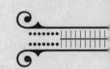

Ivy

NEW YORKERS MOVED so quickly. Pitched forward, chins leading the way, they dashed to and from destinations I could only dream about. The whole city was like a wild horse chomping at the bit—as if the island of Manhattan would soon tear itself away from the surrounding land and bolt for the wide-open sea of the future.

Jimmy, a broad-chested, raven-haired Irishman, was proving a prince of the city streets. He maneuvered the large vehicle with casual ease, pointing out restaurants and museums, secret taverns and notorious alleyways, in a voice that dipped and rose with the lilting song of the Emerald Isle. Rose disapproved—her grumblings buzzed around us like flies we casually swatted out the window. I knew what she was thinking. *So new off the boat his cuffs are still damp,* but even if it was true, Jimmy knew Manhattan as well as any travel guide. He also smelled deliciously of tobacco and bay rum. I perched my bottom at the edge of the jump seat and nearly got popped in the nose as he excitedly gestured at the imposing Arch of Washington Square Park.

"I live right here in Greenwich Village, and I'll tell you it's a place like no other," Jimmy said as we motored past a couple embracing under the Arch. The man was bent over the girl, his mouth at her neck, his steadying hand at the curve of her back. I felt a growing sense of anticipation. Was that what it was like to live here?

"Have they no shame?" Rose muttered. Another complaint, but I was glad she'd stopped crying and started looking out the window.

"Maybe they do, but have no use for it," I countered.

Jimmy turned onto MacDougal Street. "You'll like Empire House," he said. "It's in the thick of things, a good choice if you're in the city." The buildings on MacDougal, connected to one another and built in the Federal style, lined the street like painted soldiers. Jimmy eased into an empty space in front of one washed in a muddy blue-gray color, its elongated, latticed windows rowed in groups of four. Red azaleas rested in stark white window boxes and the front stoop appeared freshly swept. The door, familiar from Asher's photo, was glossy black, and the bronze plaque next to it shone in the sun.

EMPIRE HOUSE

"Don't let the landlady intimidate you," Jimmy said as he jumped out to grab the bags. I followed, leaving Rose in the car to sort out the money situation—I didn't have the head for it.

I squinted up at him in the noonday sun. "I don't let anyone get under my skin."

He laughed. "You've never met Nell." Jimmy hoisted

Rose's enormous trunk and carried it up the front stairs and into Empire House. Once he was safely inside, I could stop flirting and start eyeballing our new neighborhood. A few of the buildings had street levels that spilled open-air cafés onto the sidewalk. Colorfully dressed patrons leaned over small tables, speaking intensely about matters I could only wonder at. The scene was perfect for an artist's eye, and I felt a pang, wishing my father stood beside me with his sketchbook.

I curled my hands over the wrought-iron bars protecting the garden level of the building next to Empire House. The windows were shuttered, however a sign on the muddy door said, Republic Theater, Revolutionaries Welcome. My pulse quickened. It certainly wasn't the staid, cavernous auditorium in Albany, but then, this city was a different beast altogether. Theaters could pop up anywhere.

"Save your money. Whatever play they're hawking will be closed down before you can blink twice," Jimmy said, his breath tickling my bare neck. He'd come up without me noticing.

I turned to him and smiled. "I'm an actress," I said, not bothering to mask my pride. "I'll be looking for work."

"You and half the girls in Manhattan," he said dismissively. "But if you're looking for theater work, you'd best stay away from these anarchists."

The word turned my insides to jelly. Anarchists? Revolutionaries? This was going to be fun.

Jimmy laughed. "Don't be such a tourist. You can't walk around here with stars in your eyes."

As we walked back to the car, Jimmy continued his lecture. "Empire House attracts the more ladylike types, but it's still a boarding house. Always hide your best things, but don't shove all that you own under the mattress—the girls will think you don't trust them. Walk with a set of eyes in the back of your head, and if you're going out at night, make sure you don't get caught coming in late. But if you do—" here he had the most delightful twinkle in his dangerously blue Irish eyes "—run over to my place on Christopher Street and I'll give you a warm bed to sleep in."

I thought about the woman under the arch, and the man bent over her. I stepped closer to Jimmy. "Do you often leave your door unlocked?"

"If you're wearing that dress, I'll give you a key."

I silently congratulated myself for my fashion choice that morning. I twirled once to give him a better look at how the dress dipped low in back. "A new dress for my new home," I said. Technically, that wasn't the truth. The dress was old. But I had a feeling that little fibs were necessary in this town and shrugged off the lie.

With a wink and a tip of his fedora, Jimmy climbed back into the driver's seat. He drove a few yards, stopped suddenly and backed the vehicle up with a jerk.

Rose.

I'd forgotten all about her. I yanked open the passenger door and stuck my head in. Rose sat inside, an open book on her lap. "Did you tip him already?"

She nodded curtly. "Everyone's hands are outstretched in this town. This is a greedy place." There was a catch in her voice that told me she was trying not to cry.

A good kind of sister, a Jo March or Elizabeth Bennet, would have reached out, drawing Rose to the comfort of her solid bosom, coaxing the tears that so desperately needed shedding. But I was not a good sister. Jimmy made a sound of impatience, and embarrassment sharpened my words. "He's got places to go," I hissed. "Come on."

"I can't," Rose whispered, her expression pained. "Maybe this was a rash decision. Let's discuss this."

I scooted in next to her. "Get your nose out of that book and take a hard look at this city, Rose. Can't you feel it? All the opportunity? We can be *in* this world. We can make money and find Asher and have an adventure while we do it. So, please, get out of the car."

Rose placed her book inside her travel bag, but otherwise didn't budge.

"Why aren't you moving?"

She closed her eyes. "Give me a moment, Ivy."

Rose had spent a lifetime choosing stillness over action. When the Gilbert boys pressed their noses to our screened-in porch, shouting, "Come to play!" I ran outdoors. Our ragtag gang leaped into the cold river, scoured the earth for arrowheads and climbed the best mulberry trees, smearing the juicy berries on our faces until our skin turned purple. We hooted and hollered and lived. "Take it all," my father laughed when we'd roll in the door like tumbleweeds. "It's all yours if you want it, you little scalawags!"

Rose never joined us, preferring to stay inside, the egg tucked most firmly in the nest. She learned to knit and sew while sitting in a circle with our mother and her lady friends, who spent a few minutes discussing the women's vote, but mostly passed the time clucking at bland, country-kitchen gossip, mundane stories that all sounded vaguely alike. Rose grew up with the mild buzz of their conversations in her ear, something that really dug at my father's craw. "A child who grows up too closely aligned with adults assumes knowledge of a life she hasn't yet experienced," he always complained.

After mother died, father sent us to school in town, where Rose outshone our classmates in natural intellect, quietly assuming the top spot on the principal's most-honored list. The teachers had high hopes for my sister, but when they offered a place in the new business class for women, she demurred. I got no offers, but took advantage of everything I could wiggle my way into—voice lessons, bit parts at the local theater, dance-a-thons, beauty contests. Rose accepted her diploma with a nod and retreated back to run Adams House. She cooked and cleaned and budgeted. The townspeople spoke kindly of Rose's devotion to our family, but what begins as sacrifice can eventually become foolishness. My father would have said as much, but in the back of Jimmy's car, I saw Rose gearing up to say the one word he hated, and my sister lived by—*no*.

One moment turned into two, then three. "You don't have a choice in this," I finally said, and before she could protest further, I grabbed her hands and pulled her onto the street. She fell into me, and I kicked the door shut and shouted for Jimmy to hit the gas. He did, peeling down MacDougal in a cloud of exhaust.

We sat on the curb to catch our breath. A row of silver beads had come loose from my dress and spilled onto the pavement, rolling haphazardly in different directions.

"Did I do that?" Rose said.

"I think so."

"Well, I'm not sorry," she snapped, but there was a faint amusement surfacing in her expression.

"Oh, you'll fix it for me anyway," I tossed back.

"Yes, but I'll send you out here to search for every bead on your hands and knees."

I burst out laughing, and the sound coaxed a genuine smile from Rose. I wasn't the least bit sore at her. How could I be? We were in New York on a sunny, charming street in Greenwich Village. I gazed at Empire House, its front, aging yet dignified, and felt my father's hands at my shoulders, pushing me forward—*go, go, go!*

Rose stood and dusted herself off. "Well, I suppose we should get ourselves a room before thieves run off with our trunks."

We walked up the stoop together. I pulled the bell and the door flew open, creaking on its hinges. A street urchin answered, a young girl not much taller than my waist. Her small, heart-shaped face was dirty, but her dress, a cotton slip covered in primroses, was clean. She wasn't wearing any shoes.

"Customers!" she shrieked, and pushed past us, sitting atop Rose's trunk. "Are you moving in for good?" she asked, patting its brass lock.

"Definitely not," Rose said, attempting to soften her words with a smile that quivered at the edges.

I crouched down, eye level with the girl. "Will you watch our trunks while we speak with the house manager?"

"Maybe," she answered.

I nudged Rose and she dug a coin from her purse. With a sigh she placed it into the urchin's tiny palm.

"I'm Claudia," the girl said, pocketing the coin. "And there ain't much you can buy in New York with a wooden nickel." Laughing, she patted at the mass of orange-soda curls springing from her head like coils from a spent mattress. "Miss Nell is inside. Keep walking until you find yourselves in the kitchen. The cook made the coffee too strong again, so look out for flying cups."

I watched Rose's eyes follow the girl as she disappeared into the house. I knew my sister better than she thought. She was seeing herself in that girl, and the confused look in her eyes told me she was trying to make sense of why someone so young could put her hand out so easily. Rose didn't know that she recognized the behavior, because she was doing the same thing in coming to New York— holding out her hand with the hope that Asher would put a nickel in it. If we could find him, that is. I wasn't exactly sure what our odds were, but I knew one thing for certain—this city would offer us a thousand different paths toward a thousand different futures. We only had to choose the stepping-off point, and New York would take care of the rest.

We followed Claudia into the building. The sound of a woman's complaints, imperious and disdainful, contrasted with the cheerful, feminine interior of Empire House's front parlor. The wood floors gleamed, throwing light around a room that already sparkled with charm. Delicately etched paper—white with fine gold stripes—covered the walls. The rugs, bleached by the sun, held the faint outlines of delicate Victorian flowers, reminding me of my father's drawings. Broad-leafed plants, green and glossy, stood tall in Grecian urns, their stems curving slightly toward the open windows.

"Well, what do you know," I marveled. "Not so bad, is it?"

Rose's eyes traveled over the room, lighting up when

she noticed the floor-to-ceiling bookcase covering the back wall. "I suppose this will do," she said.

I felt a surge of triumph.

The kitchen took the whole back of the house. We stood in the doorway, watching a haughty-looking woman harangue a tall, good-looking man wearing a white apron. The woman nearly crushed the man's toes as she stepped forward, straining her neck to meet his eye. Neither of them broke away when we announced ourselves with exaggerated clearing of our throats.

"You cannot take cigarettes away from the working man and you cannot take strong coffee from the working girl," the man shouted. "Basic human understanding!"

"We cannot afford to run through coffee like a bunch of Italian widows," the woman growled. "Basic accounting!"

"Maybe some new tenants will offset the costs," I interrupted.

They glared at each other for just a moment longer, and then turned toward us in unison. The woman had a regal face—a patrician nose, icy-blue eyes and a precisely painted mouth bracketed with fine lines that hinted at a lifetime of secrets. She was attractive, and anyone could tell she'd been a looker once upon a time, which probably made middle age a real wet blanket on a dry bed.

The man was a different story altogether. His features—from his neatly trimmed dark hair to his surprisingly thick-lashed eyes—were outlined in humor. His gaze danced over us, and he smiled graciously. "I'm Sonny Santino," he said, and pointed to the bright, airy kitchen. "Welcome to my hovel."

"I'm Ivy, and this is Rose," I said, grinning back at him.

"Ah! The friends from Albany."

"We're sisters," Rose said.

He laughed. "Sisters? You look like a pair of mismatched bookends."

"I'm Nell Neville," the woman said, studying us with intelligent eyes. "I hope the trip down was comfortable."

Rose opened her mouth, but I pressed my foot against hers. "Fine and dandy."

Nell's mouth pulled into a smile. "Will you be looking for work here in the city?"

"I'm a capable seamstress," Rose said. "I can do both tailoring and alterations."

Nell turned to me. "I'm an actress," I said. "Both tragedy and comedy."

She nodded, unimpressed. "Your telegram said you were also coming to New York to find a lost relative. Is that still the case?"

"Yes," Rose said quickly. She dug into her bag and pulled out her book of poetry. Inside was Mr. Lawrence's file. "My father was Everett Adams. This is his son, Asher. Will you take a look at this photograph and see if you recognize him?"

The woman snatched Asher's portrait from her hands, but only took a quick glance before passing it to Sonny. He studied it, his expression softening while Rose explained our mission. "Unfortunately circumstances have caused an estrangement from the family, but we are desperate to find him for legal reasons. Do you recall his face?"

"It's my job to keep young men away from my door," Nell said. "I own Empire House, but I manage it, as well. Any male on the premises endures my careful scrutiny.

If I'd seen him, I'd remember." She took the photograph from Sonny and gave it back to Rose. "I'm sorry we can't be of help in that matter, but we can get you settled into your room. If you'll come with me, we can address the paperwork."

After tossing a final glare Santino's way, she ushered us out of the kitchen. We followed Nell's straight back down an adjacent hallway lined with faded fleur-de-lis wallpaper and framed photographs of hunting dogs dressed in country attire. Rose looked at me with a raised brow, doubt flooding her eyes.

"Yeah, she's an odd bird," I said lightly, "but aren't we all?"

Rose sighed. "Speak for yourself."

Nell's small office smelled of onions and rose water. A dusty brown ledger lay at the center of a circular table. "You're lucky we had a vacancy," she said, turning open the book. She fussed at a drawer and extracted a fountain pen. "Sign here."

"Could you be more specific about the rent and amenities?" Rose asked.

"You could walk three blocks and find a dozen other boarding houses that offer the same or worse," Nell said, bristling. "There are a hundred places for girls in this city. You're free to find one to your liking."

I hated talk of money. I just wanted a room. The day was growing hotter, and I longed to stretch out in front of an open window with a cool cloth on my forehead.

I signed the ledger with a flourish and handed the pen to Rose, who reluctantly added her signature.

Nell separated one key from a ring holding countless

copies. "You get the penthouse, top floor. As soon as you agree to the rules, you may have the key."

My head snapped up. "Rules?"

"Oh, darling," Nell said. "There are always rules, even in a city like this."

EMPIRE HOUSE
RULES FOR TENANTS

Curfew is strictly enforced. The front and back doors will be locked at 10:00 p.m. nightly. On Saturday nights, the lock turns at 11:00 p.m. SHARP. (After this hour, no knocking, screaming, crying or howling will be tolerated. Sleep in the garden and learn your lesson.)

Hot showers cost fifteen cents and should last no longer than five minutes. At three cents a minute, you're barely paying for the coal—quit your complaining. There is a timer on the small table outside the bathroom. It will be set.

Laundry services are available, but management is not held to any time constraints. You'll get it when you get it.

Breakfast is served at 7:00 a.m.; dinner at 6:00 p.m. There is no luncheon. If you are here in the middle of the day, then you have most likely lost your job and have more pressing things to do.

Excessive noise is prohibited. Talking, singing, laughing and loud coughing are not acceptable after midnight.

No one is allowed to sit in the parlor. Ever. No exceptions.

Absolutely no consumption of alcoholic beverages.

The Feds say it's illegal and so do we. Have a nice
cup of coffee instead (Five cents a cup and be sure to
wash it out when you're done).

As we gained the upper part of the house, I realized with
a growing sense of unease that Empire House was only elegant at ground level. The higher we went, the shabbier it
got—frayed carpet, holes in the plaster, a pervasive damp-
ness in the air. After climbing what seemed like countless
flights, we reached what I thought was the top floor, but
then Nell led us to a door, which housed a narrow staircase.

I peered up, though I couldn't see much. "Are we sleeping in the attic?"

"It's really quite lovely," Nell said, dropping the key
into my hand. "This is for the bathroom. You won't need
any other keys. I lock up the main door at night." With a
quick smile, she began her descent back to the first floor.

"What'll we do?" Rose asked, panic in her voice.

I shrugged. "We explore."

Rose and I came up the stairs to find ourselves standing
in the middle of an airy loft, marooned in a sea of cast-off
furniture and puffs of dust.

"Our front door is a hole in the floor!" Rose said, aghast.
"We might sleepwalk and tumble down the stairs!"

I didn't want to admit I'd had a similar thought. "It ain't
the Ritz, but it's not so bad," I said, but I was throwing
her a line—it was one step above a flophouse. One slim
window faced MacDougal Street, and sunlight weakly
filtered in through a dirty skylight, casting strange shadows on the two twin beds, huddled like starving children
in the middle of the room, and an old-fashioned dressing
table with an overlarge mirror. The walls were painted a

leaden gray. Our trunks sat on a frayed rug. Leeched of all color, it covered a small section of well-used oak floors.

"We have roommates," Rose whispered, pointing to a closet cut into the middle of the far side wall. Through it another room could be seen. I spotted two female figures moving to and fro, but it was like I was peering at them through the wrong end of the telescope. The gals noticed me and squealed, and they both darted through the slim passageway, fluttering into our room like birds escaping the nest.

One had brown hair that would be mousy, had it not been cut in the most precise bob I'd ever seen. She introduced herself as Maude. The other's hair was blond, not golden, like Rose's, but honey-colored, as though she'd started off light but darkened with age. She had the kind of eyes—keen and electric—that missed nothing. This was Viv.

"How'd you gals get stuck with the penthouse?" Viv asked.

"Just lucky, I guess," I said, keeping my tone jokey. "What's there to do for fun around here?"

Maude winked. "Oh, anything you set your heart on. Anything at all."

Rose glanced uneasily at the corridor linking our rooms. "We were hoping for a private room. We're paying a steep sum—"

"Don't worry about us," Viv interjected. "We won't bug you unless you ask for it."

Maude rolled her eyes. "Don't mind her. She's still working off a bender."

"But isn't drinking against the rules?" The words had tumbled from Rose's mouth, and she colored, instantly aware of her mistake. "Oh," she said, her voice soft. "It must have been your birthday."

"Nope," Viv said. She sat on Rose's trunk and began to brazenly readjust her stockings. Maude joined her and began to study her own seams. There are always leaders and followers, I thought, and it only took a minute to figure out which was which.

Viv focused her attention on my sister. "Tuesdays are Tom Collins nights," she explained. "I figure it's a neglected day of the week, why not give it a distinguishing characteristic?" The girls erupted in laughter.

Obviously unsure of how to respond, Rose looked at me in silent appeal. "You gals been here awhile?" I asked, changing the subject.

"Long enough to know what's what," Viv answered.

I caught Rose's eye and gave a little nod. Once again she extracted Asher's photograph and placed it on the trunk. "We're looking for someone," Rose said, and I noted a change in her voice, a sadness. Was she already feeling defeated? "That's him. Does he look familiar?"

Viv picked it up first. She held it very close to her face, and I realized she must need glasses. "No," she said, handing the portrait to Maude. "But if he shows up, be sure to send him my way. He's a looker."

"He's my half brother," Rose said quietly.

"I was just kidding," Viv said by way of apology.

Maude returned the photograph. "He looks familiar, but so do half the mugs in this city. I'm sorry I can't say for sure, but if you want to ask about someone, I'd go see Nell. She's been here since the Dutch waltzed down Fifth Avenue in their fur coats."

Viv barked a laugh. "If you can catch her on a good day."

"We've already asked her," Rose said.

"Well, that's that, then," Viv said, her tone growing friendlier. "So, since we're going to be sharing the penthouse, let's get acquainted. On this little island you're either a party girl or a workaday drudge. Which are ya?"

Rose brought a hand to her cheek. "Are those the only choices?"

Maude laughed. "In this city, it's one or the other." She appraised my sister with new eyes. "Hey, you're a kick. I hadn't realized."

"But she still hasn't answered the question." Viv's smile was mean. "Drudge it is."

"There's nothing wrong with a good day's work," Rose said tightly.

"Now that's the bald-honest truth," Maude attested, and Rose shot her a grateful look.

I stepped into the conversation, hand on my hip. "We're looking for work, but we never turn down a party."

"Well, now that we've got that settled, let's talk the lay of the land," Viv said, standing up. She patted Rose's trunk. "That half-baked closet in between us might be as wide as a cigarette case, but we're lucky—the girls downstairs hang their clothes on a line in the hallway. None of our rags ever go missing. The girls downstairs are fortunate if they can hold on to a dress more than a season. The smart ones keep their good dresses pressed between their mattress and box spring."

"Don't forget Claudia," Maude interjected. "She lives here, too."

Rose smiled, and I watched the straight line of her back give a little. "We met Claudia downstairs. Is she a relation of yours?"

"Claudia's a street rat Nell took in," Viv explained. "She sleeps in that narrow room, tucked under our dresses. The wall juts out, so she's got her own spot under the eave."

"Lucky her," Rose said with a sigh.

"You bet," Viv said, misinterpreting her sarcasm. "In fact, it looks like it's everyone's red-letter day. Daisy moved out around three weeks ago. Nell thought she'd have to put an ad in the *Daily* if she couldn't rent this place soon." She paused, taking in the grimy walls and bare mattresses. "I have no idea why it's so hard to let."

"Oh, it ain't so bad." Maude sniffed. "We're lucky to have it."

I studied our surroundings more closely. The room could be charming with a little bit of spit and polish. Daisy had either been a slob or she'd been in a hurry. She'd left some handkerchiefs on the floor next to one of the beds, hairpins and magazines on the dresser and some restaurant cards stuck to the mirror. Those might come in handy, give us a lay of the land. "Daisy blew out of here pretty quick, huh?"

Viv smiled knowingly. "She's either headed to the convent or the preacher."

"So old Daisy was a party girl?" I said with a wink.

Maude's eyebrows lifted. "Daisy was a workaday drudge," she said, obviously still marveling over that shocker. "A seamstress. And you wouldn't believe—"

"Perhaps we could discuss Daisy's indiscretions later," Rose interrupted, exhaustion creeping into her voice, "after we've unpacked."

Viv pulled at Maude's collar. "Let's leave the girls to their new home."

"We're going out for a stroll if you want to join us,"

Maude said as Viv pulled her down the narrow staircase. "Be downstairs in ten if you want to tag along!"

I sat on one of the beds after they'd left. The mattress felt like it was made of slate. I watched Rose unpack, her movements slow. Mouth compressed, eyes slightly unfocused, she was lost to the thoughts inside her.

"What's eatin' you?"

She took Father's painting of Empire House from her trunk and placed it on the dresser. She contemplated it for a moment and then sat on the bed opposite me. "Do you think they're all telling the truth, Ivy? I have an odd feeling."

"When your instinct talks you should listen. Wouldn't father have said the same?" I thought for a moment. "I did wonder why Nell barely gave Asher's photo a glance. I thought she was impatient, but maybe there's something else? Maude did say Nell's been here the longest, so if anyone would have come across him it would have been her."

"Maybe," Rose said distractedly, but then her eyes sparked to life. "I know what's bothering me! That cook downstairs. He didn't say if he knew Asher or not. He didn't say anything at all after looking at the photograph."

I grinned at my sister. "Reading all those books is finally paying off! Maybe we're barking up the wrong tree, but if someone's keeping a secret, I can't imagine it would stay buried for too long around here. We're going to find Asher before you need to change your dress. I know it."

"Ivy?"

"Hmm?"

"Have you ever considered what might happen if and when we do find him?" Rose was staring up at the skylight as she asked the question. The light played across her worried face.

I got up and wordlessly helped her unpack her books. I wanted to say I'd thought the whole thing through, but I hadn't. Rose was trying to prepare me for disappointment, and I couldn't consider that. Not for a moment.

"You've got something to write with in that trunk, dontcha?" I asked, changing the subject.

"Are you feeling self-reflective?" Rose teased while sifting through her things. "Has Greenwich Village already turned you into a philosopher?"

"Now wouldn't that be a kick?"

Empire House
June-something-or-other, 1925
Dear Mr. Lawrence,
As time is money and all that, I'll cut to the chase: No one here knows of Asher.

Rose and I arrived safely at Empire House in two whole pieces, untouched by the savagery of the city. Empire House isn't exactly the Waldorf Astoria, but the place has a certain gritty bohemian charm. Rose asked about Asher the minute we arrived, but every gal claimed she didn't recognize him. The more I think about it, the more I suspect Asher did more here than simply pose on the doorstep. I realize lawyers don't put much stock in intuition, but actresses do, and my gut tells me someone here knows where he's living and breathing. My gut is also telling me that said person won't open her trap unless I do some real arm-twisting, so I'm gearing up to do it. I spent my girlhood pounding the stuffing out of the Gilbert boys next door, so I am capable of twisting until something pops off. I will be subtle about it—she'll not notice until someone else points out the blood.

At this point you're most likely wishing the other sister had taken pen to paper. Well, Mr. Lawrence, you are decidedly out of luck. While our dear Rose is trying to catch her breath, I've decided to take charge and be the responsible type. Don't you dare laugh. On second thought, go ahead. I bet you could use it—you don't strike me as the type who goes through life har-har-har-ing away.

In closing, we intend to keep our promise to inform you of any developments, and expect you to do the same. Hopefully, more specific information will be forthcoming.

Sincerely,

Ivy Antoinette Adams

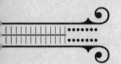 # CHAPTER 5

Rose

AFTER IVY DASHED off a quick letter to Mr. Lawrence telling him of our safe arrival, she took a few more books out of my trunk and searched our attic space for anything she could use as a bookshelf. She had yet to answer my question about Asher, but I knew she was thinking about it. I wanted to press the issue, but I also didn't want to be a naysayer about everything. I decided it was something we could revisit, and instead apologized for being gruff with her new friends, Viv and Maude.

"I'm sorry if I was rude. I promise I'll be nicer the first chance I get. It's just... Ivy, there's so many things happening all at once. I'm afraid this isn't quite what I expected."

"A little different than the way crowded city streets play out on the page?"

"Much," I said.

She walked toward the window with my books. "Why

not put some here, leaning on the windowsill between our beds?"

"The sun might fade the covers...."

She dropped the books on what I supposed she'd decided was my side, and threw herself on the bed closer to the door.

"I know it's not what you expected," she said. "Hell, it's not what I expected. But we have to make the most of it, Rose. Okay? I mean, that Sonny character...he's got eyes for you already. And mean old Nell, I think she likes you, too. We could spiff up this Penthouse of ours. We'll find Asher in no time."

"I don't mind the attic," I said.

"You don't?"

"No," I said going back to my trunk and pulling out my copy of *Sara Crewe*. "Have you ever read this? It's delightful, really. I think I'll read it again. She was sent to an attic room. If she could make the best of it, so can I. It's the rest of it...the chaos. There's a bit of Sara in you, Ivy. You're taking all of this in stride."

I went to Ivy's trunk next and opened it. My careful packing had been upturned by some kind of last-minute addition she must have thrown in.

"Dear God, Ivy! Everything's in a knot! I spent so much time trying to make sure our things were safe. When did you rummage through it, and why were you so careless?"

"I guess that's the end of your improving mood," said Ivy, staring up at the sloped ceiling above our beds and playing with a strand of beads around her neck. "One of them is lying about knowing Asher," Ivy said, "but which one? It's like that Agatha Christie novel."

"They could all be lying."

"What should we do about it?"

"Absolutely nothing. We'll try to become closer to them. You've already started that, and I was wrong to be so cold. I'll try harder, and maybe we can gain their trust."

"I think you should start with Sonny."

"Really, Ivy. I don't have any idea what you're talking about. If he was looking at anyone, it was you."

"Nope. I know a flirt when I see one. Trust me, sister. Go to him. He might be the first chink in the armor, you know?"

"Maybe…"

"Well, I'm going downstairs. It's stuffy up here, and I want to explore a little. Will you be all right? Would you like me to bring you some water?"

"No, I'm fine. I feel better up here."

"I don't think I'll ever understand you, Rose," she said and then skipped down the stairs. I held my breath, afraid she'd fall on those heels of hers. But then I heard laughter and greetings…and I knew she was safe. I heard a gaggle of girls leave the building, slamming the double doors behind them, so I went to the window between our two beds that faced the street. She was walking arm in arm between Maude and Viv. They weren't so bad, those girls. They were just…new. I looked up across another set of streets beyond the rooftops of the shorter buildings. One good thing about the penthouse was its bird's-eye view. I'd always enjoyed being alone and seeing things from a safe distance.

The attic was stuffy, though. So I struggled to open the window, and when it finally screamed its way ajar, the breeze that blew in smelled like baking bread. And in that moment I was back in my own kitchen. My past came rushing over me like the sounds of the city outside. The days of Mother and Father having academic talks on the porch with friends. I remembered staying up late and listening—so late the crickets almost drowned out their voices, as they talked of Father's drawings and Mother's work with Suffrage. And then, after Mother died, all the lovely meals I'd made and the dresses I'd sewn. I realized that I was without a chore for the first time since I was fifteen. And then I wondered over the thousands of days that Papa had to tell us about Asher, and yet never did. The thousands of days that our father had not been a father to Asher yet could have. How would Asher ever forgive us for being the children that Father did choose to raise? I was just as afraid of finding Asher as I was determined to get my house back. And I couldn't do one without the other.

Looking out of windows can make so many things clear. The city stretched out in front of me like a tattered quilt. I propped the window up with a splintered piece of window frame and then went to my trunk and finished unpacking. I took Ivy's idea and placed my books on the wide window ledge. They looked pretty there. I thought I'd go find a flower or two to spruce up the rooms, and maybe wash my face, as well. I felt so dirty.

As I went to the door that led downstairs, I looked into Maude and Viv's side.

That's when I saw a little bed tucked under an even-steeper gable. I knew right away that it must belong to Claudia, that lovely little girl who seemed to work so hard. I'd go find her…not Sonny.

The washroom was a floor below. It wasn't anything special, and I noticed it was clean. I splashed some water on my face from the basin and left quickly, my heart beating fast, terrified someone might walk in on me. I don't think I'd realized how many people would be sharing one space. I thought of taking a bath in the chipped porcelain tub. What if someone came in then? I looked for a lock and was horrified to see a tiny hook that could be unlatched on the outside by anyone's finger.

I'd returned to the hall when I heard Ivy's heels clicking on the stairs before she rounded the corner and found me. She was simply glowing. I supposed she'd been on a walk embracing the city already.

"Rose! You've come down! Here's your water. I know you said you didn't want it, but Sonny simply insisted." She placed the glass on the landing, not even handing it to me. "Now, I'm off to a party! We've both been invited. You should go through my trunk and pick a dress, then come downstairs."

A party?

"Ivy, I'm in no shape to go to a party. And I don't have a proper dress, and yours won't fit! I'm taller than you. Your dresses go up to my knees!"

"All the better!"

"Please, give my apologies…I'm simply not prepared."

"It's not until a little later. Maybe you could spruce up something you have?"

"I don't think so, Ivy."

"I told you you'd try to ruin everything." I could tell by her eyes that she didn't want me to go with her. I was a burden to her, and I'd only just noticed it. "Fine, do as you must. But me? I'm going to soak up the scene. Tomorrow you're gonna be calling me Sherlock."

"Be careful, Ivy. We don't even know these people." Even if I'd wanted to go, I wouldn't have at that point.

Why ruin her time by saddling her with a broken, old-fashioned girl? She'd be embarrassed by me.

"Rose, you're going to have to decide to live a little."

Ivy was always jumping headlong into any situation regardless of the danger or consequence. If she'd given me a flicker of real desire… If she'd told me that she needed me by her side to be brave, I may have gone. Instead, she threw up her arms and yelled, "Suit yourself!" as she ran down the stairs again.

"Remember who you are and where you come from," I said.

When she'd left, I returned to the penthouse, leaving the glass of water and my decision to try and gather some flowers behind me. Half of me wanted Ivy to stumble on that glass when she came back up.

Once upstairs I had second thoughts about that party. I didn't want her in the corrupted heart of this city without me. She could get into all sorts of trouble.

I unpacked as much as I could, and then curled up on my bed with *Sara Crewe*.

As the sun set over our first day in New York City, I could hear the gathering party outside and then I noticed a small ray of light that shimmered from behind the dressing table at the opposite side of our half of the room.

Where is that coming from? I asked myself. I walked to the dressing table and peeked behind to see a thick layer of curtains.

I pushed at the dressing table, and it moved more easily than expected. I placed my back against it and pushed harder. It slid a few feet to the side, bumping into another beam near what looked like the entrance to a crawl space.

There they were, the curtains. More fabric than anything tailored. I yanked on them and they came down, *pop, pop, pop,* as the small tacks affixing them to the walls sprang out of the wood. The fabric fell to the floor.

There was a window. A small, round window that looked out over the back gardens of the four buildings on either side of Empire House and the next block over. Decrepit, unkempt gardens.

People were gathering for the party that we'd been invited to. Lanterns glowed, glittery dresses flew past like fairies. I noticed that the window had a small platform on the outside, so it must be some kind of fire escape, though who could fit in or out was beyond me.

I couldn't see Ivy in the crowd.

Turning back around, I picked up the fabric that had fallen. There was a heavy velvet overlay. Rust colored and damp. Then, underneath…reams and reams of orange chiffon that despite the terrible color were in good shape.

*Daisy was a seamstress…*I thought, remembering what Viv and Maude had said about the woman, our next-best clue to finding out about our brother.

If she was a seamstress, there may be a sewing machine.

"Miss?"

I heard the voice from behind. It was the little girl, Claudia, who'd met us at the front doors of Empire House. I was happy to see her.

"Hello."

"My name is Claudia. I didn't know if you'd remember, because people got all sorts of different kinds of memories around here."

I laughed. "I remember. Hello, Claudia."

"How're ya settlin' in, miss?"

"I don't think I belong here," I said, confessing my deepest fears to a strange girl in a strange world.

"No one does, miss. This place is for people who got nowhere and no one. Then, we try to make a safe place for each other. Only the truth is, *safe* in't a word that means much."

"You are a wise little one, aren't you."

"I just came up to grab an apron," she said and went to the little bed area I'd seen before.

"Are you comfortable there, Claudia?"

"Yes, Nell gives it to me for my work. It's not much, I know, but better than sleepin' on the street."

"Where are your parents?"

"Gone."

"Where is your family?"

"Got none."

"Who takes care of you?"

"I do."

She retrieved a clean apron and came back near me. She took my hand, walked me to the bed and sat me down. She unloosed my hair, and for some reason, I let her.

"You got grand hair like Mary Pickford. You seen a moving picture? Sometimes they still play the flickers for ten cents down at Washington Theatre. Don't cut it, miss. It's so pretty."

"I won't, Claudia."

She picked up my book. "What's this about?" she asked.

"Oh, you'd like it! It's about a little girl your age, who comes to a school for girls. When she arrives, she's very rich. But when her father dies in the war, she has no money and she's forced to live in the attic and clean the house."

"Does it have a happy ending?"

"Why don't you read it? You may borrow it if you'd like."

"I can't read."

"You can't read?"

"A little, maybe."

"Would you like to learn?"

"Oh, yes! Would you teach me?"

"I'd be honored," I said, going to my trunk and taking out my pens, paper and ink. "Let's start with that alphabet."

Just then we heard "CLAUDIA!" from downstairs.

"I gotta go back down or Nell will slap me silly." She looked at the fabric on the floor. "You sew?"

"Yes, I do. But I need a sewing machine."

"Over on the other side of my bed I have a trunk. I keep things people left behind—you know, trinkets and such. I nabbed Daisy's sewing machine. You could have it. It's takin' up too much space anyhow. There's some spools of thread in there, too."

"Thank you," I said. "She left her sewing machine behind? What made her leave that way, Claudia? Do you know?"

Claudia shrugged her shoulders noncommittally and looked all around the room, trying to avoid my gaze. But it was such an exaggerated effort that I couldn't help but laugh.

"What's so funny?"

"You are," I said.

She laughed with me. "Daisy was a nice lady. Don't let anyone tell you any different, miss," she said.

She smiled then hopped down the stairs, counting to herself.

I went to the trunk she spoke of. It was a large steamer

trunk with the top slightly open because of the size of the sewing machine. I lifted it out, heavy though it was, and brought it over to my bed knocking over the ink and paper I'd taken out to write down an alphabet for Claudia. If I cursed, I would have cursed then. I looked around to find something to mop up the ink, but couldn't find anything so I picked up the bottle and the ink began to spill over my hands.

I flew down the stairs with the ink and went into the washroom, throwing the bottle out in the small wastebasket next to the tub.

Ink was everywhere. On my hands, a bit on my cheek and all over the front of my dress. The more I tried to scrub it off, the more the stains spread. Old-fashioned though it was, it was the most modern dress I had, and I'd already seen enough to know I'd need a less-modest dress to blend in. I would have nothing suitable at all to wear in the morning.

I washed the ink off my hands and face and went back to the penthouse. Orange chiffon would be ugly, but at least it would be something.

I pulled off my stained dress and sorted through my things I'd brought along, finding a long white nightdress that had once belonged to my mother. I loved that one; it looked and smelled like home. I pulled it over my head and loosed the last two pins from my hair. I then placed the sewing machine on the floor, hoping it would work without the stand, but it didn't.

The crawl space. Maybe Daisy had left the rest of her larger belongings in there? I walked past the window and that's when I saw Ivy.

The party was underway with starry lights glimmering

roughshod over the poor man's festival. Tattered people gathered there, one looking more broken than the next. There was a pretty feeling to the center of the gathering, but if you looked toward the edges you saw the darkness creeping in.

I focused on the crumbling brick of the garden walls, waiting to see the specter I'd created in my mind, when there, in the center of it all, stood Ivy...smoking a cigarette.

I leaned on the window trying to pry it open.

"Only fast girls smoke," was something both Mother and Father used to say, and I couldn't let Ivy become "fast." She was speeding toward disaster since the day she was born, and now, it seemed, we'd reached it.

I couldn't open the window, so I banged on it.

I saw her see me, but she looked away, that ninny of a girl. The look in her eyes, though... It made me ashamed, I must have embarrassed her...but if I was her cross to bear, it didn't matter to me. I had to stop her before she fell head-long into all the vices the city had to offer.

Frantic to stop her, I knew I had to go downstairs. It'd gotten very dark, so I picked up a hurricane lamp that was next to my bed, shuffled through Daisy's things for a matchbook and lit the wick.

I rushed down the rickety staircase, one hand on the railing, the other holding up the lamp by it's thin wire handle.

Just then, a man—I could tell by his footsteps, heavy and booted—bounded up the stairs toward me. He couldn't see me as he rounded the corner and so even though I tried to move aside for him we were both going too fast. We collided.

I started to fall, but he caught me. Only he was at a poor

angle so he fell forward. What happened was a graceless heap of two bodies intertwined, knocking the lamp askew, as well. The man reached over me to right it before too much oil spilled. I felt his cheek brush against mine, the stubble there so rough on my skin. I felt his arms try to sit me up… How strong they were, holding me, making sure I wouldn't fall again. He had to touch my bare arms in order to get me on my feet again. Calloused hands swept past my face, smelling clean, of lemons and earth…gardens deep inside the ground full of fresh, growing things.

My God, what is this feeling? I thought as my head inched past his.

He asked, as breathless as I felt, "Are you a phantom?" into my hair as I moved upward, my lips open, not realizing I'd brush the side of his neck with them as I stood on my own.

And then sank back down because my ankle had twisted in the fall.

He reached for me again, but I backed away from him. There was nowhere to go. He was now blocking the staircase up, and I didn't want to go down anymore.

"You're hurt, and I'm frightening you," he said. "Please don't be frightened. We've already met. It's me, Sonny. Santino." It was then that I got the courage to look up at him.

Shadows speak louder of a person than sunlight. He was handsome. A strong nose and even stronger chin.

Mother always said that a strong chin meant a strong character.

"Are you drunk?" I asked him. "You ran so fast, I could have died here!"

I wanted to say, *What was that, that thing that just occurred…what happened there? Did you feel it, too?*

"Not drunk yet," he said…and I felt he answered me. *No, that was nothing….* "I'm still cooking. I was coming to check up on you, actually. And here you are, my phantom." He laughed. It was a warm laugh, not mocking. Not like when I said silly things, and Ivy would laugh at me.

"You are so very pretty, Rose."

I was happy for the dim light of the lamp so he couldn't see me blush.

"Well, you look terrified, so allow me to escort you back upstairs. Only to your own steps, of course. We wouldn't want to seem improper. You are a lady, Rose Adams." He held out his arm, and I took it.

I began to walk but stumbled on my sore ankle.

"If you'll permit me, I'll carry you. I promise, no more awkward falls. I'll not mistreat you, Rose."

"Only if you promise to stop Ivy from making a fool of herself with the cigarette she's smoking."

"Agreed," he said, and picked me up and carried me back to the penthouse. I felt lighter than air. He smiled at me. He had a smile like my father's. One that lit up his eyes as well as his mouth.

"Perhaps we will meet on the stairs again," he said. Then he gave a small bow and went back to the party.

I'll admit, by the time he was gone, my ankle had stopped throbbing altogether, and I wondered if some alternate person inside of me had wanted him to lift me up. Then shook the thought away.

I rushed to the window to see if he'd do as I asked.

There he was, next to Ivy and taking the cigarette out of her hands.

Santino. A wonderful name. Exotic and full of mystery.

I went back to my original objective and found, as I knew I would, the sewing table crammed into the crawl space.

It took some time, but before I knew it, I was sewing myself a dress out of orange chiffon, thinking of home, summers by the lake and Santino.

When Ivy finally came back upstairs with Viv and Maude, they were obviously drunk.

She'd have to learn the hard way, my sister.

I pushed more filmy fabric through the machine and felt confident for the first time all day.

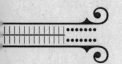 

CHAPTER 6

Ivy

I SAW MY sister in the window.

Rose stood there like Rochester's forgotten attic bride—hair loose, ghostly white nightgown billowing about, palms pressed to the glass. The calmer, more relaxed demeanor she'd exhibited earlier was gone. Her eyes scoured the patio with a desperate look, the angel of practicality prepared to rain judgment upon us, if only she could get the darn window open. Rose pushed at it, hit the frame with the flat of her hand, but the thing wouldn't budge. When I caught her eye Rose shook her head—*no, no, no!*—but I ignored her. There isn't a girl on the planet who wants to be told not to do something right after she's made the decision to do it, and my must-do list was a doozy—smoke a real cigarette, get roaring drunk, kiss somebody. I'd crossed off the first one and planned on knocking out the rest of the list that night, my worrywart sister be damned.

But that wasn't the whole story. Between the heartache

of the past and the razzle-dazzle of a gin-soaked present, I chose the here and now. Empire House was a brace to the system. Something new to forget something old.

"Give me a drag of that lipstick," Maude said, deftly taking the cigarette from my hand. She'd given it to me when we arrived at the party, to "slay my nerves." I wasn't the neurotic type, but I could see what she meant. When a gal's hands are busy the rest of her looks pretty occupied with life. It helps when you don't know a soul, and I didn't. I didn't trust Viv much, or Nell, but I did take an instant liking to Maude, and my instincts were pretty steady-eddy. Still, I wondered if she did remember Asher. Had he been a trusted friend or a boy who broke her heart? I supposed there were a number of reasons to skirt the truth, and not all of them meant the person wanted to lie.

"You okeydoke?" Maude asked. She sucked on the cig and drew the smoke so far into her body I expected it to come out her pores. "You look a little green."

Dizzy from the smoke, my head felt like it had turned into a zeppelin, ponderously circling the party in search of a place to land. Still, I flashed my teeth. "Fine and dandy."

"Viv will be back soon. She went inside to help Jimmy with the hooch."

My zeppelin head went down in flames at the name. "Jimmy?"

"He's a real harp—face looks like the map of Ireland. The girls like him, though." Maude leaned in. "My tastes are more refined. I want a gent to take me to Mouquin's for escargot. You know, someone cosmopolitan, refined."

I took in her long, plain face and simply nodded. "So… the rule about drinking liquor is loosely enforced?"

Maude took another drag and shook her head. "Rules don't apply when Nell can make a buck."

We stood there, companionably listening to the sounds of nighttime in Greenwich Village. The rest of the city popped like the gunshot beginning a footrace—*go, go, go!*—but the Village spoke in musical whispers, the sound of ideas taking form, and the soft slide into the delicious vices that make one's head swim. Maude slipped the cig back into my hand, and I readied myself for another smoke. I lifted my hand and brought only my fingers to my mouth. Santino, the cook, had taken the cig while passing. He clucked his tongue and crushed it in his bare hand.

"You ain't her father, Sonny!" Maude shouted after him. "Stick to making meatballs!"

I watched him slip back into Empire House. "What was that about?"

"He was in the war," Maude gave in explanation. "Those guys think because they've seen a few ghosts, they know everything." She shrugged. "Forget about him. What do you think about sharing a house with the rest of the crew?" she asked, gesturing to the gals moving about the patio. "We're a touch removed from the action up in the penthouse, but these baby dolls are your neighbors."

The other girls were a candy box assortment—plump and thin, brunette and blonde, tall and short, but they all looked like they knew where the world had wanted them to go, but ran in the opposite direction as soon as they got the chance. Modern girls. They clustered in small groups on the garden patio, candles in Mason jars circling their feet, tittering in anticipation of what the night would bring. A few of them sat cross-legged in front of a low slate bench, their attention drawn to the woman sitting on it. She didn't wear a dress, but a simple shirt made of light green silk, paired with a day carpenter's white canvas trousers and Chinese slippers. The odd combination somehow worked in her favor, though I suspected no one else should dare attempt it. In the dusky candlelight, her face was smooth and ageless—she could be a girl of twenty or a woman of forty. I wanted to look at her in the harsh light of day, but still I wondered if it would make any difference.

I was used to being the object of curiosity, but this woman, with her pale, fine-boned face and shock of white-blond hair, held every eye as though she were a hypnotist by trade. In this crazy city, maybe she was.

I nudged Maude. "Who's that?"

"She has far too many admirers already," Maude huffed. "Don't add to her roster."

"Are you going to answer my question or not?"

"Cat LeGrand," she answered, after making me wait a moment.

"Is that her real name?"

"What do you think?"

I took a few steps toward the bench, drawn as moth to flame, Maude dragging behind me like an iron prison ball. "I want to meet her. Will you introduce me?"

"Do I have a choice?"

I laughed. "I don't really want to give you one."

"All righty, but don't say I didn't warn you."

"You didn't! And anyway, what's the crime in being popular?"

Maude rolled her eyes. "Spoken like a true babe in the Greenwich Village woods."

We approached slowly, arm in arm. If Cat noticed us

homing in she gave no acknowledgment. A round-faced girl sat at her feet like a supplicant, telling a story with broad, expansive gestures, attempting to elicit a reaction she simply wasn't getting.

"Cat," Maude said, her nasal voice interrupting, cutting into the girl's enthusiastic ramblings.

Cat's bored expression dropped from her features, replaced by an avaricious grin. "Maude," she said, looking at *me* with glittery dark eyes. "Have you brought a party favor?"

"Possibly," Maude said, "but not for you. I'm merely making introductions."

Cat brought a hand up. Her long nails were painted the deep, pure fuchsia of my mother's peonies. I slipped my hand in hers, surprised at their roughness.

"Ivy Adams," I said, wincing a bit as her hand gripped mine.

Cat studied my face as though she were committing each feature to memory. "Are you the seamstress?"

At that moment, I wanted to be, more than anything. "No," I replied. "I'm the actress."

Her lacquered mouth drew into a pout. "Oh, pity. I can't use one of those."

"My sister can sew," I said, suddenly overcome with the need to please. "Maybe she can help you out."

"Maybe," she mused.

"Oh, jeez," Maude groaned. "Head count."

The party's attention shifted to the patio door, where Nell stood, dressed formally for evening. With one arm draped over the railing and a thin, knowing smile, she looked inscrutable as a sphinx.

With great efficiency, Nell began to work the crowd.

She hit the outskirts of the party first, but then changed course, heading in our direction. "Prepare to be fleeced," Maude muttered.

"Two dollars tonight, ladies," Nell said in lieu of a greeting.

In a flash, money exchanged hands. So distracted was I by the swiftness of the transactions, it took me a moment to notice that all eyes were on me, waiting for my contribution.

I felt myself go pale. I had a dime in each shoe, and nothing else. "If I can, I mean, if you'll allow—"

"If you don't have it," Nell said briskly, "you'll have to leave."

"Don't give her the business, Nell," Cat said, thrusting two more dollars at the old woman. She turned to me. "You owe me one."

Nell frowned. "And your sister?"

"Rose is tired," I said. "She decided to turn in."

If I'd blinked, I'd have missed the quick glance between Cat and Nell. It was a simple meeting of slightly widened eyes, but the timing of it set my senses on high alert. How easily my suspicions took root—was I taking lessons from my bookworm sister?

Maude let out a breath and laughed a little. "You look like you need a drink," she said. "I'm eager to get at it, too." We started toward the house, walking a few steps before we noticed Cat hadn't left the bench. "You coming?" Maude asked.

Cat tilted her head toward the inky night sky. "Gin comes to me," she said, her voice like silk, "not the other way around."

"Well, I'm happy to chase it," Maude whispered, pulling me away from Cat. "If I waited for it to find me, I'd die of thirst."

We entered a shadowy stairwell, bypassing the kitchen, and exited on what I thought was the second floor, but was actually a landing with a room attached. The door, marked Washing Room, was closed, but Maude walked in anyway without the courtesy of a knock.

The heady scent of pine and oranges nearly knocked me over. Jimmy straddled a copper tub, carefully tipping a large glass bottle into a cocktail shaker. When he noticed us standing there he gave a wink, and my heart jumped in my chest. "Next batch is for these two lovelies," he called to Viv, who stood at a folding table squeezing the dickens out of an orange.

"Orange blossoms tonight," she said excitedly. "You're going to want more than one of these." Jimmy gave her the shaker and she went to work, adding a dash of orange juice and a scoop of chipped ice before agitating the mixture in three slow undulations.

"Aren't you supposed to shake it up?" Maude asked.

Viv poured the liquid into two porcelain teacups. "This is a delicate drink. A *ladylike* concoction."

"Oh, brother," Maude said under her breath.

Viv distributed the drinks. "Run and get me some more oranges, Jimmy," she said, surveying her supplies. "I've only got one left."

Jimmy stepped over the tub. His shirtsleeves were rolled to the elbows, revealing thick forearms swirled with black hair. "Come with," he said to me. "I need someone to help me carry the bounty."

"I only need a couple," Viv said sharply, "not a case."

Jimmy ignored her and ushered me from the room,

closing the door on the whispering girls behind us. Once in the kitchen, he seemed to forget why we'd come, and set about investigating the knives lining the walls. "Sonny would chop off my hands with these if he caught me in here," Jimmy said.

"And what would he do to me?" I said, hand on my hip, the words braver than I felt.

Jimmy tossed me a dark look and didn't answer. I knew he was joshing, but the uneasiness I felt on the patio kicked up a notch. I changed the subject. "Do you often make gin in the washing room?" I hated the way I sounded, prim and practical, like Rose.

"That tub hasn't seen a scrap of fabric in years," Jimmy said. "The whole place stinks like a juniper and sweat."

I dipped a finger into my teacup and placed a drop of the ice-cold liquid on my tongue. "Doesn't taste like sweat— I'd say more like sunshine."

Jimmy moved closer, leaving his fascination with the knives behind. He stuck a finger in my drink then ran the gin down the slope of my nose. "We're alchemists," he said softly. "You've got magic in your glass."

There was a mere hairbreadth between us. I could smell the pine scent of juniper, and the something else, something warm and inviting. "Now that's a golden line," I said, smiling up at him. "Does it usually work?"

"I don't know if it does or it doesn't," he said softly. "I'm just trying it out."

Jimmy had a small scar bracketing the corner of his eye, and one at the edge of his mouth. His nose was slightly crooked, as if it'd been broken and reset badly. His face grew more interesting the closer I looked, and more dangerous, just like this crazy city I was only beginning to understand.

"It's starting to work," I said. "Give it time."

"No one's got much of that," he said. He leaned toward me, and my pulse hammered with anticipation.

"Jimmy," Maude said. She stood in the door frame, a strange look on her horsy features. "Viv doesn't want to wait all night."

Jimmy grabbed two oranges from a bowl on the kitchen table. "Go easy on the gin," he said, grinning as he stepped backward toward Maude. "There's a party every night if you want it. And ain't that what life's all about?"

An eerie kind of silence filled the kitchen after they left. I felt odd about following Jimmy and Maude, and I was fearful Sonny the cook would return to find me nosying around his kitchen with a cup of gin, so I rejoined the others on the patio. In the few minutes we'd been gone the party filled out, shifting from picturesque gathering to raucous bash.

The candles had been kicked to the side, so only the moon and stars lit the patio. Shifting bodies heaved unsteadily, strange elbows and shoulders knocking me to and fro. I downed the gin before it spilled. Someone called something that sounded like my name, but the darkness swirling above swallowed the sound.

A hand clutched my arm.

Before I raised my eyes, I thought about who I wished it would be. The dead? The missing? The map of Ireland?

No, I realized with a start. I wanted the girl trapped behind glass. The one upstairs, worrying.

"Hey," the owner of the hand shouted. It was the round-faced storyteller, the one we'd interrupted. "Got a light?"
I shook my head and melted into the crowd.

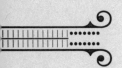 CHAPTER 7

Rose

I AWOKE TO music and laughter. I got up, pulled my nightdress up to my neck and peeked into Maude and Viv's side to see Ivy sitting on one of their beds holding slices of cucumber over her eyes.

"I don't see how this will work." She giggled.

"You can't go over to Cat's place with big circles under your eyes. She likes pretty things."

"She saw me last night!" said Ivy.

I walked over to them.

"Hey there, sleepyhead," said Viv. "You'd think you were the life of the party, the way you snored away."

"I don't snore," I said.

They all laughed.

"We need to get dressed and go find work, Ivy."

"I am dressed," she said and stood up. She was wearing a scandalous dress. Light blue with thin straps, a dropped waist. She didn't have on any sort of corset, which was usual for Ivy, but what I found most distressing was how her whole spirit seemed to be pulling against the fabric. As if her body, free from its constraints, was beginning to be as bold as her mind. One party, one night, one cigarette. Had I lost my sister?

Well, I thought, *I'll just find her again.*

Because, to be honest, she looked lovely, like a wild-flower. But, instead of saying so, I rolled my eyes and returned to our half of the penthouse.

I grabbed the dress it took me half the night to make, tried to hide myself as best I could behind one of the lower beams.

Ivy came over to me, pouting. She has the most beautiful mouth, and she's used it wisely since she was a little girl. Her pouts, even the fake ones, could get almost anything out of our father.

"I think this dress is lovely, and you know how I feel about fashion," she said.

I walked out from behind the beam and went to pin my hair up in front of the dressing table mirror. "I do, and I also know you don't care about my opinion. I'm worried about how people will look at you when they see that dress. They'll think you're a harlot. Where did you get it?"

"Viv gave it to me. I think it was Daisy's." Ivy was playing with her beads and not looking at me. I wanted to stomp my feet and get her attention. I wanted her to notice what I'd made.

"Ah, the mysterious Daisy," I said.... And she looked up.

"You made that?" She walked over to me and fingered the hem at the arms. I'd made the sleeves three-quarter inch, and hadn't used any under satin because I'd run out.

"Well, thank heaven she was a seamstress, or I'd have

to go on the streets looking like a beggar. I spilled ink on my dress last night and had to make this rag out of the curtains I found.

"You look beautiful," she said. "Like a butterfly…"

"Thank you," was all I could muster. "It will have to do until we can buy something. The color is atrocious."

"You are so silly. Have you learned nothing of the newer fashions? This dress looks absolutely new, Rose! All the girls are wearing their dresses shorter now. You're in style. How about that?"

I wasn't convinced. She went to her small trunk and pulled out a pair of black heels. Not boots, little strappy heels.

"At least our feet are the same size. Wear these," she said.

"Where did you get them?" I asked.

"Father bought them for me in Albany before…well, before. Put them on," she said.

After, she and those ninnies we lived with tried to put some rouge on my cheeks and lips but I wouldn't let them. Which, I have to admit, led us to a small romp of light-hearted fun…we even laughed a bit. They chased after me with a pot of rouge. Then the music stopped and Maude put on another record.

I always loved the way the scratching sound of the phonograph sounded in our living room.

"Oh, listen to this. I just love this ragtime. Let's dance, girls!"

Ivy took my hand without thinking, and then the four of us were dancing on the wide wooden planks of the attic, giving whoever lived beneath us quite a headache, I'm sure.

I couldn't help but remember us dancing and laughing together another time—it felt like a million years ago.

We were ten and eleven years old, respectively. We'd had dinner and were in our drawing room, as usual. That night, though, when father put the record on the new phonograph, Ivy got up and began to dance. Father and Mother looked at her with such love, I got up, as well. I took her hands and we started spinning around. Our hair spreading every which way. When we stopped, we fell to the ground in a dizzy, laughing heap.

"That was fun!" she'd said.

"Let's do another spin," I'd said.

We were out of breath, but danced on, the two of us, still so small. Our hair down, flying around us, mingling light strands with dark. Our fingers still laced together. Smiling.

"What happened to us?" I asked.

"What do you mean?" asked a grown-up Ivy. That's when I realized I'd said it out loud.

"Nothing," I said, not knowing how to explain the feelings welling up inside of me. "I'm just *deeply* ashamed that we look like loose women."

"Oh, let's just go. We're going to be late," she said.

"Late for what?" I asked.

"Late for our job interview!"

"You've found us work, Ivy?"

"Well, not really. Just an idea."

"If it's an idea, how can we be late? You can't be late for an idea."

"You can be so difficult," she said, pulling me out of our room and down the narrow stairway so quickly that I had to yank her back so I wouldn't fall down and twist my ankle again on unfamiliar shoes.

"Have a great day, ladies," said Maude as we left.

"Be safe out there…" said Viv, and the two fell into waves of laughter. It was a quiet comfort, having someone noticing that we were leaving. I couldn't remember when anyone—joking or not—had thought twice about where I was or what I was doing. That's what happens when you are the one in charge. Everyone always assumes there is a reason why you do the things you do. It felt good to not be in charge.

"So, where are we going?" I asked as we rounded the landing on the fourth floor.

"To Cat LeGrand's dress shop. She's the bee's knees, Rose. I don't think I've ever met anyone like her!" she said, as we made our way down two more flights.

"What kind of woman is she? If I read a story where there was someone named Cat LeGrand, I'd think she was a terrible villain."

Reaching the foyer first, Ivy stopped, placed her hands on the newel post and spun on her heels, the fringe of her dress reaching out around her like tendrils of smoke.

"Stop it now. Don't you dare, Rose. I mean it. Don't judge her before you meet her. This is our opportunity. As soon as we get on our feet financially, we can start a proper search for Asher."

"For who?" asked Nell, who rounded the doorway of the dining room at that same moment.

"For our brother, Asher," repeated Ivy.

"Ah, the elusive brother. Don't bother yourselves with that task, girls. People come to this city to get lost, not be found."

I walked to the entry table where there was a beautiful bouquet of fresh flowers in a crystal vase. Out of habit, or perhaps nervousness, I began rearranging them as I spoke.

"Well, we don't think he came to the city as a visitor. We think he was born here. That would make it an entirely different scenario, wouldn't it?"

"Is there something wrong with that arrangement, Ms. Adams? Perhaps you think you could have done a better job?"

"Well, actually, Mrs. Neville…the fern would look better dispersed. Sometimes an arrangement looks more creative when you let the flowers mimic the way they look outside."

"It's *Miss,* and you know a lot about things like that, I assume," said Nell, looking amused.

"My sister knows a lot about everything domestic. It's rather boring. She took over our entire household after our mother died," said Ivy.

"Is that so? In that case, seeing as I just let another useless woman go, I could use a new housekeeper. Santino, Claudia and I can't run this entire building ourselves. How would you like to work here, Rose?"

I turned around to face Nell. Ivy was behind her mouthing the word NO.

"What is the pay?"

"I could offer a barter. You work in exchange for your board."

"For both of us?"

"Don't be silly. Just your portion. It's a fair amount. But I'll need your answer right away, because I'll have to put an advertisement in the paper today if you decline."

Ivy came around to my side. "I was just going to bring her to Cat's to see if we could get jobs there. See this dress?" she said, pulling at my sleeve. "My sister made this dress last night. Out of a curtain. She's very talented."

Nell moved in for a closer look. "Yes, I see. The seams are tidy…the design is well thought out. I can arrange something with Cat. You two go meet with her, and I'll call ahead. Impressive, Ms. Adams."

"Thank you," I said, unused to any sort of compliment.

Ivy took my wrist, and we moved toward the front doors.

"Oh, Rose? Santino left this for you. I almost forgot." She fished a white envelope out of a deep dress pocket.

I took it. LADY ROSE ADAMS was printed across the white expanse in bold handwriting.

"Oh, looky looky! Rose, what have you been up to?" asked Ivy, grabbing the envelope and beginning to open it.

"It's mine," I said, taking it from her hands. I opened it as we wandered into the dining room.

"Aren't you going to read your letter?"

"As we walk. That way I won't have to look at the filth that surrounds us."

"You're such a stick-in-the-mud, Rose."

We walked out into the stunning sunlight, and I was glad for a moment that I no longer had a high collar or laced-up boots. The day was already hot. Besides, the city was about to get much more interesting.

"It shouldn't be very far. Viv even drew me a map," said Ivy as I followed two steps behind her, opening my letter. She was rushing. Usually I'm the one ahead, with her lollygagging after me all transfixed with whatever beautiful, shiny new thing she saw.

We'd only just left Empire House, so I wondered about where we could be going. We passed the throngs of people in the streets. Everyone seemed to stare at Ivy. There was a store on the corner, Gilda's Sweet Shop, and I made a mental note to purchase a sweet for Claudia when I made a little bit of money. It would be a good bribe to get her reading.

"So, what did you learn at the party last night?" I asked.

"Not much…"

"That's it?" I asked.

"The party was riotous! Even you might have enjoyed yourself. These people are so much fun."

"Did you ask about Asher?"

"In a way."

"What do you mean?"

"I think we're right. They're all giving us the business, Rose. I just don't know why. We need to tread carefully with these people. At least that's what my gut's telling me."

"Well, Papa always said we had to listen to instinct."

Ivy's smile faded, and I was sorry I'd mentioned him.

"I feel there are a lot of secrets hiding in that attic, though…" I said, trying to lift the mood. It worked.

"Oh, yeah. There's secrets a plenty at Empire House. And I'm gonna figure it all out. Starting with that note of yours!" she said, grabbing for it again, forgetting I was much taller. "Come on! What does that letter say? I'm dying!"

"You're tiresome," I said, unfolding the paper and tucking the envelope into my wrist purse. It was a poem:

I met a phantom on the stairs
With flowing hair and lamp-lit eyes
I'm glad I bounded up
And captured that surprise
I do so hope she's not upset

To cry with lamp-lit eyes.
New friend, gladly welcome now
A poem in disguise
A flower under glass
A set of lamp-lit eyes
Come see me, phantom
In my dreams
On lakes and boats and corsets gone
Through miles and miles of endless trees
Through sorrow tides and windswept seas
I'll be where flowers cannot grow
Meet me there, at dusk's last stand
Perhaps you'll let me hold your hand.
—The Poet

"It's a poem," I said.

Ivy was quick. She waited for me to lower my guard, and the paper, and then took it out of my shaking hands, reading it as we stood on the street. I didn't even try to get it back, such was my surprise at its intimacy, and my reaction to it. Like a hot poker in my abdomen. Who was this Santino fellow, thinking he could write such things to me? And what was the longing inside of me that the words evoked?

"Rose! It's lovely. When did you meet him? Is this a real story? Was he on the stairs?"

"Be quiet," I said. "It's not your business, really. And he's a brute to have written such things."

"I'd die happy to have words like this written to me. He's handsome, you know. Might not be so bad, having an Italian Lover."

I grabbed the note from her and walked briskly past.

"That's a horrendous thing to say," I said, but folded the paper up and put it in my purse, as well.

"And where do you think you're going, sister? I'm the one who knows the way...."

She walked ahead of me again and continued to tease me.

He could corrupt you!

You could have an illicit affair!

Maybe you'll go back to Italy and have a boatload of dark-haired babies.

I was relieved when she started to take a sharp left down a dark alleyway. But then paused before turning, like it was a gaping mouth ready to eat us. There were broken bricks at my feet that almost looked like teeth.

As if she read my mind, she said, "Come on, nothing is going to eat you."

"I'm fine!" I yelled after her. "Just adjusting this hateful dress."

I wouldn't let her know I was afraid. I was the caretaker not the coward.

I made sure I had my straightest back and walked into the mouth of Manhattan.

The shop was in the alley itself. Almost like a magical door to another world.

A beautiful ornate sign that read Cat's Dress Emporium with gold letters on a deep green background hung next to the large windows filled with the most colorful dresses I'd ever seen. And they looked expensive. Too fine for our budget.

"It's closed," I said, pointing at the sign on one of the double glass doors of the entrance.

"Closed for another half hour, but open for us," Ivy said

as she opened the doors. The smell that wafted out was spicy, orange, rose. Heady and confusing.

A bell sounded as we entered.

It was cool inside the shop.

"Do you think Papa would be proud? Look at us, not a full day in the city, and we have work and a place to live…." I said.

I could tell by the way Ivy was fiddling with the hem of her sleeve that she didn't want to entertain thoughts of our father at that very moment. Besides, a stunningly beautiful woman had walked out from behind a set of garnet curtains. I'd seen her the night before in the garden. It was as if she'd been holding court. Up close, though, she was even more beautiful. Not an ordinary beauty, either. It was the kind that startled you and brought you to another place in time. She was layered with mystery.

"Ivy, so glad you could come," she said, walking toward us. As she walked, her tall graceful body leaned backward, not straight up. It looked as if part of her was lunging at us. She held a cigarette in a long holder in one hand that swayed back and forth as she walked.

I'd never seen anything like her. And I couldn't decide if I was intimidated or interested.

Ivy met her, and they kissed each other on the cheeks.

"Rose," she said, "this is Madame Cat. Cat, this is my sister, Rose. She's the seamstress. She sewed the dress she has on while she was cooped up in our room last night."

"Wonderful," said Cat, spreading the word out for many more syllables than was necessary, as she looked me up and down.

"You look like someone I knew a long time ago," she

said. "Do people often say that to you? Have you grown bored with it?"

"No. Not at all. It's helpful, really. You see, we are looking for our brother, Asher Adams. Could that be the person you think I resemble?"

"I don't think so. I'd remember a name like Asher."

"Our father was Everett Adams. Do you happen to remember him?"

"Doesn't ring a bell."

"Are you certain?"

"You have style, Rose. And I think I like you, so don't push me any further. You've asked your question and I've answered it."

I looked at the interior of the shop as I mulled over whether Cat had lied to me.

Soon, Ivy and I would have to discuss a less-direct way of finding Asher. These women sure knew how to shut down conversations with a wave of their pretty hands. What were they hiding? I found myself agreeing with Ivy. We did need to be more careful in our approach.

Cat's shop was as beautiful and exotic as its owner. Chandeliers hung everywhere, all different shapes and sizes, and the way they threw the easy light against the walls was magical. A million little prisms.

The dresses lined the walls and were also displayed on mannequins throughout the long, narrow shop. There was a long oak counter with a glass top that held gloves and jewelry.

Cat saw my interest.

"It's obvious you can sew. This dress is charming. Are you looking for employment?"

"I think I may have just gotten a job at Empire House."

"Yes, I know. Nell phoned ahead. But I can offer you sewing work. You can sew clothing when you're not the new housekeeper. How does that sound?"

"How much do you pay?"

Cat let out a hearty laugh. Ivy giggled, too, and then Cat offered her a cigarette from a golden case. Who was this woman?

She turned to offer one to me but I put up my hand. I wouldn't start sinking so quickly. Ivy had always been weak when it came to danger. I was strong.

"How much do you require?" she asked, and for the first time I could hear a soft lilt in her voice. One that gave away her origins. I had a feeling that Cat LeGrand may not have come from Grand Stock. Her words were carefully chosen to cover up a less-than-stellar education. But it was only a guess.

"Ten dollars a week," I said.

"You are interesting, Rose," she said, circling me. "Refined, insecure…hardworking. Determined, yet not too aggressive, a good judge of character." She stopped to take a long puff of her cigarette.

"You will alter clothing and replicate patterns for new clothing in the store. I will have all the fabric and notions dropped off. When you are done with what I've sent, you will bring the garments back here, and I'll pay you. How does that sound?"

"If I finish quickly, will I earn a bonus?"

"I don't like rushed work, but if it's fine sewing, your bonus is more work and quick payment."

"If I sew you original garments, will you pay me a commission?"

Cat laughed. "You are a businesswoman, too, I see. Of

course, but only if they sell. And you'd have to provide the fabric yourself."

"You have yourself a seamstress," I said.

"Wonderful. Now, seeing as you're here, you can take your first pile of rags yourself. Usually Jimmy will bring you things, or I'll send you back with things when you come to collect your pay. Go into the back and gather the alterations I left there. The shop opens in twenty minutes."

Ivy stood up then, and with her best come-hither voice asked, "What would you like from me?" Then she proceeded to extol her virtues. I agreed with "I can act," but when she got to "I'm a hard worker," I had to stifle my own laugh.

Cat walked through a set of velvet curtains at the side of the shop.

"Is the ridiculous little bluebird going to follow me or not?" asked Cat. Then she turned back to me, flashing a bright smile, and clinked her beaded earrings together. "Oh, Rose?"

"Yes?"

"Do tell me how your search goes for that brother of yours. I enjoy a mystery."

They left together, and I knew they were walking down a staircase, hidden from view, because of the echo of their footfalls.

I gathered the garments and patterns slowly, because I didn't know if I was to stay and wait for Ivy, or if I was to leave.

When Cat came back up to the store there were people clamoring to come inside already. Cat's Dress Emporium seemed to be quite popular.

"I have a busy day ahead of me, Rose. So you must

go…but before you do, let me just say that I don't think you know how talented you are. And also, I think it's very brave…the way you are handling all of this…how shall I say…new," she said. "I don't like a lot of people, Rose. But I like you, so I'm gonna give you a little tip."

"What's that?"

"When you ask questions, it's important to make sure you will be satisfied with the answer you may get."

"Well, I'd be happy with a straight answer," I said, shocking myself with my bold behavior. But for some reason, I liked her, Cat. I liked her a lot.

"If you're determined, you might just get one. Be prepared, is all I'm saying. And one more thing."

"Yes?"

"I heard what you were saying to Ivy when you both came into the shop. And I think any father would be proud of two young women with such moxie."

"Thank you," I said.

Cat walked toward me and pushed a strand of hair out of my eyes. "Those eyes," she said. I could tell she wanted to say more, but didn't.

"When should I expect Ivy?" I asked.

"Ivy will be working late into the night, kitten," she said.

I didn't want to know what that meant, but I had my suspicions. Cat must be running a speakeasy in the basement. Father told us about such establishments, especially in larger cities…but to think of Ivy working in one made my skin crawl.

"I'll be making ten dollars a week," I said to myself over

and over again as I made my way back to Empire House alone. And though I thought I'd get lost…I knew the way back by heart already.

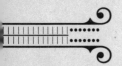 # CHAPTER 8

Ivy

I'D NEVER WANTED something as badly as I did a job at Cat's. I tried to hide my desire, dulling my eyes, turning the edges of my mouth down—anything to not appear desperate, anything to keep her from getting a leg up.

Who was I kidding? She had more than a leg—she had legs, arms, that long elegant neck and crown of white-blond hair. Her superiority shimmered around her, a phosphorus glow most visible at night.

What really took the cake was how quickly Cat hired Rose. My sister slid into Cat's glittery life like she was the trusted seamstress to the queen, while in the end, I had to beg for a job. Mr. Lawrence had been straight with us about the tenuous nature of our financial situation, and though practicality was not my strong suit, the city offered so much to those with a few dollars in their pockets and so little to those without. Living cost money. Maybe someday I'd give the Barrymores a little stiff competition, but

I had yet to visit the theater district much less take it by storm. The farthest I'd gotten was peering into the dusty window of the Revolutionary Theater next door to Empire House. I'd sneaked past a sleeping Rose in search of a newspaper stand to buy cigs, and was again distracted by the sign calling for actresses. Even at the early hour, people were inside. Three men and a woman sat on a rug in front of a small stage, eating garbanzo beans out of a shallow bowl placed between them, conversing intently. A knock on the window startled me, and a realized a woman was swabbing the dirty windows with a rag. She was a sweet-faced, sentimental blonde, the kind whose photograph ad men slapped on canisters of oatmeal. Her dress was black and cut in a bohemian style, with lace at the collarbones. The girl smiled and gestured for me to come in. "Don't be shy," she said, holding the door open. I stepped inside. The theater was cool, much cooler than the street, though it was only half-underground.

"Are you an actress?" I asked her. I don't even know why I asked it—all I had to do was take one look at her lovely face. Of course she was.

"Sometimes, but mostly I sew costumes and clean up around here. I'm Natasha."

Natasha? More like Mary or Betty or Sue Ann, I thought. "I'm Ivy."

"Are *you* an actress?" she asked. "I'll tell Bertrand, the director. He's always looking for new voices."

I glanced over at the stage, bare and waiting, and the small group of sophisticates sitting in front of it, and shook my head. "No. I was just curious. You have a lovely theater here." The words came out too stiff and formal. What was I doing? I gave her a shaky smile and backed out onto

MacDougal, my body trembling. Why didn't I say yes? I had no trouble auditioning back in Forest Grove. But this was different somehow, and I didn't want to think if the difference was in the venue or in me.

"I told you to stay away from the communists," a man's voice said. I whirled around to see Jimmy, parked curbside, giving him a front-row seat for my humiliation. He had the windows open, a cigarette hanging precariously from his lips. I should have noticed him, but then Jimmy seemed to blend into the background with ease. I'd stayed at the party very, very late the night before, but I hadn't seen Jimmy after our interlude in the kitchen. Then, as I was about to stumble up the back steps, he appeared in the garden, smoking and sipping an orange blossom as though the New York night had dreamed him up. Had he spent the entire evening in the washing room with Viv? Had he gone off in search of other temptations? I had no idea.

Through sheer force of will I managed to look him in the eye. "I thought you said they were anarchists."

"Same difference." He spat ciggy butt on the street. "That's not the job for you."

"Oh, yeah? Have you got one lined up?"

"I saw you talking to Cat last night. Play your cards right and she can be a real friend. And Cat's always got opportunities for her friends to make a buck." He laughed when he saw the look on my face. "Not that way. That's not what I meant at all."

But what had he meant? The dress emporium, elegant as it was, had dark edges, like a cracked frame surrounding a beautiful painting. What was I getting mixed up with? Would a similar fate befall Rose? She'd let a tiger stretch out across her lap if it smiled up at her. If she was going to work for Cat, then I was, too. Jimmy said she'd provide opportunities. I wondered if we defined that word the same way.

"Okay," Cat finally said after I extolled my virtues. "You can do all those things, but can you keep a secret?"

"Is the day long?"

"Too long," she said, and smiled wryly. She told Rose to gather up some dresses from the back room and brought me down a narrow hallway to a door hidden by a heavy red velvet curtain. I half expected to see Dante's words emblazoned over the entryway—"Abandon all hope ye who enter here."

I didn't change my mind once the door opened. A dim tunnel led to a crumbling cement staircase, the air turning musty and damp as we descended. "You breathe a word of this," Cat said, "I'll have Jimmy make hooch out of your melted bones."

Cat knocked on the door at the bottom of the staircase in five quick raps. When it opened, the round-faced girl from the party stood gawking at us. "What's she doing here?" the girl said, thrusting her chin at me.

"Ivy, do you know Bessie?"

I met Bessie's glare with a smile. When in doubt, father always said, kill 'em with kindness. "I do. We met at the party at Empire House."

"Ivy will take Lola's place," Cat said briskly.

"But Lola isn't gone," Bessie protested.

"Not yet," Cat retorted, and stepped past the open-mouthed girl, tugging me behind her.

I'd been in a speakeasy once before. My father, flush with a check from some naturalist magazine, took Rose and me shopping in downtown Albany. After wandering around the city, we found ourselves in a bowling alley across the street from the capitol building. Not a single soul was in it; the pins stood clustered in groups like abandoned bouquets of flowers. My father walked past the lanes, through an empty kitchen and directly into the ladies' room. Rose and I followed to warn him of his mistake, only to find ourselves in a room full of men. They didn't appear startled to see girls our age, but I was sure shocked when my father walked up to a bearded old curmudgeon and asked for a glass of beer. He ordered the root variety for Rose and me, and we sat in the corner near a quartet playing cards. The men nodded in acknowledgment as we passed, mumbling my father's name, and I realized he'd not only been there before, but was a known entity. Rose, eyes wide and face blanched of color, had obviously come to the same conclusion.

"This is against the law," she whispered.

"Laws are made by man, and anything made by man is subject to fallacy," Father said boldly, taking a sip of his beer. He leaned forward, warming to his topic. "What if a law causes more harm than good? Should it be obeyed?"

I didn't need to ponder the question. "No."

"You're wrong," Rose said quietly. "If those judgments are left to individuals, we no longer live in a community. Standards must be upheld or the world unravels like a spool of thread."

"You're being too literal," I said.

"Have you ever tried to rethread a spool?" Rose asked, and her face flushed crimson, a sure sign her spirit was up. "It's impossible to make it as neat and tidy as it was originally."

"Maybe I don't like neat and tidy."

"Girls," Father interrupted, his voice crisp. One of the cardplayers said something to his companions, and they shared a laugh. Rose and I kept our heads down, and focused on finishing our root beers. We said little but pleasantries for the rest of the afternoon, but every so often my father winked at me, and I knew he was silently telling me he agreed with my perspective. When he looked at Rose I saw a more complex array of emotions play over his features—frustration, pity, puzzlement. At the time I was angry with her for displeasing him, but as Cat brought me into the jewel-toned speakeasy that smelled of smoke and vice, I wondered if he'd approve of how easily I slipped into an underground life, just as Rose acclimated to her role behind the sewing machine without skipping a beat. Had he thought too much of me? Had he missed something vital about her? Had I? I wondered if my father could have found a way to be proud of both his daughters as we began to wrestle with this city, if he could see what was slowly becoming clear to me.

Cat's speakeasy was nothing like the sawdust floor room behind the bowling alley. Velvet tapestries hung from low ceilings, with rust-colored exposed brick peeking through, glimpses of the basement's rough-and-tumble past. In the center of the space, black-and-white linoleum tiles created an octagonal dance floor, where people tangled limbs under a canopy of paper lanterns. A raised stage fanned out from a back corner, and I giggled to think of the house drummer trying to do his job wedged firmly between two walls.

Bessie disappeared into a small room behind the bar and exited with a package wrapped in plain brown paper and tied with a hemp cord. "Your uniform," she said, and handed to me.

I opened the package to find a silk, two-piece pajama set with a mandarin collar, in line with the vaguely Asiatic theme of Cat's joint. Though soft as water, the material was sturdy, and the bright jade color would stand out in a sea of bodies.

"Maude and Viv are the other girls," Bessie said, a note of bitterness in her voice. "Now that Lola's gone."

It didn't surprise me that Maude and Viv would work for Cat. This big city was getting smaller by the minute. I did wonder what transgression had sent Lola packing, but didn't press the issue. I determined that with this crowd, questions had to be broached carefully, like searching for a pickle in a barrel full of sharks.

"Should I put this on?" I asked instead, itching to try on the uniform.

"Have you got a cleaning costume?"

"Nope."

"Then put it on, but be careful. Cat doesn't like us to look a mess."

Cat didn't like any kind of mess, apparently. I spent most of the afternoon mopping the dance floor, washing the bar down with vinegar, and spot cleaning mystery stains from the hanging tapestries. I wore a cotton smock over my uniform, but that didn't keep my silk hem from regularly dipping into the sudsy water.

"Roll up your cuffs," Bessie said, exasperated. "You'll wreck the silk." She knelt at my feet and showed me how. "Tuck 'em in twice and they won't fall. Don't you know nothin'?"

That was a pretty fair assessment, but there was no

way in hell I'd admit it. "Thanks," I said, but she shook her head.

"We don't have to like each other, but we got to stick together down here."

Later, as the club got roaring, I still wasn't sure what she meant. Other than a few pinches on the bottom, I hadn't any trouble with the customers, and the girls didn't have time for pettiness or squabbles. Cat's place was hopping with cheerful, noisy Greenwich Village denizens thirsty for homemade gin and watery beer. The waitresses relied on each other to keep the drinks coming, and, according to Maude, we'd split our tips evenly at the end of the night.

My feet were screaming at me when the joint finally started to clear out. A few lost souls clung to each other on the darkening dance floor, and I was tempted to join them, to find someone to lean against and close my eyes.

"Cat wants this place spotless," Viv said as she passed by, bumping my shoulder. "The night's not over yet."

I started clearing tables, my movements sluggish, like I was underwater. As I slowly walked to the bar with an overflowing tray, Bessie came up next to me and lifted it from my hands.

"Thank you," I said, exhaling with relief. My arms had started shaking, and I wondered if I'd reach the bar without having to balance the whole thing on my head.

"I told you we stick together," Bessie said. "You'll do the same for me."

Something, possibly the late hour, possibly Bessie's friendlier tone, made me brave. "Is that why Lola got the boot? Was she a lone wolf?"

Bessie pointed to the glasses stacked against the mirror

behind the bar. "See that glass there? How's it different from the one next door?"

One was a standard martini glass, the other a special crystal glass reserved for the customers who scored the front tables, the politicos, theatrical folk and Park Avenue men about town. I'd learned that fact after a few harsh words from a real swell with a chip on his shoulder. "There's a world of difference between glass and crystal."

"You got it," Bessie said. "Lola didn't. She thought she was crystal, but we're all glass. If you break, there's another to replace you lickety-split. We've had a string of 'em who got the dustpan—Sophie, Rebecca, Daisy and now Lola— all gone." She returned to her place behind the bar and handed me a crystal short glass and a clean cloth. "I stick around," she said, pride evident in her voice, "because I keep my head down and get the job done."

From what I'd seen, Bessie's opinion of herself was a tad inflated. She gabbed plenty, but I didn't mind. I began to clean the already-spotless glass to keep her talking. "We're in Daisy's old room at Empire House," I said, hoping she'd spill something juicy. "Boy, she got out of there in a hurry."

Bessie rubbed a hand across her freckled chin. "That one surprised me. I thought she was ladylike and classy, as fine as Hungarian crystal, but it turned out she was common as any of us."

"She got into trouble with a fella?"

"That's the skinny. He must have been a real beast 'cause in the three years she worked here, she never brought him round." Bessie began to wipe down the cocktail shakers. "Cat knew what was going on—those two were thick, though you can never really tell if Cat trusts someone. Maybe the old lady at Empire House."

"Nell?"

"That's the one. She's a piece of work, isn't she?"

They all were. New Yorkers were shaped by action, noise and the poke in the eye of competition. Asher's eyes burned with the fire of the city, with the wit and wager of a challenge. I wanted to look like that. I wanted my brother to show me how it was done.

"Daisy ever mention her boyfriend's name?"

"Not to me she didn't," Bessie said, then caught herself. "I don't know what business it is of yours."

"I'm looking for a fella named Asher," I said, keeping my tone light. "He's a relative. When we last heard from him, he was in this neck of the woods. My sister and I think he might have gotten into some trouble. You said Daisy had gotten into a bind, and I just—"

"You just nothing. Don't go looking for things in here. In the city, yeah, take what you can grab, but this is Cat's place. Private property. You gotta learn what that means." Bessie picked up a common martini glass. "And if you don't—smash! Into the dustbin you go."

I returned to Empire House late that night. We each gave Sonny a dollar to keep the back door unlocked, and Viv and Maude, still jazzed up after our shift, stayed put in his kitchen to swipe some hot cocoa while I tramped upstairs. When I poked my head through the floor, the room was still lit, and I spotted Rose at the hidden window again, wearing our mother's nightgown, her expression alternately dreamy and distressed. I was used to my changeable moods—they swept through me like small tornados. I rather enjoyed them, those dramatic reminders that I was alive, but in Rose, usually so placid, it was disturbing.

"Hey-ya!" I said too loudly, and she jumped. "Can't sleep?"

Rose drew the collar of her nightgown tightly around her neck. "My thoughts are racing," she said, but didn't offer a reason. She smiled in an attempt to mask the disappointment in her eyes. It wasn't me Rose was waiting to come up through the floor. Only later did I realize I should have asked. I should have settled in next to her and offered her a listen, drawing her out. Instead, the familiar spike of irritation ran roughshod over any tender feelings.

"While you were off staring into space," I said, "I was acting like a regular Mata Hari."

"What did you find out?"

"Well..." What felt like real juice in the speakeasy felt like failure in the soft, quiet glow of the attic.

Rose frowned. "Well, what?"

I told her about Daisy's mystery boyfriend, and of my suspicions regarding Cat and Nell. "And Daisy worked at Cat's for three years. Even if Asher wasn't her guy, she had to have run into him at some point."

"I suppose," Rose said distractedly. "But there's got to be a reason why Nell and Cat would lie. It makes me uneasy, Ivy. Why deter us?"

I shrugged. "All I know is there are a lot of mysteries attached to Cat's Place and Empire House. We know Father was connected to this house—we have his painting—and it stands to reason Asher's story fits in somewhere. Since Daisy left under curious circumstances, it makes sense to start with her."

"I agree," she said, and went to the dressing table, pulled

out the top drawer and dumped out the contents onto her bed. It was a treasure trove of Daisy.

Rose spread the menus, theater tickets and assorted odds and ends on the floor between us. "We don't have much to go on," Rose said, picking up a matchbook, "but we might as well start with what we've got."

I smiled and dug in, relieved Rose's innate practicality had resurfaced. I brushed off any lingering concern about her and focused on the remnants of Daisy's life in the city. The girl knew how to live it up. She'd been to the theater on Bleecker Street for a matinee of *The Thief of Bagdad* and spent a whole night's tip money on a ticket to *Desire Under the Elms* at the Greenwich Village Theater. She'd dined at the Mandarin Palace in Chinatown and kept the fortune from her cookie: "Time is precious, but truth is more precious than time."

That was a kicker. I would have held on to it myself. These small pieces of Daisy's life were a nice introduction—I was starting to wish she hadn't left.

"Here's something," Rose said. She'd flipped open the matchbook. On the inside was written: 3 p.m. A—Dr. Harold Spence, 67 Oleander Drive. –D."

"Do you know where that is or what it may mean?" asked Rose.

"There are many reasons a woman sees a doctor," I said, though my mind immediately went to one.

"Yes," Rose said, lowering her eyes briefly. "But what about that A? What if it's for Asher? Maybe this is about him, not her."

"Let's investigate this doc further," I said. "And keep asking around about Asher as best we can."

Rose placed the matchbook to the side. "Ivy," she said

while placing it in the discard pile, "can you press Cat for more information?"

"I can try, but she's not exactly forthcoming." I didn't want to put the squeeze on Cat. I'd never felt intimidated by anyone before. When she was around I felt like I'd swallowed a stone.

"Maybe not in front of others, but if you caught her alone…maybe," Rose said. "She seems different speaking person to person."

"That might be true up in the dress shop, but I'm not sure that's the case down in the dungeon."

"Maybe you haven't given her a chance. She asked me a number of questions today, and seemed very interested in Mother and Father, and even Forest Grove. I almost wish we'd had more time to talk."

Rose touched my hand ever so briefly. "Caution usually isn't your first choice in any situation, even when warranted. Care to tell me why?"

I didn't want to scare Rose, or reveal too much of my own fears, but I had no idea if she also felt as though we'd walked into a play in the middle of the story, enraging the actors who'd already set their marks. I'd never felt unwanted before, and it was an unfamiliar feeling. Though Cat had employed us, and Nell had given us a room, I couldn't shake the fact that they'd done so grudgingly, as though our mere presence was an insult. My confusion unsettled me, and my usual impulsiveness, something in which I took great pride, suddenly became a detriment. Tread carefully, Rose was fond of saying, and it was becoming increasingly apparent that she had a point. "I'm simply being careful."

Rose smiled. "Perhaps this city is having a good influence on you, sister."

"Possibly," I said. "But I'd rather talk about how it's influenced you."

"Oh, posh."

"I think a certain Italian war hero could tell me a thing or two."

"War hero? Where did you get that?"

"Maude said he fought. I might have embellished a little bit."

"I'll ask Nell again about Asher soon enough," she said, eager to change the subject. "I've not much experience spotting a liar, but I am familiar with a break in pattern. If she acts strangely after my question, I'll know something is amiss."

Something was already amiss, I wanted to say. But I was used to the erratic and had no experience with patterns. "Good plan," I said, and placed my hand over her warm one, threading my fingers through hers, dreading the point where she'd pull away, where I'd have to let go.

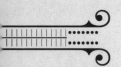 CHAPTER 9

Rose

IVY'S HAND WAS warm yet tentative. I thought I might pull my hand away, as we'd not been clingy sisters, even when we were little, except for the occasional "cuddle up" as we counted the seconds between lightning and thunder to estimate the distance of a storm. But something told me she needed me. And her eyes, they said a thousand words. She'd changed, somehow…that night working in God-Knows-Where.

I felt the city encroaching ever nearer to my heart. It was rain pouring out from a hole in the ceiling as Viv, Maude, Ivy, Claudia and myself ran for buckets and laughed as Viv tried to sing us to sleep over the incessant tapping the drops made at the bottom. I felt it in the way I was waiting, every second, to run into Santino again. I even lingered in the stairway for much too long, every time I went in or out of Empire House. Not to mention my clothes… The city was so hot. It had been officially declared a heat wave in

June, one that would last the summer. That heat made me choose loose clothing that exposed more of my skin than I'd shown since I was a child. The heat itself was running in tandem with our search for Asher. I started thinking of it as "Devil's Breath."

So, that night…instead of taking her hand, I pulled it away and said, "Let's go to sleep and sort the whole thing out tomorrow." I'd barely got the words out before Ivy passed out cold.

She fell asleep fully dressed. She must have worked so hard.

But doing what?

We rose early the next day and dressed quickly so we wouldn't miss breakfast.

Ivy wore another outrageous mix of some things she'd brought from home. Clothes she wore when she'd create her theatrical pieces. A blue chiffon blouse and a short white skirt with a frill near the bottom. To finish off the look, she had a black silk flower pinned to her short hair, like a Tahitian doll.

She scurried ahead of me like a child, but I couldn't get our beds made properly, the sheets were too big and had to be tucked under just right. "Leave it, Rose! What do we care?"

"I don't know…pride in our surroundings? Do we have any of that left?" I asked, but she was a flight down and an imagination away from me already.

When we got to the dining room it was already full. There were two seats, however, with clean plates, and Nell was right there waiting for us.

"Come in! Sit down The coffee is hot and the bread is fresh," she trilled.

"And the bacon is fatty!" said Maude.

Nell held out a starched white apron. I went to take it and then she pulled it back so quickly I thought the strings might snap.

"I suppose you can eat breakfast before you begin working. But please note that in the future I'd prefer for you to come down earlier, eat with Santino and Claudia in the Garden, and then help with the meal. Will that do, Rose?"

We sat down facing the group, and Claudia approached us. "Would you like coffee, miss?" she asked us both.

"God, yes," said Ivy.

"Yes, thank you," I said as the girl struggled with the heavy-looking silver pot.

"Let me help you, sweetheart," I said. She looked at me with gratitude. Ivy looked at me like I was keeping a secret.

"No, miss, today you sit. Tomorrow I'll let you carry the whole pot."

We laughed a little together. Ivy eyed me even more suspiciously.

"We've had a conversation, Claudia and I, I'm not keeping anything from *you*. I'm teaching the girl how to read," I said.

"And who gave you permission to do that?" asked Nell, whose hands were now on my shoulders.

The room had gone quiet. Everyone was looking at me, and Ivy shifted her chair away from me as she put her cloth napkin over her face. I'd embarrassed her again.

"I didn't think it would harm anything," I said.

"*Harm* is an odd kind of word, Rose Adams. Some things can seem the best intentioned, yet turn out to be the most damaging kind of thing. We don't need anyone selling this girl hopes and dreams. Do we, Claudia? Her life will be difficult. She needs to learn about that right now. She's tough, this one."

"But why wouldn't I be able to teach her how to read?" I asked.

Ivy kicked me under the table. Claudia smiled, and Nell sighed, clapped my shoulders once, dropped the apron on my lap and walked away.

"I think I won that one, Claudia!" I said.

"Eat your food, Rose," said Ivy.

Santino, who had waltzed in gracefully from the kitchen, was making sure everything was just so on the platters. *He's quiet and quick,* I thought.

Santino took a spoon to a water glass. He clanged on it until the room grew quiet again.

"Everyone? We have new tenants here at Empire House. Let's do a little introduction, shall we?"

"Hear, hear!" shouted Maude with a mouthful of bacon.

A large, overdramatic sigh came from the end of the table where three chubby women huddled together. Their conversation rapid and in another language…

"Adams sisters, meet the female politicos. All they do is plot to overthrow the government—it's tiresome, really. Don't call them by name. They don't believe in differences. Call them Sisters in Arms, one, two, three. Don't try to open the door for them, either. Everyone is equal, don't you know."

The Sisters in Arms were not laughing, however. They gathered up a pile of what looked like newsletters and left the room in a group. "You're a shit, Sonny," said one of them as they left.

"Didn't you notice we've evolved already?" asked Santino to their backs. "We've won! Relax, suffrage was a decade ago."

One of them turned around. "We've won nothing yet, and it's only been five years!" one of them said, and they left, slamming the front doors behind them.

"We actually have lovely talks when we've been drinking," said Sonny.

"And you've met Maude and Viv, obviously."

Viv just raised her eyebrows at me from over the table. I could tell she didn't like the attention Santino was giving us. "Other than the factory workers who leave early, come home late and are moving in and out of this place like transients, I believe we are all accounted for, so, what do you think, ladies?"

"'Life is but a stage, and all of us, merely players…'" said Ivy. "Thank you for introducing us to the cast of Empire House, as if we didn't already know everyone, Sonny."

"This is Rose's first breakfast with the entire 'cast' as you put it. Which was clever, by the way."

Ivy got up and bowed. She's so open, my sister. Ready for any and all situations.

I was the one who made the breakfast awkward.

"Do you prefer Santino or Sonny?" I asked. Everyone stopped laughing. I realized there'd been a rhythm of sorts to the previous conversation, and I'd clapped on the offbeat.

"It doesn't matter to me, not when I'm in the company of such a beautiful woman. I'd like to think that I could find the poetry that lives inside her," said Santino, staring straight at me.

"And I like to think I can find the bull that lives inside handsome cooks who are Casanovas," said Ivy.

Jimmy was waiting for me in the foyer of Empire House as we finished breakfast and I put on my apron.

He had a large basket with fabric in it. There was a note, as well. "This is for you," he said, dropping it at my feet.

I picked up the basket, confident I could do the work, and felt important.

"Poet around?" he asked.

As I unlocked the doors I said, "Santino? The chef? Yes, he's in the garden. But he's busy. Working. Now, who do *you* work for? Nell? Or Cat?"

"Both, really. Sometimes I drive, sometimes I work here. Whatever Cat and Nell need. I'm a handyman of sorts."

The Handyman of MacDougal, I thought, *would be a great name for a new poem, Edna.*

We were standing in the dim foyer playing an odd game of chess without knowing why. I will admit that I was not happy to be alone with him. Yet he might be the key to unlocking Asher.

"You're a looker, you know. Not like your sister—she's a loud kinda doll. You're a quiet looker. Always more dangerous. Santino better be careful if he's got his eyes on you."

"I'd think that would be the other way around, if you were any sort of gentleman."

"Well, I'm not. But he is, so be careful with him. The Poet's my friend. Don't go messin' with him."

"I couldn't even consider it! He's a loon!" I said too loud, too high-pitched, too nervous. "Besides I don't think I see an Italian Cook in my future. I'm trying to get my house back and get out of the city."

"Ohhh, I see. You don't know," he said.

"I'm really getting tired of talking to you," I said.

He lit a cigarette and handed it to me. "Trust me, you'll need it."

I don't know why…but I took it, inhaled and began to cough.

Jimmy laughed and came around the counter and hit me on the back.

"Look," he said. "He may be Italian, but he's done a good job savin' all his money. And he won awards in the war. Besides, he's educated. I know, that shocked me, too."

Different layers to Santino were not helping with the rising heat I felt whenever I saw him, or how I'd read and reread his poem a hundred times. I couldn't think about it, so I asked him about Asher instead.

"Have you ever met a man who could very well look like me, and whose name is Asher Adams?"

"You're a direct one, aren't ya? Sort of different than the other day when you wanted to stay in my car."

"Please, Jimmy…if you know anything…"

"Used to be a guy that might have looked like you… long gone, that one."

"Never mind," I said. I wouldn't get anything from him, either. But at least the questions got him to leave.

I went up to the penthouse, where Claudia helped me set up a little sewing room of sorts off in the corner, under the eaves. Too soon, I was sewing, and I didn't see anything but fabric for hours.

By the time I realized I'd finished the last garment in the basket, I saw the day was gone. The sun was a honey-gold color, and its rays reached in and encased our attic in the most delightful glow.

Knowing there was a chance I could get paid that very night, I picked up the basket and ran down the steps, losing a few pieces of trim and feathers here and there in my rush. I wanted to get back to Cat's Dress Emporium before she closed for the day.

I flew out the front doors and down the street, not even caring how it looked to others. I pushed past people returning from work and those who might be on their way. Everyone was busy in the city. Busy with their very own lives, mysteries, jobs and dreams. I was running, it's true, but I was noticing that perhaps it wasn't that I felt invisible at all. Perhaps it was that for the first time, I was being noticed.

Cat was just closing the doors to the shop when I rounded the corner of the alleyway.

"Wait!" I said.

"Rose?"

"Yes!" I reached the doors and she opened them for me. I tumbled inside, placed the basket at her feet, and then fell onto the couch to rub my sore arms.

"Why on earth were you running?"

"I wanted to make sure I got here before you closed."

"Why?"

"I finished the batch Jimmy brought over, and I thought I might get paid."

Cat sat next to me and began going through the work.

"I see. I hope you didn't rush…no…I see…oh, Rose. You are talented. I may have been blowing some smoke with you earlier, you know. A girl's got to have some self-esteem if she's gonna make it in this town. Have a straight back and a good smile that can take a few hits. So I thought I'd give you a set of compliments to make you feel good. Now? Now I can see I was right. These seams are simply perfect. And I love the notions. Wait here…" she said as she gracefully got up and floated to the back of the store. "I keep the cash in the safe."

I felt flushed with pride. I bit my knuckle out of pure excitement and leaned on the counter where a stack of papers stood too high. And because I'm who I am, those papers spilled out onto the floor and weren't papers at all. It was a stack of mail.

Sorting through it, I found our first solid clue as to Asher's whereabouts.

It was a postcard depicting a roller coaster in Coney Island. I don't know why I turned it over, really I don't. I'm not normally a snoop. Fate? Maybe…all I know is that the back wasn't blank, there was a note.

"It's best this way. Please don't worry.–D." The same script as the matchbook in Daisy's things.

And then, in smaller print at the bottom of the card, "Coney Island Cards & CO."

I slipped the postcard into my apron pocket.

"Is everything all right, Rose?" asked Cat, who emerged again, reaching out toward me with an envelope. The way she looked, just then, reminded me so much of Nell that very morning with the apron that I thought she might pull back, as well. Only she didn't, and soon I was holding real money in my hands. New York was proving to be kinder than I'd imagined.

"Now, will you show yourself out? I have some terrible bookkeeping to get straight."

"Do you need help?"

"Don't tell me you're good with bookkeeping, too?"

"Yes. As a matter of fact I always…"

"Yes, yes, yes…Rose. You need to learn how to breathe. I'll enlist your help another time. Try and get back to Empire House and enjoy your evening."

"May I speak with Ivy?" I asked.

"Of course. Just… Well, go through the magic curtains, my dear."

I had to tell Ivy about the postcard. And I wasn't a thief, so I thought I'd tell her while she was working so that I'd be able to put the postcard back on my way out. Besides, I just knew that we'd find an Oleander Drive in Coney Island, and I was eager to tell my sister.

I looked at the red velvet curtains where Ivy'd disappeared the day before.

I thought of going back to Empire House and waiting for her, but she might be drunk when she returned, or too exhausted to try and plan what our next move would be. I walked to the curtain and began to push it back, wondering for a moment if I'd return as changed as she'd seemed to be. Was I ready to take that step into the unknown?

"It's still daytime," I said to myself out loud. "They're probably still setting up. I can simply go down there, show her, figure out what we should do then go back to Empire House. Easy."

I took a breath and walked through the curtains and down the rabbit hole.

When I reached the bottom I realized what a mistake I'd made. Stupid Rose… It's always nighttime in a speakeasy.

I stood there and felt the entire bar go quiet. It wasn't at all like the speakeasy our father took us to a million years ago—it was fancier. And much more dangerous. There was no natural light at all; the entire room was dim, overcast with smoke and thick red hues coming from damask-covered lamps that stood on the tables and adorned the walls. There was a sultry sort of air that beckoned to me and heightened whatever sense of freedom and fast ways lived deep inside my soul. I tried to fight it.

I thought of how I must look. My dress, pretty though it was, wasn't at all as revealing as the other girls were wearing. I still had a pencil stuck in my hair, which was pinned up in my usual bun, but messier because of the heat and the flurry of sewing.

I saw Viv and Maude staring at me, both holding trays full of drinks. Maude looked sorry for me, but Viv, on the other hand, looked amused.

Ivy was standing next to a piano on a small stage.

She's singing, I thought with pride and horror. She'd been put on display. She looked at me and then quickly went center stage to begin singing. It took her a moment to see me, and when she did, she looked at me, dead in the eye. I couldn't figure out if she was pleading with me to sit down and get out of the limelight or leave.

Jimmy and Sonny were there, too, sitting at a small round table near the front of the stage. They were beckoning me to sit with them. Jimmy wasn't working; he was there with Sonny to relax. I remember thinking, *it must be nice, relaxing.*

"Go on," said Viv, who walked past me. "Don't want to make Ivy any more uneasy than you already have, do ya?"

"No, I…"

"Just grab a seat, fancy face. She's just started her set. She's good, ya know. You should be proud a' that one."

An unexpected surge of anger went through me that I thought I might throw myself on Viv and tear each hair out of her thin bob. Instead, I tried to smooth back my chignon, tucked the postcard in my shirtwaist and went to sit with the boys.

"Look at the newest Empire Girl! You are a vision. Tell me, dear lady, what brings you here to the dregs?" asked Sonny.

"Why aren't you at Empire House? Isn't it dinner?" I asked.

"Dinner's easy. Unless Nell is having a party, I set up the meal and Claudia serves it."

"He's got the best gig on the block," said Jimmy.

"You keep saying that, Jim…but every time I try to get you some work that doesn't involve breaking the law, you laugh at me."

I could tell the two of them were close. They had an easy, trusting friendship between them, and I liked seeing them smile at one another. *Like brothers,* I thought.

Santino looked so handsome. He was clean-shaven, and his perfect smile was alight with the drinks he'd already had. I blushed simply looking at him.

"I didn't mean… I was just coming down to see Ivy before I left for the day.…" I stammered, and wanted to slap myself for not being more confident.

"Here, you might want to take notes *later,*" said Jimmy, reaching over and taking the pencil out from behind my ear.

"Thanks. I'm kind of unprepared for a night on the town," I said.

"You look great, doll. You Adamses could win a beauty contest wearing pants," he said, but he was looking at Ivy, who was getting ready to sing. "Charming, that's what you are. All three of…"

"Shut it, Jimmy," said Sonny. "Not now."

"Three?" I asked.

"Yeah," said Jimmy. "You, Ivy and this guy over here…" He pinched Sonny's cheek.

"Nice," said Sonny.

"Shhh…she's gonna start. She sings like an angel, that sister of yours," said Jimmy.

Viv walked by with a short-stemmed glass full of clear liquid. "On the house," she said, and winked at Jimmy.

"I shouldn't…"

"Just drink it. I know how to make a drink, and it's not strong. You think I'd do that to you? Just want you to fit in, is all."

I took a sip as a peace offering. It didn't taste bad, citrus and some kind of bay, maybe. Liquor for sure, but not too strong.

It was then that my sister began to sing "Always." Father had loved that song.

She was wearing a beaded cap over her bobbed hair that shimmered under the spotlight. Her dress, black and too slinky to be called a dress at all was a little big for her small frame and the straps kept falling off her shoulders. She gracefully used her arms to help her not only "act" out the words of the song, but push the straps back up at the same time.

Her voice, more beautiful than I ever remembered it to be came ringing out soft and low, then grew. And in that voice I felt an ache that I didn't know existed inside my sister. Where I thought she was shallow, there was pain.

I finished my drink, and Viv was there with another. And another, I was smoking a cigarette.

By the end of her set, five songs I think, I was…intoxicated.

Ivy came to sit with us. She plopped herself in a tired heap across from me and lit a cigarette. I noticed Jimmy didn't offer to light it for her.

"Some kind of a gentleman you got there, Ivy," I slurred. I was slurring. I had to get out of there.

"Are you okay? What have you been drinking?" asked Ivy.

"Damn it, Jimmy, what did the two of you give her? You said it was light." Sonny was angry.

"Come on," said Jimmy. "Lighten up, Poet. We just wanted to see what kinda' moxy this one had hidin' underneath her proper, ya know?"

"That is not funny," I said, wagging my finger back and forth and then looking at it so close that my eyes crossed. It seemed like I had seven fingers on that hand instead of five.

"Ivy, I have this psstard. This pstcrd…this mail I have to show you came tday for Cat. Think she's lyin…can't seem to figure out…do I have sevn fingrs?"

"Good lord," said Ivy.

I was embarrassing her again. I pushed the postcard toward her and waited until she placed her hand on top of it. Then I got up, spilled my drink and made for the stairs.

I was glad I didn't fall down. I looked up the flight I'd walked down not a half hour earlier—or was it hours and hours? I couldn't tell—and got dizzy. Sonny was there again to catch me before I fell.

"I'm so sorry. That was a cruel trick, but I will say that I could get used to catching you. God, look at you."

"Who do you see when you look at me?" I asked.

"Shhh...don't talk," he said, and I realized he was drunk, too. He pressed his forehead against mine. "Just answer me, about catching you. Will you let me do that, Rose? Catch you, once, and twice, then again and again?" His face was so close to mine, too close.

"Kiss me," I said. "You know you want to."

He leaned in and his lips brushed against mine. A shiver went through me that gave me the single moment of clarity I needed to get myself up the stairs. I slapped him. Then ran to save my virtue.

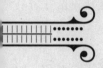 CHAPTER 10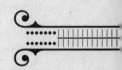

Ivy

"WHEN THE CAT'S away—" Maude said.

"The mouse sings torch songs," Viv finished. Their smiles weren't completely insincere as I wiggled into a black dress I nicked from the rack in Cat's Dress Emporium. Only widows wore black in the middle of June, so I figured I'd put it right back when I was done and no one would be the wiser. It was cut too big for me, but if I held my arms up like Bessie Smith, I'd not break any decency laws.

Earlier in the day, after I'd rubbed spots out of my millionth cocktail glass, the trumpet player for Cat's house band, a skeletal fella in a peg-leg suit, beckoned me over to the small stage in the corner. "I hear you can carry a tune," was all he said. He didn't have to go any further.

"Name it and I can sing it," I said with more bravado than I felt. I'd walked away when the sweet-faced girl beckoned me into the Republic Theater. I wasn't about to make the same mistake.

"We'll see about that," he said. "The name's Stan."

"Ivy."

I didn't know who told him I could sing, and I didn't care. Stan tugged me onto the stage and we ran through a couple of numbers, the guys letting me pick the tunes. I faced them to start, making connections eye to eye until I felt each musician could see into every part of me and knew I wouldn't lead them to nowhere.

"Tonight," Stan said when I finished. "I can't promise more than that."

I smiled at him. "It's enough."

Viv, Maude and I decided a singer needed a dressing room, so we commandeered one of the small storage closets behind the bar. After I dressed, Viv gave instructions to Maude for something she called "liquid insurance." It involved gin, honey syrup and lemon juice and would supposedly keep my throat from catching on fire. She didn't say what it would do to the rest of me. Viv settled me onto an oak barrel and then dug into her pockets, pulling out a pocket mirror and pot of lip rouge. In the glow of the yellow, overhead lightbulb, she applied the makeup to her lips with keen precision, and smoothed the spit curls leading to her precisely bobbed hair. A kohl pencil appeared from inside her sleeve. She rimmed her hooded eyes, took one last glance in the tiny mirror then turned to me.

Theater folks know that a bit of grease paint and colored oils can transform an actor into a character, but I was not prepared for this new Viv. She was pretty before, but now her face would turn the head of a prince. Viv's eyes burned with a dangerous excitement, the dark kohl high-lighting the green and gold in her hazel irises.

She tentatively placed her strong hands on my shoulders and stared at my face. "I've never painted anyone's mug but my own," she said after scrutinizing my features one by one. "So I could really do a number here."

"I trust you." *With makeup,* I thought. *And only makeup.*

"You do? I wouldn't."

"My hands are shaking too hard to hold that pencil."

"You? Miss Razzle-Dazzle? You'll knock 'em off their feet, especially after I'm done." She took a breath. "Now close your eyes. Those peepers need to be seen in the back of the room."

Viv went to work. After she finished lining my lids, she relaxed enough to start chitchatting again. "Your sis coming to watch?"

"Naw, she's working back in the penthouse."

"You two don't get along, do ya? Has it always been like that?"

Had it? Our lives in Forest Grove had been mostly separate. When we did bump into each other, Rose did everything she could to pluck every nerve in my body. I couldn't remember what it was like when we were young girls—the past was cloudy as a dirty martini.

"I suppose we've never seen eye to eye," I finally said. "It's been worse here in the city, or maybe it's the same only I notice it more in such close quarters. Rose belongs in the country—anyone can see that."

"Maybe not," Viv mused. "Maybe you need to let her have a little fun."

"No one's putting the brakes on her."

"Maybe she sees you living it up and thinks there's

nothing left for her but the scraps." Viv pinched my cheeks, hard.

"Ow! What was that for?"

"You needed a little color. I ran out of cheek powder." She stepped back, evaluating her work. "Perfect. Now go out there and bring the house down."

I walked back to the bar with trembling legs. All my life I wanted to be onstage, and now that the opportunity presented itself, my insides had turned to jelly. Maude passed me a drink and I downed it, the honey coating my vocal cords in a protective film.

"I'd say knock 'em dead, but we need these folks alive and thirsty," Maude said, giving me a forceful shove. "Get on up there before the band boys change their minds."

To my relief the fellas started up with "My Man," the first song I'd chosen during our practice session. I could tell it wasn't their usual kick, but they were game and I gave it my all. The room was full, but the guys and gals paid attention, clapping with more enthusiasm than I'd hoped. One pair of hands sounded louder than the rest.

Jimmy.

He'd taken a seat slightly to my left, out of my line of vision but in clear sight of the stage. Sonny sat next to him. Empty glasses littered the table.

I couldn't look at him. I sang to the room, to the bar, to a gangly gal in the front row who grinned joyously over the red froth of her sloe gin fizz.

I tried to focus on the music. *My Man…he's not much for looks…*

And no hero out of books… Who was Asher? Had he been a villain or a hero? My brother was made from my father.

He had to be good. He was what Rose and I had left, not a house, but blood.

Or was I fooling myself?

I dived back into the song, my voice giving me courage, and met Jimmy's gaze.

My man…

He sat, still and watchful, those Irish eyes burning my skin, making their mark. Sonny signaled to someone—Maude? Viv?—and the song ended. I took a bow, careful to only let the dress gape a little in the front, and then the band started another, jazzier number, then another, finally leading into "The Sheik of Araby." The audience laughed, unused to a woman singing the tune, and I took advantage of their surprise, shimmying across the stage, bringing them to a roar, making the most of it. I forgot about Jimmy and Sonny, Viv and Maude. I even forgot myself.

The band, picking up on my mood, transitioned back to a real torcher. I searched out Jimmy again, unable to help myself, and nearly lost my footing when I saw who was about to join his table.

Rose. Gaping at me with those eyes she shared with our brother.

Rose sat flush between Jimmy and Sonny, gaping at me with those eyes she shared with our brother.

It felt like someone turned me inside out. I wanted her to go, but I also wanted her up onstage, her solid presence holding me steady. Those conflicted feelings went into the song, and I finished my vocals with a sigh. The trumpet player tapped me on the shoulder as the applause rose around us. "You want to take a breather?"

"Yeah," I said, wiping the sweat stuck to the back of my neck. I went to the bar first, and Maude handed me another glass of honey liquor. "You're doing all right there, missy. Keep it up."

"Move your shoulders a little more," Viv said as she speared olives with jade-colored toothpicks. "That dress sparkles if you stand in the center of the stage. Make the most of it."

I thanked her, but my attention darted to Rose. She laughed at something Sonny said, but both men leaned in close over the tiny table. Rose's pale complexion and blond hair caught the light better than my dress ever could. In fact, Rose was aglow. She commanded attention.

"I've been thinking about what you said before," I said to Viv, feeling mean. "Bring my sister one of your gin rick-eys, on me. On second thought, bring her two or three. It's a long set. She wants to have some fun tonight, and I want to help her out."

"Is that right?" Viv, stone-faced, looked at me long and hard.

I stared her down until she shrugged. "Long as you take her home," she finally said. "This wasn't what I meant by letting her live a little, but I guess it couldn't hurt."

I went back onstage and belted out a few more jazzy numbers. I kept my attention away from Rose's table—too much of a distraction. I couldn't hear Jimmy's loud clapping at the end of each song. I thought he might have left, but I didn't want to glance over and appear overeager. When Stan gave me the eye, I knew the guys wanted to do an instrumental piece. I skipped back over to the bar.

"Old Viv's been mixing your sister some real hoochie-koo," Maude whispered. "It's doing the trick."

I looked over at Rose. Her posture was sloppy. She

moved to push a stray lock of hair from her forehead and poked herself in the eye.

"Oh, brother," I said, handing my empty glass back to Maude. "Thanks for the warning shot." I felt a pinch of guilt.

Jimmy didn't bother to get up when I approached the table. He didn't light my cig, and he didn't shower me with compliments. What he did do was hook a finger into the slouching fabric of my dress and slowly pull it up over my shoulder, brushing the damp skin with rough fingers.

"Let's get out of here," he whispered.

Rose was trying to tell me something, but her mouth crushed and garbled the words before they could form coherent thoughts. Finally, she pushed a postcard forward. It showed a man sitting in a metal car, climbing the steep incline of a roller coaster, the interminable wait until gravity took over. Halfway to the top of the crest, he seemed completely unaware of the perilous drop on the other side, the fall into nothingness. "What's this supposed to mean?"

Rose looked like she might vomit. Wild-eyed and embarrassed, made a run for the stairs back up to the shop. I slid the card into my bosom and stood to follow her.

"No," Sonny said, a gentle hand on my arm. "Let me. You've got a set to finish."

He was gone before I could respond.

"Take a load off," Jimmy said, and I sat down heavily, stunned by how quickly and fully the liquor affected Rose. Jimmy signaled to Maude, and she brought a pair of drinks.

"Can you hear your voice when you're singing?" he asked, breaking the solid wall of silence forming between us.

"What?"

"I'm wonderin' if you can hear how good you sound." Jimmy lifted his glass. "To talent," he said. *"Slàinte."*

"Slàinte," I repeated, and took a small sip. My thoughts turned to Rose again. "Will she be all right?"

"You can trust Sonny," Jimmy said, his expression turning uncharacteristically serious. "He's never given me reason not to."

"You're not a twenty-two-year-old girl."

"True enough," he said. "But I've known him for years, if that says anything."

"How long have you been in New York?"

"I left home more than a decade ago, only returned once when I was fighting overseas in the war. My mother sent me here. Trouble were brewing—with her right eye she saw Sinn Fein wanting to make me and with her left she saw Germans heading toward our potatoes with pickaxes. It made sense to put me on a boat."

"Really? You've been here that long? You sound so…"

"Irish?" Jimmy laughed. "Once you learn something you don't unlearn it. Get many foreigners where you're from?"

"Only if you count the fortune-teller from Poughkeepsie."

His laughter was interrupted by the shrill, earsplitting sound of a whistle. Viv stood on the bar, blowing away. "There's been a raid at Sullivan's down the block! Four squads!" She didn't look overly worried.

Jimmy grabbed my hand. "Come on."

"Will we really get raided?"

"Maybe, but it's not the coppers I'm worried about." He gestured toward the narrow staircase leading outdoors. People crowded into it, pushing and shoving, shouting insults to each other. "These folks lose their heads faster than their dollars."

There was a thickening in the air, a dense fog of panic and fear. Jimmy held his hand out again, but I paused and found myself knocked to the floor for my hesitation. Someone kicked my side and a pair of wingtips trampled over my dress. I curled forward to protect myself, but strong hands lifted me up, and my back was pressed to Jimmy's broad chest, his arms protectively folded over my body. He shuffled me away from the scuffle, down past the dressing room I'd used earlier, farther into the basement, into a damp corridor smelling of earth and water, as though we were burrowing ourselves underground.

"How much farther?"

"Turn to your right."

I was in a root cellar, or at least that's what it would be, come late fall. The bins were empty. The musty air felt cool on my exposed skin, and the single electric bulb hanging from a wire above our heads didn't add a bit of warmth. Jimmy overturned an empty barrel and perched me on it. I thought of Viv, painting my face with such determination. It was only a few hours earlier, but the memory was already watery at the edges.

Jimmy rooted in his pocket, drawing out a handkerchief. It was surprisingly white and crisp. He held it in front of his mouth for a moment, paused and then placed it inches from mine. "Spit," he ordered. I did what he said.

"You should see yourself," he said, rubbing at my face with the dampened cloth. "You look like a bootblack."

The edge of the postcard stabbed at my bosom. "I should go home," I said quietly. A panic had been rising, slowly and steadily, since Rose ran out of the speakeasy. What had I done to her? Had Sonny caught up with her? Was it better he did or was Rose better off alone? I had a quick image of her running, frightened and bleary-eyed, through the streets of Greenwich Village. "I really do need to go."

"Come on, now. Don't be like that," Jimmy said. He tucked my hair behind my ear. "Nell won't let you in the house looking like you went a few rounds with Jack Dempsey."

When Jimmy teased me his brogue came on thicker, and I thought about him living so far from his home. I also wondered if he had little brothers and sisters back in Ireland, pale, raven-haired children who missed him desperately or thanked the heavens he left when he did. As Jimmy dabbed my cheek with the linen handkerchief, sweeping the dirt away with soft, gentle strokes, I thought it surely must be the latter.

I forgot everything else for a moment and closed my eyes, relishing his touch. I could feel the heat of his fingers through the thin fabric. The handkerchief brushed my throat, collarbone, the swell of my breast.

I opened my eyes. Jimmy dropped the cloth. He moved closer to me and tilted my chin up with one finger. "I'm going to call you Beauty," he said, his eyes darkening. "Does that lack a certain poetic grace?"

"I'd expect something more original from an Irishman," I joked, but it came out a whisper.

His mouth on mine was a revelation. I grasped at his shoulders, the muscles of his arms, wanting more, greedy and desperate.

He brought his mouth to my neck, and I thought of the couple under the arch at Washington Square Park, the way the man devoured the woman, the way the woman tilted her head back, welcoming him. I pulled Jimmy closer.

"Say yes to me," he murmured. *"Say yes tonight."*

And wasn't that the way of this city, say *yes, yes, yes,* and keep saying it because there was no end to what it had to offer. *Yes, yes, yes.*

He'd moved to my shoulder, the front part of my dress falling to my ribs. With an intake of breath he paused, plucking the postcard from the fabric and tossing it to the floor. I looked down and didn't see the man on the roller coaster, but the other side. –D. Daisy.

"I…I need to go."

For a moment it was like he hadn't heard me, but then he lifted his head, eyes glassy and features soft. "Now?"

"Yes."

Jimmy straightened up. "There aren't any girls in this city, Ivy," he said quietly. "Do you know what I'm telling you? Only women live here."

"There are plenty of girls," I countered. "The women warn them about men like you so they stay away."

Anger pulled at the corner of his mouth, just for a moment, and then he laughed. "True enough. Come on, I'll walk you home," he said. "Keep you safe from the wolves like me."

"That's not necessary."

"Now, Beauty," he said, lifting my dress to a modest height, "I don't want you tellin' those other girls I'm not a gentleman, do I?"

The kitchen was quiet when I let myself into the back door of Empire House. I crept up to the penthouse, only to hear the sound of retching as my head popped up through the floor. I got the basin under her chin just in time.

"I'm so sorry," Rose whispered. Her features collapsed in misery. "So, so sorry."

"No," I said, wanting to cry. "I am."

She heaved once more, emptying her stomach. I smoothed her damp hair and rubbed circles on her back. "Did you see it?" she mumbled as I tucked her back into bed. "Postcard…match."

I drew the postcard from my bosom and placed it next to the other one, along with the matchbook we found in Daisy's things. The images were identical. I felt a rush, a need to run out the door, but Rose was in no state. "I do see it," I said. "Now go to bed. We can talk this through in the morning."

I brought the full basin to the Washing Room, but it was locked. The kitchen was still dark, so I headed down, wondering how much of a crime it was to dump what I had into the sink.

Sonny's kitchen was spotless, smelling of lemons, so I didn't have the heart to soil it. I ended up tossing the basin into the bushes outside. When I passed the garden on my way back in, I saw the cherry-red glow of a cigarette behind a lilac bush.

"What's good for the gander is not good for the goose?" I called. "You owe me one of those."

Sonny stepped onto the patio. He looked older in the moonlight, not haggard but weary, as if my request was another in a long line of things that disappointed him. "Smoking is not good for women." He sighed.

"Now that's a tired line," I said, holding my hand out.

"I'd say liquor does more harm, given the state of my sister upstairs."

"Would you know anything about that? Viv kept those drinks coming more often than the A train."

I didn't respond.

"I would've stopped it if I'd realized it was going to her head so quickly," he continued. Sonny passed me a cigarette and lit it. "I personally don't find that kind of prank funny."

I shrugged. "Nobody's perfect," I said, which wasn't admitting or denying much of anything.

Sonny gave me a pointed look.

"Did you put her in bed?" I asked, going on the offensive.

"I walked her in the house. That's it."

"Good, but I want you to remember—do her wrong and you'll have to deal with me," I warned. "And our brother. He could pound you flat before you even raise a fist." I didn't know why I said that. I meant to say our father would, but it hadn't come out that way. Mentioning either of them was childish and made no kind of sense. I picked up the cigarette and noticed my hand was trembling.

"I was under the impression you hadn't found your brother yet." He didn't smile, but there was sympathy in his voice, an understanding that embarrassed me deeply. He noticed, and was kind enough to change the subject. "It's Sunday morning already. What do you have planned for the day?"

I smiled at him, grateful. "I'm going to grab a few hours of shut-eye, then I'm going to eat a fabulous hot cake breakfast prepared by you."

"Is that right?"

"Yep. Then I'm going to put on the dog and start exploring this city with my eyes wide-open."

Sonny lit another cig. "Just don't get anything stuck in them. There's a lot of garbage blowing around these days."

"You're a real ray of sunshine, you know that?"

He shrugged. "You caught me on an off day."

We stood side by side in the moonlight, smoking. The silence wasn't companionable—he had something to say and whatever it was took some gearing up to spill.

"You taking your sister?" he finally said.

It hadn't occurred to me. My plan didn't include meandering down Fifth Avenue like a Sunday tourist; I was going to get all dolled up and drop in the Republic Theater and demand an audition. Rose would probably try to talk me out of it. Would Sonny? I figured he had the same attitude toward the revolutionaries as Jimmy. "I think Rose is sticking around Empire House tomorrow. It's hard to get that girl to leave the attic."

Sonny tilted his head toward the still-dark sky. "Did you even ask her?"

"I'm taking her to Coney Island next Saturday to stroll the boardwalk. That's more her speed."

"On the subway?"

"I don't own a chariot."

Sonny shook his head. "You'll be packed like sardines. Boiling sardines, in this heat. I'll have Jimmy drive you."

He wasn't asking a question, so I couldn't say no. How had he done that, made an order sound like a kindness? I didn't want to face Jimmy after what had happened in the cellar, but I guess I'd only have to stare at the back of his head. "Okeydoke," I agreed, regret immediately pooling in my stomach.

But it was a week away. I shrugged it off and put my hand out for another cig. We smoked next to each other, both of us looking at the moon, and then I trudged upstairs.

Empire House
June 7 (or maybe 8?), 1925
Dear Mr. Lawrence,
Wasn't it Friar Lawrence the wise monk who sagely advised Romeo and Juliet in a fruitless effort to avoid tragedy?

Okay, it was Friar *Laurence,* but maybe you could still give me a bit of wisdom and we could avoid the tragic part?

I did a lousy thing tonight. I got my sister roaring drunk. I feel guilty about feeding her the gin, but I don't regret it. Confusing, right? If I had the chance to do it again, I might. Does that make me a degenerate? Tell me, great Friar!

No Asher yet, but I do have some good news: Rose and I are both gainfully employed. Our dear Rose has gotten a job slaving away at a sewing machine making dresses for a la-de-da ladies emporium. I've found less taxing—but infinitely more amusing—work as a waitress. How do you like that?

I wish we were getting along better. I'm alternately angry with her and worried for her. I want her to go far, far away, but then I want her waiting for me when I get home, even if she's just in the bed next to me, snoring away. In some ways, I'd like her to go back to Forest Grove, completely erased from my new life here in New York, but then I think of living alone, and I'm learning I'm probably not cut out for the solo ride. Each day Rose's independence grows like a wildflower, while I swat at my encroaching fears buzzing around my head like angry wasps.

Why do those thoughts give me such turmoil? Is there something wrong with me? Wait...I'm not sure if I want you to answer that question....

Sincerely,

Ivy

PS: I may have had a little nip myself tonight. I'm going to sneak out and post this before I give it a second thought.

June 10, 1925

From the Law Offices of J. W. Lawrence:

Dear Miss Adams,

For your information, I do spend many an afternoon har-har-har-ing until closing time. My clients find it most peculiar. Your note, incidentally, prompted the faintest snicker, at most. If you'd like a guffaw—try harder.

Empire House sounds, if not suitable, then comfortable enough. I was relieved to hear you'd found employment. Bringing food to hungry people is a most noble profession, but hardly a profitable one. Please let the other Miss Adams handle the financial matters while you organize the hunt for your brother.

I do have information to share, information which may prove distressing, which is why I am glad it is the unshockable Adams sister with whom I am corresponding. I've got an old acquaintance working in the archives in Washington, D.C., a fellow I regularly caught glancing over my shoulder during law school examinations, so I felt no hesitancy in asking him to peek into our nation's military records. It appears Asher John Adams served in the 308th in the war, commonly known as the Lost Battalion. As he survived Argonne, more information was not recorded. Take that for what you will—I'm certain you've heard stories of that rough-and-tumble—and heroic—group of men. Keep in mind that I've learned in my profession to reserve judgment until the sketch of a person's life is filled in at least halfway, and even then the blank spots can only be shaded in context.

Please keep in touch.

Sincerely,

J. W. Lawrence

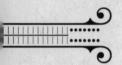 CHAPTER II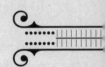

Rose

HERE'S WHAT I remember: my sister's beautiful voice and the peculiar desire I had to get onstage with her and sing a duet. I remember Santino's breath on my face. I remember running out ahead of him, and I remember he was standing next to me outside again. The night air was simply beautiful and cool. I started to wonder about the fact that I liked the nights in Manhattan better than the days. A lady, a true lady, would like it the other way around. And she wouldn't have gotten drunk in a speakeasy or felt her body pulled, as if by a magnet, to a man she barely knew.

"Rose…" His voice trailed off as I tried to walk ahead of him down the alleyway using the brick walls to keep me standing.

"I told you to leave me alone, didn't I?"

"Actually, you didn't. Look, I'm just going to walk behind you and make sure you get back to Empire House safe. You don't need to turn around or anything. You don't even have to talk to me."

"Good, 'cause I don't wanna…" I said.

He was a gentleman and did as he said. He didn't bother me at all, simply made sure I got into Empire House safely.

The disappointment that I felt shocked me. I'd wanted him to talk to me, to kiss me, to hold my hand. I wanted him to follow me up the stairs at Empire House. I wanted things I didn't even understand, and I was frightened.

Here's what I don't remember: anything else.

I woke up with a terrible headache, a sore throat and my sister saying, "Get up, sleepyhead—we got ourselves a ride to Coney Island. It won't be till next week, so you can thank me later. We'll see the diving horses, ride some rides and maybe even find our brother. That's some kind of clue you found. Well done. Now, what do you say, my little gin blossom?"

I burst into tears the way I used to when I was a little girl, a fierce flow of crying that came out of nowhere and had no bounds.

"What is it? What's the matter?" asked Ivy.

I couldn't speak. I sat up in bed, and she sat on the side of me, trying to soothe me as I cried.

"Okay, let's do this. I'll ask a question and you nod yes or no. Okay?" she asked.

I nodded yes.

"Are you upset about last night at the speakeasy?"

I shook my head, no. And then, of course…nodded yes. And then no again.

"I get it," said Ivy. "Let me try again. Is it Asher? Because we'll find him. Maybe even today."

I shook my head. No.

She took a good long look at me. Up and down, before she asked the next question. "Is it Sonny?"

I didn't have to answer or nod. I just cried harder.

Viv and Maude were cackling over something on their side of the penthouse. Were they laughing at me? I couldn't even bear it, so I cried harder.

"Shut your traps a second," Ivy yelled at them. "Did he hurt you? Rose, did he touch you? Because I'll…"

"No, nothing like that," I said, finding my voice to protect him. What was the hold he had over every single one of my emotions? "I made a fool of myself, Ivy. And Santino…I don't know what is stirring inside of me. What could this be? It hurts me to look at him. I don't know who I am anymore."

"Is that all? Jeez, Rose, I thought you were in trouble!"

I threw myself back under my covers.

The week drew out long and hot before me. My days were filled with sweltering, attic sewing binges, clinking dishes, playing chase with Claudia and trying to avoid falling headlong into Santino's ill-hidden stares.

Though each day brought the dreaded "newness" with it, I was not afraid of the city anymore. I began to enjoy my new routine and the easiness that came with it.

A few trips back to Cat's and I had a nice sum in my money box. Those trips usually ended up with Cat bringing me downstairs to hear music and keep an eye on Ivy waiting tables. She also wanted me to join her for a drink.

"I don't think so," I said the first night she offered.

"Pish posh. Don't be dull," she said, escorting me across the dance floor, her beaded dress sparkling in my eyes like stars, and in my ears like raindrops. Her long fingers seemed permanently attached to the cigarette holder, and her advice fell on eager ears.

"Lighten up, Rose. That night when you tossed your cookies, Jimmy and Viv were havin' a bit of fun with you is all. Have a drink with me, and I'll make sure you keep your wits. A girl does need to know how to drink if she's to survive the city. Think of it that way, Rose. It's survival!"

She had a point.

I didn't overdo it until the night before we went to Coney Island. There was a party at Empire House, and that was one I wasn't going to miss. I wanted to feel the way Ivy must have felt on our first night in the city. The evening started off light with music and dancing. The garden glimmered with lanterns, candles and bubbling laughter. Before I knew it, I was tangled up with both of my new-found favorite intoxications, gin and Santino. Through a smoke-filled haze I watched my Ivy arrive, but I didn't care. I wanted to keep dancing.

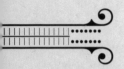 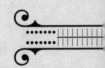

CHAPTER 12

Ivy

ON FRIDAY NIGHT the old thermometer wouldn't take a dip below steaming, and all but the whirring fans came to a standstill in Manhattan as folks tried to stay cool. For once, Cat's place was nearly cleared out as the clock hit ten. The hard-core drinkers of Greenwich Village, rendered listless by the heat, slowly floated up the stairs in search of relief. The basement speakeasy had somehow sucked up the night's feverish air, the tapestries turning the room into a kiln that glazed every one of us in sweat.

"They all wanted water," Maude complained. "I told them we ain't a fountain. No reason why they can't head over to the park and take a dunk."

"Maybe we should have made gin ice-cream floats," I said, sighing as I emptied the tip jar. Our take wouldn't buy a block of ice.

Cat appeared from one of the tiny rooms behind the bar, looking remarkably fresh in a bright chartreuse-and-aqua-striped slip dress. She crossed the empty dance floor, scowling at the band as if its desolation was their fault. "Go home," she said, waving a dismissive hand. "I'll get more fans in here tomorrow night. This heat is unbearable."

Sweat had completely wilted Stan's suit, and he sighed in relief. He nodded to the guys and they disassembled their instruments quickly, most likely grateful they were heading home to cold-water flats. Maude and I placed cool cloths on the necks of the few remaining rummies slumped over the bar. "They'll sleep here," Maude assured me. "It wouldn't be the first time."

Cat collected the cashbox and dismissed us, too. "Leave before you melt all over my floors," she said, and Maude and I scrambled for our things, bolting up the stairs before Cat could change her mind.

Being outdoors only improved our situation slightly— the night couldn't shake the day's heat no matter how hard it tried—but our spirits lifted on the walk home. Some kids had pried open a fire hydrant, and the water ran slowly down the gutters like a lazy river. I was tempted to kick off my shoes and dunk my feet. Heck, I was so desperate I thought I might toss off my dress and swim home.

Maude fanned herself irritably. "I don't know how we're going to get any shut-eye."

"Is the Rivoli open all night? We could take turns sleeping," I suggested. I had read in the paper that the Rivoli Theater had installed an air-conditioning machine—buy a ticket and get a free trip to the North Pole.

Maude shook her head, the damp ends of her bob sticking to her cheeks. "Forget it. The line goes around the block and then some. Got any other ideas?"

I didn't. Sighing, we turned onto a more residential street. Maude whistled. "Now, they've got the right idea."

Whole families slept on fire escapes, bare limbs dangling at odd angles. The metal structures snaked up the walls like extended bunk beds, each one occupied. Some threw their mattress down first, but others stretched out over a pile of blankets, which I imagined felt like sleeping on a waffle iron. I'd never seen anything like it. "Aren't they worried about the little ones?"

"Naw," Maude said. "Look at that doll up there."

A small girl lay nestled against another child on an iron platform two stories up. Her pale face and blond hair glowed angelic in the streetlamp. She spotted me staring and wove her fingers through the bars to wave hello.

My mind immediately went to Rose. I wasn't struck by a memory or led by guilty feelings; I simply felt something I'd never felt before—the overwhelming desire to know what my sister was doing right at that very moment. Was she broiling up in the penthouse, tossing and turning under the dirty skylight? Was she sitting in Sonny's kitchen with a lemon ice?

Was she wondering about me?

I took Maude's arm. "Let's go back to Empire House. Nell doesn't charge for cold showers, right?"

"I wouldn't count on it," Maude said, but she quickened her step to match mine.

We heard the party from the street, the sound of female laughter, light and airy and somehow cool, drawing us toward the chaos that surely awaited in the garden. Maude and I had torn through the kitchen and out the back door, nearly stumbling over the Victrola someone had dragged out of the living room and set just outside the back door, and we stood openmouthed at the scene before us. Girls danced the Charleston in bare feet, hands clutching sweating glasses of gin, while others draped themselves over benches, and in some cases, the low hedge lining the wooden fence. It was as if the crescent moon had hooked Empire House by its chimney and pulled, dumping its inhabitants, half-dressed and dazed, into a private New York jungle.

"Wowza" was the only thing I managed to say.

Maude kicked off her shoes. "You know what they say about the heat? If you can't beat it, revel in it!" She joined the other girls, throwing her long limbs in the air, her awkwardness made fluid by pure joy.

I wanted to join her, but first, where was Rose? Instinctively, I looked up to our window, but the penthouse was dark, no sister pounding at the window. Still, the sharp nudge of a warning elbowed my consciousness, the feeling that something was going on and I was about to step right into it. I studied the dance floor again and noticed a couple tripping through the fox-trot, half leaning into each other to stay upright. It wasn't Rose and Sonny, but Jimmy and Viv. He'd peeled down to his undershirt, and his trousers were rolled to the knees. His broad hand spanned the small of Viv's back. After a moment he noticed me staring and winked. I wasn't sure what that meant. *You're next?* Or... *Mind your own beeswax?*

Maude motioned for me to join her, but my feet wouldn't move. The party seemed untouchable, an abstract painting I admired but could not understand. I sat on the stairs and leaned my cheek against the Victrola, letting the music zip through me, vibrating against my ear. It should have razzed me up, but still I didn't budge. Why was I such a lump? I thought of my brother, living on the outskirts of life. *Where are you, Asher?* I thought. We could sit on these stairs and share a cig, and none of this would matter. Together we could shine.

Viv spun away from Jimmy, and he crooked a finger toward me. Part of me wanted to go to him, to run my fingers through his damp hair, to feel his hand lifting me slightly toward his expansive chest. The other part of me wanted the party to break off and spin away into the night like a wayward star. I closed my eyes, searching for an answer in the music.

"You're gonna give yourself a headache," Viv said. She stood in front of me, blocking my view of Jimmy. She plucked at her dress and hair, both limp against her body. "Your sis was in a state," she continued. "She was climbing up Sonny like a beanpole. I'd go check on her if I were you."

Escape. "Will do," I said, pushing myself to standing. I wavered, unsteady without the music to ground me. Jimmy grabbed another girl from the crowd and spun her in circles.

"I'd bring a bucket," Viv advised, smirking. "And some aspirin powder."

Again? I snagged some supplies from Sonny's kitchen and climbed to the penthouse. On the way up, I pictured Rose dancing with the other girls, arms reaching high, carefree and careless, their faces aglow with the joy of living. I saw her in Sonny's embrace, laughing and gay. It was startling how easy it was to place her in the thick of things. Had this city changed her as much as—loath as I was to think it—it was changing me?

I could hear her voice as I poked my head into our attic bedroom. A single lit lamp brought a blush to the room's bare walls. The air was heavy and damp. Rose lay on her bed, restlessly crumpling the sheets with her hands. She mumbled Sonny's name over and over.

He was crouched next to her.

The way he was looking at my sister—a potent mixture of reverence and desire—was the way every woman wants to be seen in a man's eyes. A good sister would think, *Bully for you, Rose,* but…I was not a good sister.

"I should have kept a better eye on her," Sonny whispered. "But you know what? She was having fun. She's a beautiful girl, but she's a stunner when she's smiling. It wasn't just the booze, Ivy. She was happy."

I dropped the bucket. "You should leave. I can take care of this."

He turned, and his eyes adjusted to me, switching from reverence to pity, from desire to mild curiosity. "I don't mind staying."

"I'd mind if you did," I retorted. "And so will Rose if she gets up heaving."

Sonny stood and patted Rose's hand. She murmured something incomprehensible and he touched her cheek in an effort to soothe her. "You haven't found him yet, have you?" he asked softly.

"No," I said. "And I don't know if we ever will."

Sonny hesitated for a moment, and then patted my shoulder in a brotherly manner. "You will because you have to," he said before leaving. "That's as good a reason as any."

Was it? I wondered, but there was no one to ask.

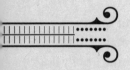 # CHAPTER 13

Rose

THE SUN WAS relentless, and Maude's music was too loud. I looked down at my bare arms and felt my hair loosed down my back.

"How did I even get to bed?" I asked, pulling a pillow over my face to drown out the day and stretching my legs out so they dangled over the side of the bed. The morning was hotter than Hades.

"Oh, forget about it," said Ivy. "You don't want to know."

"You don't remember hanging all over Sonny in the garden?" asked Viv.

"Stop teasing me, Viv. I'm too tired for that," I said.

"Too bad she's not teasing," said Maude.

I sat straight up and surveyed the room. My vision was blurry, and my head seemed to echo my heartbeat, but the penthouse, bathed in morning sunshine, depicted my sister and our roommates—who were in various stages of dress—

in the warmest of possible lights. Vignettes of Greenwich Village Girls: Viv tying Claudia's apron with a cigarette in the corner of her mouth and one eye squinted against the smoke. Maude, who patted Claudia's hair reflexively as my little friend sent me a smile and scooted downstairs. Ivy, who was placing bangles on her arms, inspecting each one carefully.

"Careful," teased Maude. "Those might burn you if you aren't careful, especially if you wear them to the shore." She grabbed some of the bracelets off Ivy's wrist and ran to my bed, bouncing me so that I thought I was seasick, and holding up one of my arms to accept the stolen bracelets. "You two need to share. That's what sisters do. Viv and I were just sayin' the other day how you don't even seem like sisters at all!"

Ivy glared at us and tied a bow on a pretty pair of black heels.

"Ivy, speak true. What happened? Should I be ashamed? Did I throw myself on him?"

"Listen, I said it before…I'll say it again. You don't want to know."

The look in her eyes spoke volumes…and too soon one memory surfaced. Kissing Santino…for a very long time.

"Get up, Rose. We have things to do today."

Then I thought of something, and popped my head out from under the pillow I'd pulled back over my eyes. Ivy was getting my dress ready.

"Who did you say was taking us to Coney Island, Ivy?"

"Who do you think? Jimmy, of course."

"Is Santino…"

She sat next to me again and pushed my dress at me. I could tell she was calming herself down so she could get me out of bed and downstairs. She spoke slow, like I was hard of hearing.

"They both have the day off today, though me and Jimmy have to go to Cat's later, but don't worry. What happened with him already happened. We can talk about it later."

"Okay," I said. My head was pounding, and even though her patronizing was making me a little angry, she was right.

When we were ready to go, she looped her arm in mine, and we went downstairs to breakfast.

We walked into the bright, sun-filled dining room together, and I flinched. It smelled strongly of fresh fruit, toast and fine coffee, all of it making my stomach heave. I walked over to the table where Santino laid out the morning meal. It wasn't the usual fare. "You aren't the only one who got the day off, Rosie," he said from behind me. "But Nell and Claudia put together a fine feast, as well."

Ivy and I sat down together, but Santino sat across from us just looking at me. Then he got back up, stumbling toward the front door, opening it for Jimmy.

"Crap, he's drunk," said Ivy, whose body stiffened. She was nervous, I just didn't know why. I turned around to face the two men who were going to take us to Coney Island. They looked like little boys who'd been up to no good, and they were giggling.

"You're *both* drunk," she said. "Boys, really?"

"Perhaps we should take the train," I offered.

"It'll take an age," Ivy said, "and I told you I have to work later. If we don't go with them, we'll have to wait another week to figure this thing out."

Jimmy walked over to the table, poured a cup of coffee and took a bite of a roll before proceeding to speak to my sister with his mouth full. He winked at her first and I felt her relax. *What is going on?* I wondered.

"Beauty, I'll admit, we were drunk a little while ago… had things to work out. But now? We're fine. You gals ready?" He rubbed his cheek, which I realized had a bruise on it.

"What happened to you, Jimmy?" I asked.

"He did," said Jimmy, nodding his head toward Santino. They both started to laugh.

"What was it about?" I asked.

"Santino was defending a certain lady's honor…" said Jimmy.

"Whose?" I asked.

The entire room broke into laughter. I understood, but didn't want to understand.

"So, ya ready or what?" asked Jimmy.

Ivy shot me a look that was excited, wary and afraid all at the same time. We got up, and she skipped ahead of me with Jimmy down the front stoop steps. Santino held out his arm, but I wouldn't take it.

He didn't take offence, but he matched me, step by step, each of his growing more exaggerated. When we got to the bottom step, we both laughed. Only I had to hold my head. Even my jaw was pounding. Ivy shot me another warning glance from the backseat of Jimmy's sedan.

"You have a handsome laugh," I said.

"Thank you," he said. "I was flattered when you told me the same thing last night."

"Is anyone going to tell me what actually happened? Seeing as you all seem to be in a fine mood, I'm put off guard."

"Well, you complimented my laugh, told me I could call you Rosie, and you let me kiss you. Nothing more, nothing less."

A wave of nausea rose unbidden and I tried to keep smiling, but sat on the bottom stair. He sat next to me.

"And by the way," he said, "last night I told you that your laugh sounds like the way water sounds as it travels over stones. Powerful and quiet at the same time."

"Rose, get in the car. God, do you think you could not sit in protest over everything?" said Ivy. Then she pointed at Santino, "And you, Poet? I warned you." There was steel under the laughter in her voice, and her eyes were clear. Jimmy didn't notice, but Sonny did.

The car was hot. I was so afraid I'd retch that I stared at the city going by and stayed still and quiet. Saturday in New York was a lovely thing. The city was always bustling with the prospect of adventure and life-altering opportunities.

Santino and Jimmy were singing in the front seat of the car, and Ivy was leaning forward and talking to them, an effervescence streaming off her that I wanted to bottle and drink. Looking at them was a mistake, because I couldn't take my eyes off Sonny.

He looked even more handsome in the front seat of Jimmy's car. He was a man who liked to laugh, and Jimmy seemed to know all the jokes. They were both so sturdy, yet complicated. Each of them seemed to be hiding something deep inside.

Santino was, to me, the more interesting of the two. I watched him talk, sing and laugh with Jimmy, but sitting in the back, I could only see his profile. He didn't turn around to talk to me; I supposed Ivy had scared him. But he looked up at me and caught my eye in the rearview mirror. His fine nose and strong chin…his eyes that always carried a searching kind of look. And again, my heart seemed to skip a beat every time he glanced my way.

I wanted to remember more about last night because the fleeting images were making my mouth hurt. The ache inside me, one I did not understand, was quietly eating away at me.

"Hey, sourpuss. We are on a grand adventure. Look! The Brooklyn Bridge… Come on, Rose, don't ruin this. We're so close…" I could see she enjoyed that little inside joke about finding Asher. I smiled at her, but I could tell by her posture, and by the way she kept trying to tangle me up in their conversation, that she was worried I'd ruin everything, and that thought reminded me of a day, years ago:

"You always ruin everything," Ivy said when she was thirteen and I was fourteen. She was having so much fun as she began turning from girl to woman. I, on the other hand, thought it was messy and strange. She'd wanted to accept an invitation to a party being thrown by the parents of a handsome young man in town.

Father had been away, and Mother said Ivy could go, but only if I went along, as well. I refused, and that's when she told me I "ruined" everything. She didn't speak to me for a month.

"Sing with us. Come on, Rose…" said Ivy, bringing me back to the present.

"Meet me down at Luna, Lena, meet me at the gate.… Do not disappoint me Lena…" Then she hummed a bit, forgetting the words, as Jimmy and Santino forgot and remem-

bered other words. It was quite funny and I began to feel more alive.

"We'll take a trip up to the moon
For that is the place for a lark
So meet me down at Luna, Lena
Down at Luna Park…"

The end was sung off-key on purpose with the clashing notes hanging in the air amidst their laughter.

Before I knew it, the four of us were leaning against Jimmy's car and staring out at the beautiful ocean. "I'd love to go swimming," said Ivy.

"There's a shop, the Seaside Dream, right next to Nathan's. They have some nice suits you can get. Only make sure you get a real skimpy one, Beauty," said Jimmy.

"We don't have money to waste on that kind of frivolity, Ivy," I said.

"You don't. But I do. I'm flush. I'll buy them. We deserve a treat, don't you think? Boys, give us a sec alone, would ya?" said Ivy.

"The way I figure it, you're both leanin' on my car…" began Jimmy.

Santino punched him playfully, and ran down the beach, and Jimmy ran after him.

"Absolute children," said Ivy.

"Why do you want to go swimming?" I asked. "We're here to find the card shop, right?"

"Right, but Rose…we have to lose them. They've all been lying to us, I think. So let's just take in the sights, and then, in a few hours we'll shake them. There's a train that goes back to the city at six. So, put on your best face and let's have some fun. When I ask you if you want to freshen up with me, that's our cue, okay?"

"You planned all of this already?"

"You slept in, remember?"

There's nothing quite like the seaside, all open and airy. I felt better almost immediately and watched Ivy relax as I smiled and laughed more. I almost forgot about finding Asher because of the way Santino kept looking at me.

The four of us walked along the boardwalk and made it to the enormous and beautiful gates of Luna Park. I'd never seen anything like it. A spectacle. With structures higher than the imagination and all sorts of things to catch one's eye. Everything covered in gold paint and sparkly glass.

"I could use a drink," said Jimmy. "What do ya think, Sonny?"

"I'm game. Rose?"

"She's fine," said Ivy. "But I could use one."

A man stood at the side of the entrance. He didn't look like he worked there.

"Rose, you're the one who looks the least likely to do anything bad. Do me a favor, would ya? Go give that guy this money," Jimmy took a few dollars out of his back pocket.

"You can't be serious," I said.

"Come on, Rose," said Ivy.

"You don't have to do anything you don't want to do," said Santino.

"Can everyone stop talking at me? You're like seagulls after a crumb, squawking. My head might explode."

I took the money from Jimmy, and walked up to the shadowy man.

He held out his hand. I didn't want to shake it. He was

dirty, as if he'd taken a bath in coal. And he was short, shorter than me. Shifty.

"Shake my hand like you know me," he said through clenched, smiling teeth.

I shook it then tried to give him the money.

"Are you crazy? Women. Can't trust 'em…" he said, grabbing me. He pulled me behind a large wall painted with animals and futuristic machines. From the front it looked like magic. Behind, it was just a bit of wood. And I was hidden with Mr. Shifty.

"Now," he said.

I handed him the money again, and he gave me a bottle from inside his jacket.

"Tuck that away safe, dearie," he said.

I walked back to Ivy, Sonny and Jimmy and said, "I've bought gin. Does that make me a criminal?"

They all looked at me, and then laughed so hard they started to cry and people began staring at us. We'd become a sideshow all our own.

That started another wave of laughter that I had to join. "Sometimes you have to laugh at yourself, Rose," said Ivy.

It felt good to laugh.

As Ivy and I were there for another purpose altogether, and our "fun day at the beach" was to be a ruse of sorts, the fun we had at Coney Island that day was unexpected and blissful. The boys put gin in lemonade they bought from a stand. I wouldn't drink any because of the debacle the previous night, but they did and it relaxed all of us. It's funny how you can be drunk on sun, sand and good company alone.

We ate hot dogs at Nathan's, which were delicious. We

hadn't had them before. And we did, in fact, buy bathing dresses. I couldn't talk Ivy out of the one that was too short. She simply glared at me. And the way Jimmy was looking at her made me a little angry.

She'd been lecturing me about Santino with her eyes and her gestures all day long, but she and Jimmy were worse! I couldn't believe I hadn't realized their attraction sooner.

We swam in the ocean. Running back and forth like children.

We even rode the Roller Coaster, which was brand-new and terrifying.

Then we went back to the boardwalk.

Ivy, sun kissed and glorious-looking, was admiring a booth where a paper moon was hanging. It was enormous and there was a line of people waiting to sit on the crescent and have their picture taken. A man working at the booth came up to us and asked, "And how are you young ladies doing today?"

"Oh, we're doing fine…enjoying the park!" said Ivy.

"Would you like to have your picture taken on the Paper Moon?"

"We sure do!" she said. "Boys, will you hold our place in line?" she asked, batting her eyelashes at Jimmy.

"Sure thing, Beauty."

"Let's freshen up, Rose. For the picture!"

There it was, my clue, and our chance to find our brother.

As I started to follow her, Sonny grabbed my arm. "Rosie, be careful, okay?"

I felt right then that he knew what we were doing. That he'd known it all along.

On impulse, I threw my arms around his neck. He returned the embrace and whispered words into my ear that made me blush. He whispered, "Just tell me you're my girl and I'll leave happy."

Now, a clever, upstanding woman like Jane Eyre or Marilla Cuthbert would have been able to craft a response that implied a shared affection at the very same time as it kept the young man in his proper place. But I was realizing hour by hour that I was never going to be either of them. I was far more Anne of Green Gables, hungry for life, always ready with a mouth that had a life of its own. So instead, I said, "Of course I am."

And chased off after my sister.

When Ivy ducked into the changing tent where we'd left our dresses, I looked back. I'd been right; they must have both known, because they'd left the line and were nowhere in sight.

"Quick, did you by any chance bring the matchbook and postcard?" she said, shimmying out of her swimsuit behind a curtain.

I smiled at her and brought them from my purse.

"Atta girl! You get a prize," said Ivy.

"Look! I knew I recognized that address. Come on, let's go."

"But I thought we were looking for the card stand."

"Yes and yes. Just get dressed and follow me."

"Hey, Ivy?" I asked while I changed.

"What? My God, you are so slow."

"Jimmy was in the war. Did you know that?"

"Nope. What does it matter? A lotta guys their age were over there. Asher, too. In France. Mr. Lawrence wrote me about it this week." She paused, looking genuinely apologetic. "I thought I told you."

"Well, now things are starting to make sense. If Sonny, Jimmy and Asher were in the war together, there's a connection. And that's what Jimmy was trying to hide last week when he started to say *three*, instead of *two!*"

"Rose, you're babbling. Just get dressed."

For the first time since we'd begun asking about Asher, I felt we were close.

Ivy was dragging me through crowds of people, dodging them and bumping into them sometimes. I felt I was saying, "I'm sorry," and "Excuse us please," over and over.

Then she stopped, and I bumped into her.

"Here we are," she said.

Cards & Co. wasn't a shop at all. It was a kiosk on the boardwalk in front of Nathan's. I hadn't noticed it, but she had.

"I even browsed while you were eating your hot dog and making moony eyes at Sonny. You need to watch yourself, do you hear me? Anyway, look."

"Did you ask the clerk if they knew Asher?"

"Of course I did."

"What did he say?"

"Jesus, Rose, LOOK."

She walked to the stand and pulled a postcard out from a display called Streets of Coney Island, which held bird's-eye drawings of different neighborhoods and streets around the park.

I walked to her and saw what she had seen. She held the matchbook cover up to the postcard.

Picturesque Oleander Drive.

I was so excited that I clapped.

"And the best part," she said, "is that it works just like a map, and we are...here."

She pointed to the boardwalk on the postcard. We were mere minutes away from the address on the matchbook.

The neighborhood past the park was quiet and lovely. I couldn't believe it was part of New York. Tree-lined streets and people walking at a proper pace.

We walked down Oleander Drive and counted the house numbers together.

"Thirty-four, forty-two, fifty-eight..." The excitement growing in our voices as we got closer.

"Sixty-seven. This is it," said Ivy very softly. We'd stopped in front of a two-story building with an iron gate. There was a metal sign affixed to the gate itself that quieted both of us.

It read:

SEACREST HOME.

The building was boarded up, but there was a man taking care of the front garden.

"Hiya, mister!" yelled Ivy.

He walked to the gate. "Can I help you?"

"Well, we were coming to meet our brother who lives here, but it seems we're too late," I said.

"Yeah, the neighborhood got bent outta shape with all those crazy people livin' there. Got some kind of petition together to oust 'em."

"What do you mean *crazy?* What kind of place was this?" asked Ivy, visibly upset.

"You know. Those ones that came back home after the war, only left most of themselves on the battlefield. Their minds, at least."

My face must have betrayed my emotions because I saw the man's eyebrows rise.

"Thought ya said your brother lived here," he said with a wariness clouding his disposition.

"Sir," I said, "we've recently found out we have an older brother. Our father has died and we need to find him. Everything we have points to this address, and any help you can give us is appreciated."

"Well, now…I sure am sorry for your loss, but to tell you the truth, I don't know where that doctor up and moved his patients to. Somewhere in the city, I think. Sorry I can't say where."

He walked away.

Ivy held fast to the bars, pressing her forehead, her eyes closed, against the metal.

"Ivy…"

"Don't talk, Rose."

"Ivy, that address may not mean anything. Why are you so upset? We'll find him. We'll shake the truth out of everyone…."

"I said don't talk to me."

She let go and walked by, going too fast.

"Ivy! What is the matter with you? We are chasing tiny tokens. We might've made the wrong assumptions anyway."

She turned around and stood in the center of the sidewalk.

"You don't understand anything. Besides, you don't care about it the way I do. You want to find him so you can go home to that dollhouse life, that bubble we lived in…. You have an *agenda,* Rose. And this would suit you fine, wouldn't it! To find out that he's mad or slow-witted. To find out he's ill…you'd write to Mr. Lawrence, get some kind of doctor's note and that would be it! Ta-da! Rose saves the day! But that's not what I want."

Her hands were in fists at her sides.

"Then tell me what it is you want. I cannot read your mind, and you don't often bare your soul to me, do you? So what do you want, Ivy?"

"What do I want? I want to find him, to get to know him, to have another person in our lives who may love us. I want to know if he likes theater and music. I want him to hear me sing…I want to stay in this glorious city and learn to live in it. Really live."

Her face was red, and as the first tear fell, she turned her back on me and began walking again. Ivy doesn't like to cry.

"Besides," she said, "that was our only real clue, so now we might never find him."

"We'll find him, Ivy," I said catching up and trying to put my arm inside of hers.

She shook me away.

"I don't want to talk to you. I don't want to look at you. I don't want to take care of you while you throw up, or worry that you'll embarrass me again."

She said it because somehow she knew it was my Achilles' heel, and even though I knew she might not even mean it, I snapped right back at her. I yanked her around by the same arm she'd used to shrug me off.

"If you could stop telling me what to do, maybe I could act the way you want me to act, or be the sister you've wanted me to be, but you just can't. You can't stand that I fit in so well to this life you expected would suit you.

You're jealous Cat asked me to work for her, and that she talks to me."

She stared at me and then turned away.

We caught the six o'clock train and parted ways silently.

When I walked into Empire House, Santino was there with two other men. Nell was clucking around them. When she saw me in the foyer she came to me. "You must be quiet, Rose. Once a week, I let Sonny meet with his writer friends in the salon. They pay me for the space, in case you're wondering. But don't disturb them. He might be famous one day, that one. I do love supporting the arts."

"You start this poem, Joseph," said Santino.

"And if the night be long..." said Joseph, a pale man who I thought might be Asher when I first walked in because of his coloring, but he was too young.

"The twinkling fade of stars that were her own..." said Sonny.

"I have something to LOAN," said the third man, thick, short and glistening with sweat.

To which Sonny groaned and banged his head on the table.

"No! Boris...it doesn't have to rhyme. Dear God, man! What is the matter with you? Honestly, I think you may have to give this writing idea up. Can't you be a mason or something? You lay one hell of a brick down with your words...."

Joseph was laughing. Boris, who I realized was drunk, tried to say something but stopped midsentence and looked at me.

That's when it happened. Santino turned to me.

"Oh lady fair, come join me here."

Joseph started to continue the poem, but Santino put his hand up in the air to stop him.

"I have a stone of nothing in my room for you to see," I said. The words tumbled out so fast and seemed to make no sense but all the sense in the world. A chill of pleasure ran through me.

"Another poet," said Nell. "Why do all the fancy literati have to work here at Empire House? Hmm? Now no work will get done. None. Write a poem about that!" said Nell and walked away.

"I have something for you," he said to me, reaching across the table for a box wrapped in brown paper and tied with string. He got up and handed it to me.

"Let me know what you think…" He was leaning against the door frame, more to hold himself up. He tried to smooth back his thick hair to no avail.

"Is it from you?" I asked.

"No. It's from Boris. Of course it's from me, Rosie! You agreed to be my girl, right?"

All three started to laugh. But Sonny stopped when he saw my face. I think he understood that something had happened to me, something too enormous for laughter.

"Are you okay? Did you find things you didn't want to find?"

I couldn't answer him. I ran up the stairs to the penthouse, but before opening The Poet's present, I had more words that wanted to tumble out from my fingers.

Dear Asher,
Your youngest sibling, Ivy, thinks I don't care about finding you. Well, that's not true. She thinks I only want to find you so that I can get back to a life we

used to live. Oh, say...a little over a week ago, yet it feels a million thousand years gone.

At first, that was true. I only wanted to find you because you were the key to my past. But now I realize she's right—you are also the key to my future.

Only when we thought we'd found you, and then had not? When we realized that if the address was really a clue to you, that you could be ill?

We had a terrible row.

Who is Daisy? Who are Nell and all those who live here at Empire House to you? Where are you, Asher?

I can't explain it, but what happened today with Ivy made me feel closer to you. Made me want to find you for the same reasons she gave me. And Asher, you really should hear her sing...I'm so proud of her.

If we find you, will you be kind?

If we find you, will the sins of our father be visited upon us? Please, if you are angry with him, take it out on me. Please release my sister from any sort of retribution. It was never her fault.

Your Sister,

Rose

I thought I'd burn the letter I'd just written to Asher, but I didn't. I put it in a small tin I was using to save the earnings we didn't spend on living expenses. We had eighty dollars. A far cry from three thousand.

Then I opened Santino's present.

It was a stationery set with roses embedded in the border. There was a new bottle of ink and a fancy pen. The best part of all was a small, leather-bound journal that was inscribed:

"To my girl, Rosie. Write down your dreams."

I held the new stationery to my chest and pulled out my new pen again.

I wrote,

Dear Santino,
Thank you,
Rosie.

And when I was sure he'd left for the night, I placed it in the kitchen by the coffeepot.

When I awoke the next morning, Ivy was still sleeping, and she looked so lovely.

I touched her soft cheek with the back of my hand, and pushed away the black hair from her sweaty brow.

She woke up and reached to touch my face.

Then she pulled her hand away.

She put a pillow over her head, and I put on my apron.

I went to breakfast without her. Maude had saved a seat for me, and there was coffee already poured. Everyone seemed to be smiling.

There was a family here. Nell shouting orders to Claudia, who was bustling around the tables. Santino tried to engage me as he put more food on the tables, but I would not comply. The politicos were sipping coffee and not arguing, for once.

Maude had taken the bread basket from Claudia, and she was chasing her for it. Playing. It was nice to see her play.

Sonny clinked a spoon against a water glass.

"Nell, I have an announcement to make. We have another poet in residence. Miss Rose Adams…"

The room applauded.

I had no idea what he was doing.

He sat down, amused with himself.

"I'd like to invite you to our weekly workshops."

"Have you lost your mind?" I asked.

"Rosie, just say yes. If I can't…well. We can be friends and start this over the right way. What do you say?"

"I'm no poet," I said.

"I don't care," he said.

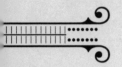 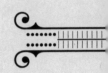

CHAPTER 14

Ivy

The Law Office of J. W. Lawrence
June 13, 1925
Dear Ivy,
Ah, Friar Laurence. Wasn't he responsible for that poor girl stabbing herself?

I generally give advice on contracts and wills, documents that have everything to do with human emotions, but the distant, dry legal verbiage greatly diminishes their impact.

Even so, I'm in the business of offering guidance, and I will not hesitate to give you some. First, I don't have any siblings but I understand the relationships formed are often fraught with conflicting feelings. Is it possible this is the norm? Or, if you determine your case is an extreme one, could you somehow find a way to modify those emotions?

You are in a large city, Ivy. New York seems a place

that cultivates loneliness along with vice. Please try to work out a way to accept your sister and make her your ally. It's the safer route, really.

Friar Lawrence has spoken.

Kind regards,

J. W. Lawrence

Empire House

It's got to be summer in this heat, 1925

Dear Mr. J. W. Lawrence,

When you get a minute, I want you to tell me what "J" and "W" stand for. At this point in our correspondence, I think it imperative I know who I'm dealing with.

Then again, you're not obligated, because I lied to you. Well, maybe that's a little harsh—I bent the truth. I'm not slinging hash at some greasy spoon. I am a waitress, but I'm serving drinks to the New York hot-to-trots in an underground speak. Cat, the glamour-puss I work for hired Rose to work in the dress shop above it—her story was legit.

Had to get that off my chest. Lies make it difficult to breathe, do they not?

More soon,

Ivy

"ROSE!"

I woke suddenly, heart pounding as I desperately tried to remember the vivid dream that had so brutally pushed me into the morning. Or was it a nightmare? The specifics lay just beyond my reach, but I knew I'd been running down MacDougal Street, bare feet tearing against the pavement. I tried to scream but nothing would come, and I'd wrapped my hands around my neck and squeezed, desperate to push out a sound. My mind immediately went to Asher. Was the dream a portent of what was to come? Was he in trouble? Would I never find him?

But how many people called out the name of the person they'd least like to save them? I was glad Rose's bed was empty and she hadn't heard. She would have come running, her eyes full of the pity that so incensed me in front of the Seacrest Home. That's what got my goat: if I was the object of Rose's pity, then Asher meant considerably more to me than he did to her. She worried for the house, and I worried for our brother. Why did she have to be so damn practical? I couldn't stand to look at her after we'd stood side by side, grasping the bars in front of the awful crazy house. I didn't speak to her on the way home from Coney Island, preferring to watch the city roll by, my eye scanning the streets for a man I hadn't yet met. I managed a busy night at Cat's, and then afterwards, sneaked into the Washing Room at Empire House with a bottle of hooch from the stash Maude keeps under her bed, and penned a response to Mr. Lawrence's latest letter. I didn't mention Asher or Seacrest. He'd know soon enough, but I couldn't spell it out for him. How does one write about heartbreak? I told myself that I'd spill the whole story once I found Asher and could evaluate his condition myself. I wasn't completely in the dark—I had a doctor's name, and I knew he'd moved his patients to Manhattan. There couldn't be more than a handful of hospitals on an eight-mile island. There was even one right on Eleventh Street here in Greenwich Village. St. Vincent's. I'd start there.

With renewed confidence, I pushed myself out of bed

and got dressed. Empire House smelled of freshly baked bread and percolating coffee, the comforting scent of Sunday morning. I sped down the stairs, barely touching them, and nearly knocked Rose over where she stood arranging flowers in the foyer.

"Ivy, you're like an earthquake," she said, her hand going to her heart. "You startled me."

Rose's dress and hair were smooth and neat as usual, but her eyes looked wild.

"What's with you?"

She shrugged. "I don't know. Feeling skittish, I suppose."

So she wasn't going to tell me. Even though I'd promised myself I'd avoid her, I couldn't help but push a little. "What happened this morning?"

"Nothing at all, except that you're speaking to me now." She pushed the vase to the center of the table and removed her gloves. "I'm sorry yesterday didn't go as planned. I've given it a lot of thought, however, and I don't think we should make any definitive assumptions." Rose sat on the bottom stair, and after a moment's hesitation, I joined her. "We should inform Mr. Lawrence," she continued, her words twisting my nerves, "but if Asher's condition can't be proven, then I don't know where that leaves us. He's still missing, Ivy, and until we find him, everything is hearsay."

My anger spiked again. She wanted to find him, but only to make smooth the legal process. That damned house in Forest Grove meant nothing to me—it wasn't our father. Asher was a direct blood tie. He was family. Why couldn't she see that one was the past and the other our future?

"I'm going to find him," I said, standing up. "I have an idea and all day to pursue it. Cat isn't expecting me until this evening." I smoothed down my bob in the foyer's mirror and straightened my stockings. They were torn, but I didn't care. I had money for the first time in my life. Not a lot, but enough to pay for my own without having to beg Rose. Enough to hail a cab or buy a plate of chop suey. Enough to feel like the city was mine, if just for the day.

I stepped out onto the front stoop. MacDougal shimmered in the noontime sun, a gemstone in the jewelry box of Greenwich Village. This is the beauty my father saw, what he tried to capture with his brush. I took a deep breath and walked into it.

"Wait, Ivy." I turned to see Rose calmly moving toward me, purse in hand. "I've told Nell I'll be gone for a bit. I'm coming with you."

There was no question in her voice—she wasn't asking me. Caught off guard, I simply asked, "Why?"

"I'm worried for him, too," she said, and all at once I believed her.

"Okay," I warned, "but you better hope Nell's patient, because we're on my timetable."

Rose fell into step with me. "Fine," she said, laughing, "but you don't own a watch."

Though we'd been silent with each other since the day before, Rose became chatty as we strolled, telling the story of Edna St. Vincent Millay's birth and how she'd been named for the hospital we were on our way to visit; the doctors there had saved Edna's uncle's life just before she'd burst into the world, and her grateful mother repaid the debt with a namesake. Rose's voice was animated as she told the story, as rich and vibrant as the cafés and art galleries that lined the streets. Perhaps I was wrong, I thought as we crossed Sixth Avenue. I'd focused so much on what

I could take from the city that I hadn't focused on what the city could offer—but Rose had. This was a different Rose. This Rose walked right up to the starched, prim nuns at St. Vincent's reception and inquired directly about Doctor Spence.

"I don't recognize the name," the nun said, smiling down at Rose from her raised desk, "however, we have a number of doctors from other hospitals on consult. It is possible he's been here, but we don't keep formal records of the doctors' comings and goings, just the patients."

"Have a number of new psychiatric patients come recently?" I asked before thinking about how to best phrase the question. The nun turned to me, her mouth pursing as she took in my bobbed hair and short dress.

"It wouldn't be in my rights to say," she answered curtly.

Rose stepped forward, her innocent face upturned toward the sister's stern countenance. "Our brother served in the war, and we have reason to believe his mind has been compromised. May we enter the men's ward to look for him? I promise we won't disturb anyone."

The nun glanced toward the heavy doors leading into the hospital. "No women are allowed in there except the nurses...."

"Please," Rose pressed.

The nurse relented, opening the heavy door and ushering us through. "The men's ward is on the second floor," she explained. "You have ten minutes. Anything more than that and I call the guard."

The men's ward was silent, orderly and half-empty. Patients lay in an endless stretch of beds, their privacy curtains pulled back, exposing healing limbs and feverish bodies. Nurses attended some; others, propped up by pillows, picked at lunch trays or played solitaire. We merited a few raised eyebrows, but most were lost to their own boredom, and, with the number of nurses bustling about, hadn't the energy or desire to engage two young women.

"I don't see him," Rose whispered.

We walked to the end of the ward and back again, just to be sure. None of those men had Rose's moonlit eyes.

"I'd like a cup of Joe when you get a chance," a voice called out. The ginger-haired man lying nearest to the door smiled in our direction. He was older than us, but barely so, his large feet sticking out from under the thin white blanket. He winked. "Add a dash of cream if you've got it."

"We're not nurses," Rose said, and he didn't bother to hide his disappointment.

"Can you grab one of them holy dames for me? I need a pick-me-up."

"Yep," I said, "but could you do something for us? We went through the wrong door. Where's the nuthouse in this joint?"

He thought for a moment. "Don't they send the crazies to Wards Island? I haven't heard of one here, but there is a charity ward on the fourth floor. Saddest thing. Lots of veterans and motherless sons."

Rose nudged me. "It's been five minutes."

I shouted the man's coffee order to a startled nun and ran for the door, Rose right behind me.

The charity ward looked identical to the men's ward below, except for the patients. Their gaunt faces and sallow skin told me these guys needed more than a cuppa Joe. There weren't any nurses visible, and Rose, clutching my arm, nearly buckled under the tidal wave of male attention. Luckily, serving drinks at Cat's speakeasy had taught me how to handle groups of men. It appeared I had learned something from the city.

I stopped in the middle of the aisle and put my hand on my jutting hip. "Hey, fellas!"

The ones that could hooted and whistled.

"Anyone know a sap named Asher Adams?"

"Who's he to ya?" one man bellowed.

"He's my brother, and I'm looking for him."

"Why should we care?"

Why should they? I racked my brain. "Don't you care about your heroes? He fought in the war. In the Argonne. The Lost Battalion."

Silence fell like a brick. Finally, one man sneezed, and the rest, grateful for the distraction, showered him with blessings.

"No need to be so glum," I said when they'd quieted. "He *lived*."

"Of course he did," the loudmouth said. "He's a New Yorker! All those guys were. It's why they lived. A buncha survivors."

"But you never heard of Asher?" I asked, hope fading.

They all looked sincerely sorry they didn't. Rose tugged on the back of my dress, and I reluctantly followed her toward the door.

"Is it true?" The man who spoke sat propped in his bed. He cradled his arm, which was a patchwork quilt of scar tissue. I walked toward him and tried not to stare.

"Is what true?" Rose asked gently.

"Was your brother in the Argonne?"

"Yes," I said. He looked stricken, but I had to ask. "Were you?"

"Not quite," he said softly. "But I served in France."

I sat at the edge of his bed. "Our brother is lost again. We don't know much about what he experienced overseas. Could you tell us about what happened there?"

"Those boys were surrounded by the Germans for almost a week. No food, very little water. Every day they must have wondered if they'd be saved, or if it'd be their last. So many didn't make it."

"Our brother did," I said, my pride surging.

The man lifted his good arm and grasped my hand. "Will you tell him I'm sorry?"

"Whatever for?" Rose asked.

"We didn't know they were there. We thought we were pummeling the Germans, not our own men! By the time we found out, we must have made their lives pure misery in that forest." The man's voice turned raspy, his throat full of tears. "We didn't mean it," he said as a sob escaped. "You'll tell him when you see him, right?"

I squeezed the pale hand holding mine. "Yes," I promised, "but I know what he'd say back to you—you're forgiven, though there's nothing to forgive."

We each took a turn kissing his cheek and left him in that sad ward, crying for the sin he believed he committed.

Both Rose and I sorted through our thoughts on the way home. Our silence wasn't bred of anger, but of contemplation.

How lonely those men must have been in that French forest! I tried to imagine their horror of discovering the direness of the situation—and the desperate need to keep the flame of hope flickering in their hearts. Did these hopeful ones survive, or was it the men who had none, and therefore acted with reckless bravery? If they were New Yorkers, it was more likely the latter. This city was full of cynics who paradoxically acted as though life was a party to be celebrated by walking a tightrope stretched across two willing skyscrapers. Was that who Asher was?

"Did you see that sign, Ivy?" With a start I realized we were already back on MacDougal. Rose had stopped, drawn to the Actors/Actresses Needed board nailed to the front door of the Republic Theater. Early in the week it had only been placed in the window. They must be getting desperate.

"I saw it."

"Why not go in?" she said. "I'll go with you. It's just what we need right now. A little diversion for me, and a little bit of stardust for you. What do you say?"

No, was my first thought. *I'm not ready.* Rose's face showed a confidence I couldn't find in myself. Could I find some kind of courage in that? "All right," I said, taking a deep breath as we stepped into the land of the Anarchists.

A couple stood on the low stage, rehearsing something I didn't recognize. Rose settled into one of the folding chairs in the front row, and I slowly walked up to the man pacing the proscenium. He wore a tattered black sweater, though it was a scorching day. His glasses were round and wire-rimmed, balanced low on his nose, and if I wasn't so nervous I might have laughed. I glanced back at Rose, and her eyes shone with excitement. She looked like a stranger.

"Yes," the man said impatiently.

"I hadn't asked anything."

"But you will."

I gestured toward the door. "You advertised for actresses. I am one. An actress, I mean."

"Isn't everybody?" he said. "But we always give auditions. You never know when a star finds its way out of a black hole." He barked something at the couple, and they slunk off the stage. "What have you prepared?" the man said.

Even in the hot room, I felt my blood go cold. I had nothing.

"She knows Shakespeare," Rose said from the audience.

My blood was frigid, but my face was hot. The contrast made me nauseous. "I know quite a few monologues," I managed to say.

"Then choose one," he said briskly. "And be quick about it."

The stage, no higher than a foot or two, seemed insurmountable. What was wrong with me? I lifted one heavy foot and then another, and turned to face him.

"Begin," he shouted.

I quickly decided on the Player Queen's speech from *Hamlet*. "'So many journeys may the sun and moon...'" I began, the familiar words tumbling from my mouth as my mind wandered to Asher and the lost men, to my father, to our lives in Forest Grove. Had he been lonely, too? Had we all? Were we destined to stumble through the dark and never find each other? The director tapped his foot and I mangled the line about fear and love, the two words catching in my throat. Tears clouded my eyes and I tripped off the stage. "I'm sorry," I whispered. "I shouldn't have come."

Once outside I tried to compose myself, but the tears kept falling. After a moment, Rose exited the theater and squinted into the late-day sun. "Ivy? I don't understand."

"I don't think you can," I said, and made a run for Empire House. Jimmy sat on the stoop smoking a cigarette. He grabbed my hand and drew me onto his lap.

"What's got you, Beauty? Tell Jimmy your troubles."

"You smell like another woman's perfume," I said, bolting inside and closing the door behind me.

From the Law Offices of J. W. Lawrence

Dear Ivy,

The "J" stands for "John." The "W" is fiction, though based in enough embarrassing fact to still turn my face red. When I was in junior high school, I was the only boy tall enough to jump up and reach the basketball hoop. My fellow students called me "John the Wonder." Aren't you sorry you asked?

And, please review the enclosure. It was in an unaddressed, sealed envelope, found in my embarrassingly disheveled file cabinet. I'm sorry to send it, in a way, because it means you have not yet met your brother. This certainly changes your situation, and I'm honestly not sure if it is for the better. If it's any comfort, it does seem your father intended to communicate with you from the spirit world, so to speak. I also found a letter addressed to both you and your sister in his safety deposit box, which the bank has finally let me open. I'll send it along to Empire House.

That letter will remain unopened until you and Rose do the honors. It was not my place to read his private correspondence, so I hope it offers comfort, Ivy. As I said, your father was an unusual man, but also strangely prescient. I hope what he's written doesn't add to your grief, but rather adds another golden layer to our memories of him.

Sincerely,
John
Enclosure:
From the desk of Everett Adams
Mr. Lawrence,
Please add an addendum to the growing mountain of papers I've asked you to collect: If Ivy and Rosemary do not find Asher Adams within three weeks of my death, management of the estate reverts to Rosemary.
Regards,
Everett
PS: Do stop by for a cigar sometime.

Empire House
Oh–I–don't know, 1925
Dear John-the-Wonder,
You do realize I am calling you that from now on. So, lawyers are like doctors, right? You can't repeat what I tell you in confidence. And what I am going to tell you is to be kept strictly on the QT.

I'm afraid of so much, and it seems this city knows it, clamoring around my head, leaving me senseless. Loneliness is not always pushed away by human proximity. I feel it working in Cat's speakeasy, while surrounded by loud, chatty souls. I feel it walking through Washington Square Park as so many bodies brush past me. I feel it while tucking my sister into her bed, her wine-soaked breath hot on my skin.

I felt it standing on stage during a disastrous audition for an actress job. It paralyzed me, head to toe. I've never felt so disconnected from everything around me.

I miss my father, miss him with an ache I've come to realize will always live deep in my bones. I dearly miss a brother I haven't yet met. As much as I hate to admit it, I'd miss my sister if she returned to Forest Grove. I will tell her about my father's wishes. I will. But can I have a minute to sit back and catch my breath?

Ivy

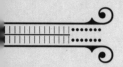 CHAPTER 15

Rose

IT'S SURPRISINGLY EASY to avoid people when you want to, even in tight quarters. Another week had passed since Ivy and I visited the wounded men, and Ivy's subsequent—and rather unusual—lackluster performance at the audition. Something was wrong with Ivy and I didn't want to think about it or face it. She made it easy...smiling at me then dashing off here or there. Too soon our silence compounded itself, and we were in a stalemate. There were so many reasons for her to be angry with me, but the odd thing was that none of them added up to the quiet, sad eyes she wore, or the moments when she started to address me, and then left the room as if haunted by a ghost. It was exhausting, so I simply started to ignore her.

I don't like to admit that without her, well...without worrying about her or about what she thought of me...I felt free. Instead of seeking out her council, I went to Santino, or Nell, Claudia, Maude and Viv. Even Cat, when

I dropped off dresses, or when she'd stop by to visit with Nell and her "Empire Girls." When we'd first arrived, I thought the term derogatory. But as my fondness for Empire House grew, I longed to be called one, as well.

It was safe, spending time among my new friends. There was drinking and weaving of words and laughter. I didn't feel as if I was under a microscope. With Ivy, I was always waiting for the next moment I'd disappoint her. Her silence had set me free.

A week after our trip to Coney Island, Ivy walked into Empire House after her shift at Cat's to find me in the Salon deep in poetry, camaraderie and liquor.

When I saw that she was going to walk up the stairs without a second glance at me—again, the drink made my tongue too sharp.

"I never knew that she, the queen of night, could be a solid ass," I said.

"The harlot chased the king across the grass…" said Joseph.

"Like Ivy growing up on solid brick, choking mortar, wisely lies," I continued, skipping Santino on purpose. I was talking to my sister, and I was being mean.

"And it can't be a flower, no matter how it tries!" said Boris, not knowing that his poor rhyme would slash both of us.

Ivy stared at me in disbelief and then stormed back out.

I felt my heart go with her.

"That's it for me, boys," I said.

"Don't worry about Ivy," said Santino. "She'll come around."

"Without a sound…" said Joseph.

Boris hit him playfully and then leaned over to throw up in the bucket Nell kept by his feet. Boris could not hold his liquor.

"That was childish of me, and you don't know my sister," I said. "Once, when we were small, I told her that I didn't like a drawing she'd made, and she held it against me for months."

Walking up the stairs, I reconsidered my actions. Besides petty things, what was I angry about?

We'd found nothing new about Asher. Our trail on Daisy had grown cold. And worst of all, I was starting to wonder what I would do if we did find Asher. The more I thought of Forest Grove, the lonelier that existence I'd planned for myself seemed to be.

For the first time since he'd died, I wanted my father. Yes, I'd grieved and yes, I'd missed him. But at that very moment I wanted to resurrect him from the grave and send him out into the city to find his wayward daughter and force her to divulge whatever secret was festering inside of her and ruining our precarious relationship.

I undressed and tried to go to sleep, but the air was becoming more and more oppressive. I thought perhaps a storm was coming. Or maybe the ghost of our father heeding my call. That thought made me sit straight up in my bed.

I needed air—fresh air, so I went to the window that looked over the garden. I opened it only to find Claudia sitting on the tiny platform of the fire escape, carefully with cupped hands taking soil from a burlap bag and pouring it neatly into little earthenware pots.

"Claudia, it's so late! Why aren't you asleep, little one?"

"I couldn't sleep 'cause it was too hot, so I was getting a head start on somethin' The Poet asked me to do. He said we should put flowers in pots so it'll look like the garden growin' all the way up the side of Empire House. I think he's doin' it for you."

"He's a love. How many pots do you have to fill?"

"Look."

She pointed down the staircase and I saw at least fifty little pots.

"That's a lot of work, sweetheart," I said. "Do you need help?"

"No. I like this kind of thing. And, miss? If ya don't mind me askin', don't you, too?"

"I guess I do. Only I never thought of it as work. I suppose I'm just realizing that I grew up in a dollhouse."

"What?"

"Nothing…I need some air. Is there another place to go? Not the garden or the fire escape. Is there a way to get to the roof?"

"Well, that depends—are you gonna go and do somethin' foolish?"

"You mean, jump?"

"I guess, or other things. Nell says the stars lie to us, promise us things they can't deliver. Make us think things can stay the same, only the stars are already burned out a long time ago. At least that's what she says, and she's smart, Nell, for an old lady."

"How about this—I promise I won't do anything foolish. Now will you show me? And, is it safe up there?"

"Safe, miss?" she said. "Is anything?"

She ducked back in through the window and walked me to a pull-down ladder hidden in a narrow, high eave across from her bed.

I walked out into the air, clearer up five stories, and

looked across the city. Feeling small against its vast expanse was a welcome relief that straightened the backs of all my bent and twisted thoughts.

Ivy would warm to me again or she wouldn't.

We'd find Asher or we wouldn't.

In the meantime, I had to live.

These were the things I was saying to myself as I sat on the roof, my back against a chimney, my knees drawn up against me.

"Whatever is meant to happen, will happen...." I said aloud to the night.

"And when the rain is pouring, I'll do my gypsy dance," said Santino, who swung his tall body around from the other side of the large chimney. He held out a flask.

"How did you get up here?" I asked, smiling and taking the flask.

He slid down the bricks next to me so we were sitting side by side.

"There are many different routes to the same destination," he said.

"Poet, sometimes a straight answer is a good answer," I said, taking a large sip. It burned all the way down.

"There's another fire escape on the narrow side of the building. Can I start again, please?"

"But of course."

"And when the rain is pouring, I'll do my gypsy dance..."

"The moon in awestruck shadows stood alone..." I said, and took back the flask.

"A Grecian Goddess, wayward made her peace..." he continued.

And so it went. Until the flask was empty and I was lying with my head in his lap.

"You're a poet, Rose Adams. You've been one for your whole life, scrawling the words out of your beautiful mind from before you could walk, with that wickedly straight back."

"Nope," I said...my lips lingering over the informal *p* and liking it. "I am not the artist...." I said it *are-t-eeeest*. "I leave that to Ivy. Forever the actress, the singer, the dancer... The light of our lives. Me? I make lace. I sew. I'm a good girl."

"A good girl," he repeated.

"Good girl..." I said again.

"Gargoyle!" we said together.

We laughed then. My laughter didn't sound like me. It wasn't tight or tinny. It was real. And loud. It was from the bottom of my toes.

"What was it like, the war?" I asked.

"It wasn't any fun," said Sonny.

"This from the man of many words," I said.

"It was dark. And the world was screaming. I can't think about it too much or I'll end up just like..."

"Just like Asher?"

He ignored my question. "We all became brothers when we stepped off those boats. And then, those of us lucky enough to step back onto them and come home... We got a new kind of blood runnin' through us."

The look in Santino's eyes told me that he'd tell me more. That he'd tell me anything I wanted to know. But I didn't want to evoke the same haunted look I saw in the eyes of the men Ivy and I visited at the hospital. Someday we'd talk of it, and maybe even write of it. But not right then. Not yet.

"Are you going to come clean about Asher? I know you know him, Poet."

"Sometimes, we have to keep promises just so we can look at ourselves in the mirror."

"Promise me, then, that if I get close enough to the truth, you'll tell me, okay?"

"I promise, Rosie. I promise."

I laid my head on his shoulder.

"Stay here, Rosie. I'll get us a bottle of wine, okay?"

I nodded.

"Are you sure?"

"Just go get it," I said.

He was back, fast, with two glasses and a bottle that was gone before I knew it.

He wound a stray curl, which had escaped my bun in the humidity, around his finger. I closed my eyes and the rooftop began to dance underneath me. We weren't even there anymore. We were somewhere else. Two people in an ancient world of words, where there were no rules. We were free. I walked to a waist-high ledge and leaned into the night air.

He must have come around behind me while my eyes were closed, because all of the sudden I felt his hands, busy taking pins out of my hair.

"What are we doing?" I asked.

"I don't know," he said as my hair tumbled down my back, and I realized he was shaking. So I turned around to face him, and he picked me up. I wrapped my legs around him. "I don't know anything anymore since I met you,

Rosie. All I see, all I think about, is you. Please let me touch you. Please, I feel like I'm dyin'."

I placed my hands either side of his face. "You already are," I said as he placed me down on the rooftop on my back, where we lay together under the lying stars.

His eyes.

His kisses. A small kiss, and then a longer one, and a longer one. Each time he pulled away from me, each time searching my eyes for some sort of answer. And then, the kiss that did not end, that touched me in a place I did not know I owned.

"No," he said, pulling away. "Not yet, not like this."

Before I could feel any shame, he reached into his pocket, took out a pocketknife and cut a thin strip of white cloth from his dress shirt. He tied it around my ring finger.

"I'm saving money, Rosie, and I don't want you to say anything to me now. Just know that when I come to you with a real ring, I'd like for you to consider the possibility of sharing your life with me. Will you think about it?"

"Of course I will."

"There is something I have tell you. Well, there are a lot of things. Sort of, maybe only two. No, three." He was talking in circles, nervous.

"Say anything to me, Santino. The sound of your voice is so beautiful that I could listen to you talk all evening," I said.

"No, don't be nice to me. Not yet… Oh, God. I didn't want to tell you. But I have to do it or we can't ever move past all this. And we have to, Rosie. We have to get on with our lives together, right?" The fear in his voice brought me out of my reverie and made me think the first terrible thought I'd had for a month.

"Then don't say it. Is Asher dead? I knew you were keeping something from me, but I don't want Asher to be dead. Please don't tell me that. A few weeks ago I'd have told you he needed to be alive because of Ivy. But now? I know I need him just as much as she does. I need my family."

"And I need *you*," he said. "I love you. I've loved you since I saw you on the stairs."

"I need you, too," I whispered, trying to remember the last time those words had ever come off my lips, if ever at all.

"In that case, let me tell you a little more of what I know about Asher."

"You don't have to…"

"I need to. Okay…" I could tell he was struggling.

"Let me help. You were in the war together, the three of you? You, Asher and Jimmy," I guided him.

He nodded.

"And you all grew up together?"

"No, not Jimmy. Me and Ash and…"

"Daisy?"

"Yep."

"Who is Cat—was she around, too?"

Sonny took a deep breath and started to talk. "See, the thing is…"

"No," I said, bringing my fingers to his lips. "You love them, and you want to protect them. I understand why you kept it from me. I won't make you tell me more. Yet."

The girl who got off the train sweating her way through Grand Central Station would have been cruel to him. She would have yelled at him for keeping any sort of truth from her. But the person I was becoming was very aware of how people interact when they care for one another. I mean, who was I to ask him to reveal secrets he was keeping for, what I could only guess, was the benefit of our brother? It was my own confusion that was making me angry. My own muddy intentions about Asher when we arrived in search of him. I'd wanted his signature on a legal document. It was a callous need. Nothing more, nothing less. These people I'd met, the ones who were becoming my family, they were right to keep Asher from me.

"You're not mad?" he asked.

"No, I am not mad. I am so grateful you shared what you could with me now, and not a second sooner."

"Oh, God, Rose, I've never been so happy to hear someone say anything. If the Virgin Mary were to come down from heaven right now and speak to me, it wouldn't make me any more relieved. Rosie, I thought you'd hate me."

"Hate you? I love you," I said.

I thought he might jump up and hit the stars.

Once he was settled, he said, "Look. Maybe I can't tell you everything I know, and it ain't much, believe me. But I can help you look for Ash. I've got an idea. Why don't we go on over to Washington Square Park? A lot of the guys who came back from overseas—how should I say this— different... They go down there to sleep. Lot of them with no place to go, no place to call home. I go every once in a while to check and see if I can find Asher. Maybe you're the lucky charm."

"Let's go," I said.

Washington Square Park in the dead of night is still a busy place. Santino and I searched each bench, each arch... under and over trash cans and other heaps lying here and there. We found plenty of men. All homeless, most of them veterans of the Great War. But none of them were Asher.

Santino put his arm around me as we made our way back to Empire House.

"I know you want to find him, but I'm glad he wasn't there."

"Me, too, Poet. Me, too," I said.

He kissed me good-night on the stoop, but before he slipped away I said, "Thank you, Santino."

"For what?"

"Tonight, I woke up for the first time in my life. I couldn't have done it without you."

"Oh, Rosie. This may be the first and last time I tell you you're wrong. I didn't do nothin'. You were well on your way before you even thought about me twice. And believe you me, I'm more than happy to hitch a ride on what promises to be a grand tomorrow."

I crept back up to the penthouse quietly. Ivy, Viv and Maude were already back from Cat's and sleeping; I could see their chests rise and fall. I was so drunk, everything was rising and falling…the room would not keep still.

I ran to the window and leaned out, thinking I'd retch… but the air hit my face and I was calmed.

Ivy woke, ran to me and slammed the window down.

"Rose? Where have you been?"

"Oh, Ivy! I've had the most wonderful night. Look!" I said, raising up my hand, showing her the small bit of fabric Santino had tied there.

"What's that supposed to be? An engagement ring? Don't fall for any of that, Rose. I hope you didn't do anything untoward."

An anger I didn't understand came up and filled my throat.

"Oh, shut up!" I yelled. "You've been quiet and strange all week, why talk now? I'm so sick of worrying about you and looking after you. I'm sick of your insolence and that way you look at me, like I'm some terrible cross you must bear! You want to know what I was doing? I was getting more information about Asher. The Poet and I even went down to Washington Square Park to look for him. Did you know that Asher, Daisy and Santino grew up together? No, that's right. You've been too busy ignoring me."

"Rose, this is not the time to argue. Remember, we will find Asher and go home, right? That's what we need to do. We'll do that. Let's get you into bed."

"And where is this older brother of ours? The one you think will make your dreams come true?" I stood up, making a wide circle with my arms and then put my hand to my forehead pretending to scan the room. "I know why you want to find him. You think he'll be like Father, and he'll love you best. Asher the hero, Asher the great! Asher the…"

Ivy picked up a book by my bed and threw it at me. It hit me square in the chest. Drunk, I began to laugh.

"What's goin' on over there?" asked Maude from her side of the attic.

"I swear, if you girls get up and come nosing over here, I'll pop you both. Leave us be," said Ivy. Then she turned her full attention to me, her green eyes filled with so much hate, I lost my breath.

"Rosemary Adams. Quiet, perfect, boring Rose. Look at you now! Out at all hours, engaged with a piece of cotton to a common cook. Is this how it goes in those books you can't get your nose out of? I have a question for you, one that doesn't need an answer. Tell me, Rose, how it is that you stole all this from me? How did you connive your way into the hearts and minds of the people who were meant to belong to me? Was that the plan from the very beginning? How long have you plotted this coup, dear sister?"

My anger had faded, and the room was spinning relentlessly. I sat on the bed not able to answer her or fight back.

"At a loss for words, finally," she continued. "You listen to me, sister. I have plans. Plans that don't include you. I don't care what you do or where this newfound awakening will take you. But there is something I know that you don't know. See, I had a letter from Lawrence, and I was trying to figure out the best way to tell you so as to spare your feelings. Only right now I'm not concerned with being careful. Mr. Lawrence discovered something very interesting, Rose. Seems like Father's papers state that if we didn't find Asher after three weeks here in the city, that the house reverted to you. So there you have it. You are free. Save up the tax money and you can go home."

I was stunned. "When did you find this out?"

"Last week."

I stood up, walked to my sister and slapped her across the face.

She didn't move an inch—standing there bathed in the moonlight. She was holding a hand to her cheek. Soon, she gained her composure and began throwing a few things into father's rucksack.

"Where are you going?" I asked.

"None of your business," she said.

And then she was gone.

★ ★ ★

What does one do when the light of day pours in and you understand that you have erred in such a way that is never to be righted?

The day after I struck my sister and found out that my original search for Asher had been a moot quest from the third week we'd arrived, I went about my duties in a daze. When the clock in the foyer struck noon, Jimmy came by with a letter from Cat.

> Dear Rose,
> She's with me, though she'd kill me if she knew I told you. Give her some time. I'll come by Empire House to visit you, and I'll make sure Jimmy comes to pick up the garments. Steer clear for a bit, pet.
> Love, Cat.

"Hey, Jimmy? Can you wait a minute? I want to reply."

"Sure, doll. I'll go bother The Poet. I hear you two may be a permanent item soon."

"Word travels fast."

"You're livin' in Empire House—no one has secrets here."

"That's the biggest lie of all time," I said.

"Yeah, maybe it is," said Jimmy.

I ran upstairs and wrote to Cat.

> Dear Cat,
> I won't ask about Ivy, not yet, and I know, between you and Jimmy, she's well taken care of. The two of you, blindfolded and drunk, could protect her better than I did. She'd have been just fine if I wasn't with

her at all. I was so worried about her getting "loose" and "fast" in the big city that I never realized it would be me who would be the one to change. If you think it's appropriate, tell her I'm not angry, and that I'm terribly sorry I slapped her. Tell her...you know.

Thank you, Cat.

Rose

It was hard to do my daily tasks after Jimmy left. I had too much to think about, so I tried to do what Ivy did when she was feeling antsy—I tried to sing. Only each note fell flat so I descended into silence instead.

That's when I realized why Ivy had been silent on the train ride back from Coney Island and in the days that had passed since our trip to the hospital. She'd been worried, too! And I thought she was steaming mad at me. She wasn't angry at me at all. She was angry at herself, and at Asher. She'd dreamed a dream so big it ate her up.

I cleaned as I thought, and I moved into Nell's office to dust off her bookshelves and desk. I brought over a small stool to get to a higher shelf and found a large, leather-bound book that reminded me of scrapbooks our mother used to keep. Curious, I brought it down and opened the heavy cover. Old photographs peered back at me.

Young Nell and a beautiful little girl in the garden. Photograph after photograph of that little girl. I realized immediately that I'd found something that could hold another clue, and the first thought...*I have to tell Ivy*...sent me reeling.

Nell walked in shaking a piece of paper in front of me. I slammed shut the album and slid it behind me. "Did you see this?" she asked.

"What is it?"

"A note from your sister saying she's no longer living here. You could have told me."

"It all happened fast, Nell. I was going to tell you when I finished dusting."

"Well, it is a bit cryptic, which worries me. And then there was the fact she didn't tell me face-to-face."

"That's not easy for Ivy. Besides, Jimmy was just here. Seems Ivy is staying with Cat."

"How very maudlin of her. Anyway, Miss Rose, we'll talk more about this later. And thank the lord you didn't decide to leave home, too," she said.

The word *home* rang in my ears as I hurried upstairs to put the album away for further examination, and then finished the daily chores.

Claudia and I were peeling potatoes in the garden while Sonny was inside cooking the evening meal. I had her alphabet primer on the table in front of her.

"Practice," I said.

"My hands are all dirty, miss."

"Call me Rosie. And you don't need your hands to read, you need your eyes!"

She rolled those pretty eyes at me and started. "*A*, apple. *B*, ball. *C*, cat…like Cat!"

"Yes, some words mean more than one thing…"

"It's confusing." She sighed.

"Everything is," I said.

She put down the small paring knife and wiped her hands on her apron to turn the page of the primer. The starch is hard to get off, so she smudged the pages a little. "I'm so sorry, Miss Rosie!"

I put my hand over my mouth to stifle the laughter.

"Oh, Claudia, all my books are stained! I think that means you love them. Don't give it a second thought. Keep reading."

"*F,* farm. *G,* gin."

"That's not in the primer, Claudia!" I laughed. She was catching on quickly. I knew she'd be reading soon."

"You're no fun," she continued. "*G,* gold. *H,* house. Rosie, tell me about your house."

"That's not in the primer, either," I said.

"I'm sick of the alphabet. Come on…tell me about your life before you came here."

I took a breath, not knowing if I was ready to revisit memories at the same time as I knew I needed to make sure I didn't push them away. Claudia had been, since the day I arrived, my little conscience. Always able to know what I needed a second before I needed it. So I decided to answer her as best as I could.

"Well, Adams House was rather big and full of secret nooks and crannies, but it was stunning and simply poured warmth and welcome out its windows. There were white painted clapboards and a picket fence. Old oaks lined the road with their leaves meeting in the middle, forming a canopy. There was a lake, too. And no sounds at night. No lights, either.

"The air out there is clean and crisp, with no notes or textures. Not like New York City at all, with its lovely, awful smells."

"It must have been nice to grow up in a place like that."

"Yes, it must have," said Nell, who had slammed into the garden armed with pinking sheers. "Away from all the vermin, beggars and filth."

"Are you teasing me, Nell?"

"Maybe so," she said, snipping a stem so precisely I could hear it snap.

"Have you ever been to the country, Claudia?" I asked.

"Nope. And I don't plan on it. All that quiet would scare me silly."

"Terrible place, the country," continued Nell. "Full of misfits and heathens pretending to be Christians. Humans forget to be human when they aren't surrounded by comparisons." She paused. "Not that you and Ivy are…"

"I know, Nell. I know what you meant. I am not offended."

That's when Nell turned pale and fell to her knees. Claudia ran to her and I yelled for Santino.

He knew just what to do. He had ice water and cold cloths. Maude and Viv had come home to change for evening shifts, and they were clucking over Nell, as well. My worry over her condition was startling. I'd felt myself growing closer to the city, and those who I considered friends, but Nell? I suppose she was part and parcel of it all.

"She'll be fine," said Santino, noticing my concern. "Claudia, take our Rosie out into the garden while I take care of Miss Nell."

"You bet, Poet."

She took my hand.

"Honey, aren't we already in the garden?"

"Yeah, but that ain't the one he's talkin' about. Come see."

We walked around the side of the building that hid a surprise—a small square, sunny and filled with wildflowers. Claudia unlatched the gate, and it moaned open to reveal a wonderful, riotous world.

"I think fairies live here," said Claudia.

"I wouldn't be surprised."

"*F, F* is for fairy."

I picked her up and hugged her tight. "You did it!"

"I been practicing…"

"Tell me, why is this garden all hidden behind here?"

"Cat likes it this way, all free. Drives Nell mad. But anyways, I gotta go finish the potatoes. Sonny won't tan your hide, but he will mine." She skipped away from me, leaving me with the flowers.

"Well, a clever girl would wonder why two women who aren't related would spend so much time together," I said to no one.

"Talkin' to yourself, Rosie?" asked Santino.

"You scared me!"

"I'm sorry, it's just… Nell's askin' for ya."

I held my hand over the wild daises. They were waist high, and I let them tickle my palm.

He kissed me. "I could kiss you in the daisies forever," he said.

"Though that sounds like heaven, we mustn't keep the queen waiting," I said, and I took his hand and led him back inside Empire House.

Santino stayed in the kitchen, and I walked down the foreign back hall toward Nell's room. I pulled up my hand to knock on the door, but heard Cat speaking with Nell instead. Unsure of what to do, I listened.

"Have they found him, do you think?" Nell asked.

"No. At first it was fine, keeping things from them. But now I feel as if they are becoming part of this family. Soon, we'll have to tell them everything."

"Not yet. Daisy was so skittish when Seacrest closed,

I'm afraid she'll abscond with him entirely. Only those sisters can walk this road gently. They're close. Give them some more time."

"Another week, and that's it. It never felt like lying before. Now it does."

I couldn't believe my ears—Cat and Nell *did* know about Asher, and had been keeping him from us all along, just like we suspected. And they were much closer to each other than they let on. I could have exploded with all the newfound clarity right there because I had no one to tell.

So I walked a few steps back down the hall and then stomped a bit before knocking.

Nell called for me to come in. She was sitting up in bed, and Cat was reading to her. The way their heads turned toward me at the same time and angle as I entered the room made me recall the ways I'd always noticed Cat and Nell's similarities. How had their relationship—whatever it was—gone right over my head? Could the little girl in the gardens with young Nell be Cat? Or was that too long ago?

"Good, you're here. I've got to get back to the shop. Hopefully, you and your sister will patch things up soon. I miss you."

"I miss you, too. Tell her…"

Cat smiled as she gently shut the door behind her, leaving the room. I was alone with Nell.

"Miss Neville, have you had your tea? I'll get some for you," I said.

"You may call me Nell. I know you do when you are not addressing me directly anyway," she said.

I went to her then and sat on the side of the bed. The memory of the last night I cared for my father was heavy on my mind.

"Tell me, Rose—what is it? What is this all about? Why has Ivy left?"

"Everything will be fine, Nell. You need to rest."

I was fluffing the pillows up behind her and easing her back into a sitting position.

"That's lovely, Rose. Honestly, you've surprised me these past few weeks. I thought you a cold duck, I did."

"I behaved like one, Nell. But lately I've been wondering about something. Did you ever wonder whether I really was that person, or if I *became* that way because you decided on my constitution before you even met me?"

"The city has given you a sassy tongue, I see."

"No, just a sense of humor, I think. Are you feeling better?"

"Just a bit of heatstroke. And my legs have been bothering me, arthritis or something. It can't be your wildest dream, this life, cleaning up after people. I suppose you can't wait to get your house back. You'll be where you are most comfortable, alone with your books in the quiet of the country."

A queer bit of nausea began rumbling in my belly. That didn't sound like a very interesting life at all. I thought of telling her right there about Ivy's revelation, only something held me back.

"Did Santino tell you that he's decided I should marry him?" I asked instead, changing the subject.

Nell's eyes grew wide, but they weren't angry...they seemed almost happy.

"Rose, don't kid an old woman."

"See?" I said, holding up my hand with the now-limp piece of cotton.

"Well, well…here I was thinking you'd cut yourself. Does this make you happy?"

"Please don't take this the wrong way, Nell. But I'm confused. Does my happiness matter to you?"

She turned her head from me and looked toward the door. A tear pooled in her eye.

"When you get to be my age, and you meet someone who reminds you of yourself when you were younger… you begin to care. If that bothers you, I have a hundred more closets for you to clean tomorrow."

I paused, wanting to know everything—wanting to confront Nell about what I'd overhead. But I knew, instinctively, that I'd have to find my way back into my sister's heart before I could unravel the rest of the mystery.

"I'll get your tea, Nell," I said, and tentatively touched her hand. She did not pull away.

The next day we were all gathered at the crowded dining room table.

Jimmy came to call. I was delighted to see him, but could not for the life of me figure out why he felt like an old friend.

Perhaps it was because he was so happy to see me. I was beginning to realize what friendship meant.

"Tell me, how's old Nell?"

"Just fine…a small bit of heatstroke is all," I said.

As if on cue, Nell entered the dining room and took her seat at the head of the table.

"I don't feel like being waited on tonight. Tonight, I want everyone to sit and eat together."

We all took turns looking at one another, but sat down as directed. The hour went by with laughter and companionship, but Nell was quiet. I could tell she had more than her usual complaints on her mind.

"After dessert I'd like to see you in my study, Rose."

"Is she in trouble?" asked Claudia.

"It's nothing of the sort," said Nell. "I swear, I am surrounded by idiots. Now, go fetch dessert, Jimmy. There's a cake in the icebox."

"It's so hot, I can't think of eating sweets," I said. "Would anyone mind if I stepped out to the stoop for a bit of air?"

"You're a free woman," said Comrade One—whose real name, I'd learned, was Bernadette.

"That I am," I said, getting up.

"Not for long," said Santino.

"Why, do you think if I marry you, you'll own me?" I snapped.

He held his hands up like I was robbing him, then smiled his playful smile.

"If I really thought that, I wouldn't have asked."

"Here," said Nell, handing me the carafe of red wine and a glass. "Stoops are lonely without something to drink. But if Sergeant Bridey walks by, remind him who paid for his billy club."

Santino followed me onto the stoop.

"I think she winked at you," he said.

"Did she?"

"You seem to have won the old broad over."

"We'll see," I said.

"I love watching the city go by, don't you?" he asked.

"As a matter of fact, I do."

I hadn't told Santino about Adams House, either. I didn't want him to worry that I'd leave him, or worry that I'd ask him to up and leave his life in The City. I needed to know more about my own intentions before I told him. Holding back that information helped me to understand, on a deeper level, his inability to tell me everything he knew about Asher. It wasn't only about keeping a promise. It was about protecting himself and protecting me, as well.

"How about we make this an evening ritual? Jimmy says Ivy talks about wiling away your youth on that big front porch the two of you grew up on."

Ivy? Thinking fond thoughts about our childhood? It made me want to cry.

"In my memory, it feels like it was always summer," I said, pouring a glass of wine. "Want a sip?"

He smiled and brought a flask out of the inside of his jacket pocket. I clinked my glass against his.

"Cheers, Poet."

Nell's study was always dark, but that evening, with the midsummer night closing in, it felt darker than ever. One lamp with a green glass shade pooled light out onto Nell's tidy desk.

"If this is about the album…" I began.

Nell didn't notice my slip. I was beginning to learn she could be deaf when she had her own agenda. Much like the girl I used to be.

"Your Mr. Lawrence has phoned with news. He tells me that he had to rent Adams House."

"He's not *my* Mr. Lawrence," I said, trying to catch my breath. *Strangers? In my house?*

"Sarcasm at a time like this? You surprise me, Rose. I thought I was finally seeing the young woman you were born to be."

"I'm sorry. It's been one shock after another recently. Is

it just a rent? Or are they wanting to buy it?" I asked, sitting up a little higher.

"Just a rent as far as I know. He needs your approval. I have to phone him back by the morning. I know this is difficult, Rose."

"Well, I'm not happy with the news, but not sad, either." I took a deep breath, ready to finally put words to Ivy's confession. "You see I've just recently discovered that the house actually belongs to me. And I'll be honest with you, Nell—I'm trying to digest the information at the same time as I'm trying to figure out why I'm not deliriously happy. Even this news of the rent. It seems to me that the money accrued from the lease would buy me more time to earn the taxes due on Adams house, and once that is done, I could go back to Forest Grove. And yet…"

"And yet you aren't convinced that is what you want to do at all," said Nell.

"Why is it so hard to let go of things?"

"Welcome to real life, my dear. Nothing we expect is ever how we expected it. And the unexpected is frequently just as disappointing," she replied, rising from her chair to rest a gentle hand on my shoulder.

By the second week of living in Empire House without Ivy, I hadn't even peeked at the photo album. It felt wrong to discover anything new without Ivy. I hadn't confronted Nell about her relationship to Cat and my growing suspicions about their relationship to Asher, either. More importantly, I had lost my journal. I spent days searching the entire building for the private words I'd kept there.

I asked Maude and Viv, but they didn't even come up with a funny response, so I knew they didn't know, or care where it was. Claudia was helping me look, thrilled that I hadn't blamed her first. "Thanks for trustin' me, Rosie," she'd said.

"You only take things that people leave behind. That's not technically stealing, honey," I said.

Santino scoured the streets all around Washington Square, where I sometimes went to write, and even Nell was going through her bookshelves. I bit my nails waiting for her to discover her photo album was missing. But all the searching was to no avail. My journal was gone.

Losing that journal started to smudge the ink from the lovely pages my mind had created. Poked holes in the peaceful life I'd been pretending to live. Because I knew that the only person who would understand how terrible it felt for me to lose anything else that close to me would be the other person in my family who experienced the same losses. Ivy.

I fell on the parlor couch in misery as a summer storm loomed. The clouds forced themselves angrily together, and I remembered what it was like sleeping next to my sister. Little girls face-to-face, breath like cold milk, waiting out long nights together. We'd cowered under the blankets, Ivy and I, whenever a storm approached. How safe I'd felt with her.

Nothin's safe, miss…

Clever Ivy always knew how far away a storm would be.

"Who will count the minutes between the thunder, Ivy?" I'd asked when she carried her dolls from our room to her new one.

"You need to learn how to do it yourself, Rose," she'd said.

I'd pretended to be brave and responsible for her. Not

for me or our mother before she died or our father, either. I'd been looking for Ivy to notice me and say, "How brave you are," or "How beautiful," or even "I'm proud to be your sister."

It's a strange creature, the beast called pride. I'd wanted to hear those words from Ivy, and when she never said them to me, I felt hurt and ashamed.

But lying there in the parlor of Empire House, I realized I'd never said those words to her, either, even though I believed, with all my heart, that she was the bravest, most beautiful sister in the world, and that I held my head a little higher for knowing her.

"You know something, Rosie?" Santino asked, sitting next to me and gathering me up in his strong arms. "When you birds came here, I knew a little about why you'd come. But right from the start, I never thought about it as the two of you reclaiming your brother...I always assumed that given the time, the two of you could reclaim each other."

His words rang with truth in my ears. "I miss my sister," I said.

Santino clasped my hand. "I know, Rosie. And I promise...when she's ready, she'll come back. And in the meantime, you could try writing to her?"

So I did.

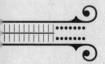 # CHAPTER 16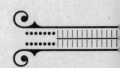

Ivy

I HAD ABSOLUTELY no idea where to go when I left Empire House, but I knew I couldn't go back. There was no room for me there, and scared as I was, I couldn't live like an unwanted houseguest. Apparently, it was Rose's home now, not mine. And if my cheek didn't still sting from where she'd slapped me, I'd give her a begrudging compliment. She'd managed what I'd failed to do.

After wandering around Washington Square Park, I hopped the A train, riding it up and down until dusk brought out the men who looked me over like I was a steak dinner on a platter. When one put a rough hand on my knee I hightailed it to safer ground and found myself down the block from Cat's shop.

"I'll need to dock your pay," Cat said, frowning, after I told her of my predicament. "It's in your best interest to go back to your sister."

"I don't think anyone else sees it that way," I said.

"This is temporary, Ivy."

"Don't I know it."

Though Cat didn't exactly welcome me with open arms, she also didn't ask a lot of questions, and for that I was grateful. She set me up in yet another small room behind the bar, one that housed an ancient feather bed in a heavy wood frame and a plain bureau, into which I stuffed my dresses and underthings. That first day, I halfheartedly made the bed with the fresh linens Cat provided and crawled under the coverlet, falling into a deep, dreamless sleep. When I woke up, I spent considerable time staring at the ceiling, content to stay in the cocoon I'd made for myself. Rose had recently become such a center of activity, and it was exhausting. I don't have to *move* much, I thought. If I took my meals at the bar, I could stay in the speakeasy indefinitely, forgetting there was a city above me. I could be in Atlantis, or purgatory or twenty thousand leagues under the sea. I could be anywhere. And when I did eventually surface, perhaps the world would be mine again.

"You're gonna get rickets if you don't let the sun hit your face," Bessie said on my third day underground. We were polishing glasses, which by then I'd realized was what we did to look busy when there was little else to do. Maude hovered but remained silent. When she discovered my hiding place she tried to talk me into returning to Empire House, but I'd held my hand up every time she opened her mouth and said, "Give me time." Isn't that what people said when they really meant, "Scram!"?

"You're being greedy with time," Maude said. "It ain't all yours. You've got to give some back soon." After that, she'd stayed quiet.

Viv didn't say much, either, just watched me with cool eyes. Every so often she'd crowd my tray with too many drinks, sending me out into the crowd with buckling knees. I didn't complain, just gritted my teeth and minded my business.

Until Jimmy caught me alone. He came in with a large group—a blur of navy blue suits and fedoras—but they disappeared into one of the endless rooms behind the bar, their deals made in the dark, even in a place where vice was brazenly courted.

Around two the place cleared out. A few lost souls hung their heads over glasses of gin, but otherwise the bar looked as bleak and desolate as I felt. Onstage, the drummer seemed not to have noticed the rest of the band had called it a night. He hit at the snare with a fan brush, the noise sending shivers down my spine.

"Pour me one, Beauty."

Jimmy slowly lowered himself onto a bar stool. His eyes looked made of glass.

"Don't you think you've had enough?"

"I wouldn't have asked for one if I did."

I fixed him a drink using the good crystal and slid it in front of him, along with a bowl of peanuts. "You should eat something."

"So now you're taking care of me?" Jimmy said. He tossed his drink back, downing half of it in one shot. "Pour one for yourself."

"Cat doesn't like it."

"That day I picked you up from the station, you didn't strike me as a girl who liked being told what to do."

I couldn't remember what that girl had been like, but I

couldn't explain that to Jimmy. I didn't want to disappoint him. "I need this job."

"Oh, I forgot," he said, his voice flat. "You ran away from home."

"This is home now."

"This ain't no home for anyone," he grumbled. "You need to find something better."

"You offering?"

Jimmy picked up a handful of peanuts and pelted me with one.

"What was that for?"

"You set small fires and then run away. That's what a child does, so I'm treating you like one."

"Are you any better? Running around with lipstick on your collar, smelling of perfume?"

"I'm living, Beauty. I've seen enough of death. I don't plan on ever sitting still long enough for it to catch up with me." He drained the rest of his glass and pushed it toward me. I poured him another, and after a moment's hesitation, drank it down myself.

Jimmy smiled. "That's my girl."

"I'm not your girl."

"Now that's the first intelligent thing you've said in a week."

My hand itched, and for a moment I understood the impetus behind a slap. The urge ran hot and swift like lightning, an electrical shock of the pure need to cause pain. Its strength stole the words from my tongue. Was that what I'd done to Rose when I'd pushed her to this point? Robbed her of everything but base impulse? I thought of the journal hidden in my rucksack and felt a wave of guilt so strong I grew dizzy. I'd taken all her words, the whole kit and kaboodle. But she'd hurt me just the same, hadn't she? She sat in the Republic Theater, quietly watching as I stumbled through the loss of my dream. She sat there, an impassive witness to failure.

I turned away from Jimmy, unable to go back and forth with him any longer. I knew he wasn't done with me, but it was still a surprise when he leaned over the bar and brushed his lips against the nape of my neck. "Fight, Beauty," he murmured in my ear. "With me, not Rose. Let's have a little fun. That's all this is, isn't it? A little fun to pass the time away."

"I don't want to fight anymore," I whispered.

"Are you done with me, then?" he asked, his voice gone cold.

"I'm just done."

"Well, if you're done fighting then get your arse back to Empire House and take care of your sister."

Why would she need my care? When I turned to ask him what he meant, Jimmy was already weaving up the stairs leading to the alley. When he stepped outside I could see a beguiling sliver of the New York night, but then the door slammed shut, leaving the ghosts of twinkling lights spotting my vision.

Exhausted, I closed up the bar and returned to my room, slipping under the covers fully clothed. I lay there in the darkness, but my brain would not slow and my eyes stayed open. There are few things worse than being wide-awake during the precious stillness of the wee morning hours, that wonderful time when we truly give ourselves over to our dreams. I gave sleep a final, sporting chance, and then, irritated, threw off the covers and reached for my rucksack. I tore a sheet of paper from Rose's journal and retrieved a pencil from behind the bar.

July 2, 1925
Dear John the Wonder,
How well did you know my father? Lately, I feel I barely knew him at all. I think about the secrets he kept, and the reasons he kept them. Papa was an unusual man, but not a cruel one—did he hope sending Rose and I on this little excursion would draw us closer? Then he was an innocent, as well, and misjudged his daughters' true natures.

Turns out I'm the scaredy cat, not my sister. I am enchanted by this city, but I'm terrified of it, too. There are so many open doors here, but the thought of crossing all those thresholds breaks a cold sweat on my brow. My father bravely chose an eccentric life. Rose allowed the city to seep into her soul. Our brother, Asher, remains a mystery, though we do know he's a survivor of the horrible onslaught in the Argonne, and it appears he's still battling his memories. He's lost just as I am, but for some reason I'm not as worried for him. He is my father's son surely as Rose is his daughter. Turns out I'm the one hiding in the corner, the odd (wo)man out. I was fearless when there was nothing to lose, and that isn't fearlessness at all.

You're a good listener, John the Wonder. Is that why my father chose you? Perhaps you are one of his final gifts, as well?
Sincerely,
Ivy

PS: Take note of the return address. I no longer re-
side at Empire House.

After finding a stamp, I left to post the letter. The city
was oddly still in the predawn hours, and I breathed in
sea air that felt fresh and new. The milkman tipped his
hat to me, and some newspaper boys whistled as I walked
by. "Watch your manners," I quipped with a wink and
a smile, and their laughter followed me back into Cat's.

I still wasn't sleepy, but I crawled into bed, dragging
the lamp off the bureau onto the floor next to me. Rose's
journal still lay on my coverlet. I drew it to me, opened
to the first page, and began to read.

I spent the next few days getting to know my sister. Was
it a lousy thing to do, reading her innermost thoughts?
Maybe. Was it cheating since I didn't have to deal with
the flesh and blood? Definitely. But it was all I had of her,
and a true introduction would be difficult in the chaos of
Empire House.

Rose's words were alive, just like the city that had
opened her like a flower. I read her poems again and again,
learning Rose's interior language, the one I never thought
I could speak. I read before work, on my breaks and before bed, her poems becoming the prayers I'd never bothered to say before. On Independence Day, after night had
fallen and the sharp crack of fireworks rumbled through
the speakeasy, I sat reading on my bed during a break from
the speak, when Cat walked in.

I shoved Rose's journal under my pillow.

"I hope you didn't waste your money on one of those
dime-store novels," Cat said. She stood in the doorway, her

deep crimson dress made celebratory by a blue-and-white striped sash at the waist. She held an envelope in her hand. "If you're looking for a little sauce just walk back into the speakeasy and open your eyes. People love to neck in the corners. Why is that? I'd think it would be uncomfortable."

"I don't think they care," I said.

She didn't say anything after that, just studied me with an odd expression on her face. The band started up a jazzy number, their new singer laying into "Somebody Loves Me" with too much juice, hitting at the notes like a punch-drunk boxer. When I asked Stan if I could sing again, he said I "wasn't seasoned enough."

"What is she, a roast chicken?" Maude said in my defense, and I loved her for it.

Cat tossed the envelope my way, bringing my attention back to her. "Jimmy dropped this off."

I couldn't imagine Jimmy sitting still long enough to put pen to paper. Curious, I ripped it open, but it wasn't from Jimmy. It was from Rose.

Cat perched awkwardly on the bed next to me. For the first time since I'd known her, she seemed unsure of herself. "Do you mind if I stay while you read?" she said, and I wondered if she had an inkling of what it contained.

"You're already sitting down, aren't ya?"

July 4th, 1925
Dear Ivy,
I look for you everywhere. I peer down the streets hoping to see a flash of beads. I listen for your laughter. I keep expecting that you'll return, slamming the doors and everything will go back to the way it

was. Only it can't…because we are not the sisters we used to be.

I think I've realized why our argument became a silent war. You may correct me if I'm mistaken, but I feel as if we both had urgent matters of our own hearts that had to be addressed. What could we have said to each other after that night? We'd experienced so much change in such a short span of time, we—or at least, I—didn't have the vocabulary to clearly express my thoughts. It's odd, this new language. Words I said before hold no meaning for me now. Words like "No," and "Ninnie," and "Disgusting." Harsh words that serve no other purpose than to sting and slash. Saying I'm sorry for the things I said to you, for slapping your sweet face, for all our years growing up, means nothing now. Because, you see, I realize that we cannot go back to the past. We can't return to who we used to be, and we can't undo the things already done.

Those first few days after you left, I was a muddled mess, then an angry tiger, then a fragile cup teetering on the edge of a high table. For so long I thought that you and I fit so tidily in the perceptions that our parents, without meaning to do harm, built around us.

Rose: the eldest child. Responsible and plain. A cold streak running through her for defense, because Papa thought I'd never marry, and would live with him, taking care of him forever. My, how the hidden urgencies of family can demolish those they love.

And Ivy: the youngest child, wild and free. An exotic girl meant for greatness.

First Mother, then Papa, locked us inside those

boxes, Ivy, and though the fragrance of those traits may have scented our baby hair, it's a shame they didn't notice how they mingled. How when we held our little girl hands tight against the world, we were infinitely stronger.

When and if you decide you are ready to see me again, I want you to know in your heart two very important things. First, I forgive you for not telling me Lawrence's confession about the house being mine all this time. If I'd known when you found out, I may never have opened my heart to Santino. So thank you. And second, I have found the most amazing clue to finding Asher. I've been so patient with myself, for I refuse to peruse it until you and I are together again. I was a thief, you know! Took a photo album from Nell's study. I'm sure it holds many answers to the myriad of questions we still have.

We'll find him, Ivy, but only if we work together. For the first time in our lives, we must be the pair we were always meant to be.

How about it, doll?

All my love, from yesterday, today and tomorrow,
Rosie

I thought the first time my sister touched me with any real emotion it was the slap, but that was just frustration. This letter was her heart meeting mine. I began to cry. Cat didn't pat my back or murmur soothing words as most women would have done, but she placed her hand on my arm, and for some reason that was better consolation.

"I never had a sister," she said gently. "But from what I gather you didn't have one, either, and neither did Rose."

"Do you think it's possible to make up for lost time?" I asked, lifting my chin to meet her eyes. She was still hard to read, but something warm melted away the frost I usually saw when she looked at me.

Cat shrugged. "Why would it matter if the future is going to be different?"

"Is it?"

"Ivy," she said, standing up, "forget about finishing your shift. Maude and Viv can manage. Go to bed and get a real night's rest. When you wake up in the morning, go see Rose. It really is that simple." She pulled back the bed-clothes, and I slipped in, conscious of the journal cradling my head through the thin pillow.

Cat switched off the lamp. "I'm not an overly optimistic person, but I do know that when you wake up the sun will be shining. Like someone stuck it up there just for you."

"Like aces high in the ever-loving sky," I murmured.

"Your father used to say that to you, didn't he?" Cat asked, her voice soft. I wished she hadn't turned off the lamp. I wanted to see her expression.

"He did. How did you know?"

But she was gone and I was tired. I closed my eyes finally and slept.

The next morning Cat was nowhere to be found. I let the cleaners in to scrub the floors and got dressed in my best-cut dress, a sky-blue drop waist. I pinned a pink summer cloche to my bob and carefully adjusted my stockings. My pulse raced so quickly I almost asked Bessie to pour me a quick nip.

"Aren't you a picture?" she said, and I decided I didn't care if she meant it or not.

"It's my day off. Why not put on the dog?"

Bessie reached into the pocket of her apron and placed a telegram on the wet bar. "This came while you were getting gussied up."

I snatched it up before the water ruined it. Was it from Rose?

Western Union
From: J. W. Lawrence, esq. , Forest Grove, New York
To: Ivy Adams, New York City, New York
Arriving on the 5:00 train. STOP. Grand Central. STOP. Meet me at the station? STOP. A country lawyer could get lost in the big city. STOP.

"I tipped the boy," Bessie said, interrupting my thoughts.

I stuffed the telegram into my purse and handed Bessie a dime. "Don't spend it all in one place," I said and rushed up the stairs and into the day.

MacDougal Street looked just as I'd left it, a patchwork quilt of old and new New York. Cat had been right; the sun was absolutely blinding, and I squinted across the street at Empire House.

I saw Nell first, shouting orders to Sonny, who smiled lazily, nodding his head but not moving. Claudia lay stretched across the sidewalk playing marbles and annoying passersby, who had to scoot around her.

Rose sat on the top stair. The sun caught her hair and skin, painting her in the golden hue worthy of Klimt's brushstroke. She wore a gypsy-cut gown in the lightest of cotton, a dress she'd made with her own hand, I could tell. She laughed at something Sonny said, but her smile was wistful.

Still, I balanced on the curb, watching the scene as if it were a play. Was there a place on that stoop for me?

MacDougal, so familiar to me now, was more than just a street to cross. It held everything this city had to offer, including my sister's friendship.

I needed her to look at me. If I saw welcome in her face, I'd run pell-mell across that street. If she didn't, I'd stay lost, wandering the city like a ghost.

Look at me, Rose. Please. Look at me.

Please.

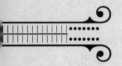 # CHAPTER 17

Rose

I SAT ON the stoop in the morning with my eyes open in a way they hadn't been before, and I was seeing things for the first time. Our attic, for example, was lovely. Where before there were only dusty floors, I saw the history of all the previous tenants. Where before, the confines of the place left me feeling nothing but fear, I looked into the recent past and saw my own bravery. Where before I'd thought there was no honesty to be found in what I thought was a cruel city, I now saw the truth hidden between each line of conversation and each glance back and forth between those I realized were now friends.

Everything looked different to me through my new eyes, including my sister, who, I realized, was standing across the street, looking back at me. From the moment Santino and Nell urged Claudia inside and I followed their gaze across the sunny street, I knew, just from seeing the way her face lit up, that she had changed, as well.

She raised her arm in a wave, but I could not get over how stunningly perfect the moment was. I was recording it in my mind. I was savoring it. I may have even closed my eyes, because when I opened them, she was walking away.

"Ivy!" I yelled, chasing her, barefoot, the pavement burning my feet.

She stopped and turned around at the corner. I saw she was crying.

"I thought…I thought you didn't want to see me. I thought you'd changed your mind," she stammered.

"I wanted nothing more!" I said and pulled her to me so tight I may have pushed the breath right out of both of us. "It's so wonderful to see you."

She was looking at me in a way I'd wanted her to look at me since we were small. The way she looked at Father, and the way she looked at The City the first day we arrived.

We held each other, daring the sun to burn our bare shoulders. We couldn't let go, because both of us knew we wouldn't be able to go home again. I was learning I never really wanted to, and Ivy was learning, for the first time, that the safety it had given her was gone, making her grieve. I hushed her. "We'll create a new family together, Ivy," I said, holding her as the busy city disappeared, leaving only us.

"I'm sorry I slapped you. I was overwrought," I said after a long silence. "Also," I said, wiping my tears, "you were right. I cry much too easily, I've found."

"You feel things deeply, Rose. There's nothing wrong with that. I don't think anything you cried over was easy at all. Unless I'm mistaken and you cry when you burn toast."

"No," I said, laughing.

"So, what do you want to do?" she asked.

"I want to find Asher, and I think I've found the last clue. Cat and Nell are in on it, and I overheard them discussing Daisy—she has to be the key. I think she's hiding Asher."

I looked at my sister for any sign of surprise, but her eyes reflected a softer understanding. Then she said, "And Cat, I believe, knew Papa very well. Only I can't put all the pieces together."

"Of course you can't. We need to be together to do that."

"And now we are," she said.

"Onward."

"Onward," agreed Ivy.

Arm in arm we walked back to Empire House. Words tumbled out over one another. She told me of her suspicions about Cat knowing our father. I told her of my suspicions of Cat and Nell being related.

"Perhaps you're right, Ivy," I said. "Maybe Nell is Asher's very own Miss Havisham!"

"Of course," she said, and hugged me again, touching my long braid.

"I like your hair this way," she said. "I'm proud of you, Rose."

"I'm proud of you, too."

As we reached the stoop, her eyes fell.

"What is it?"

"You said in your note to me that you stole something. Did you really?"

"Yes, and I haven't been able to peek at it or put it back for that matter, until I was with you again. So let's go! It's a photo album. I just know it holds the answers."

She reached into her rucksack, brought out my journal and set it in my hands.

"Is it stealing if we learn things? Is it stealing if we give it back?"

"No. It's not," I said and kissed her cheek.

"I'm glad you never bobbed your hair," she said as we walked into Empire House. "It's lovely this way. You should wear it down completely, you know."

I stopped at the foyer mirror, took my hair and un-braided it at the bottom, letting the loose layers frame my face. "Are you sure it doesn't look too much like I've been in bed for too long?" I asked.

Ivy laughed. "No, Rose, you look like a writer," she said.

"I'm not really a writer."

"Yes, you are. Who knows? Someday, you may travel to Europe and write with the Parisians."

I knew that she was proud of me.

"You look like a gypsy," she said.

"I feel like a gypsy," I replied.

We walked up the stairs together, arm in arm, unwilling to let go, and laughed at our bodies bumping the walls as we rounded each landing. We were starting again.

"I missed this place," Ivy said when we reached the penthouse.

Claudia came bounding up the stairs after us. She sur-prised me by throwing her arms around Ivy's waist, and Ivy surprised me by hugging her back. "I missed you!" said Claudia. "And I can read!"

Ivy laughed and nodded her head patiently, listening to a litany of the weeks that had gone by at Empire House.

"Can I show you how swell my penmanship is? Rose says it's near perfect for a girl my age."

"Yes, of course," said Ivy, who turned back to me as Claudia went to retrieve her notebooks. "Did a letter arrive recently, Rose? I didn't get a chance to tell you before I left, but Mr. Lawrence said he'd found a sealed letter in Papa's safety deposit box at the bank. It should be addressed to both of us."

Claudia dropped her notebooks. She stood stock-still in the middle of the penthouse. I could tell she didn't know whether to run from us or to us. "Miss! Oh, no. Miss!"

"What, what it is Claudia?" I asked.

She stepped backward toward her little corner under the eaves, and then, turning around, she reached into an apron pocket on a low hook and retrieved an envelope.

"I found it in the foyer. I thought I'd put it by your bed, like a favor. But then I must have forgotten about it."

Ivy and I looked at each other.

"Show me," I said.

"Swear you ain't mad."

"I swear!"

She brought us the letter.

"Just so you know," said Claudia, who sat on my lap, "I didn't steal it or nothin', I swear."

"We both know you didn't steal it," said Ivy.

"You're good sisters. I wish I could be one of you."

"How about we just say you are?" I asked.

"You mean it?"

"You bet," said Ivy.

We sat on my bed side by side, and I held Claudia on

my lap for comfort. Ivy opened the letter. "It's from Papa," she said.

"Read it aloud, Ivy."

Ivy read us the last chapter of our search.

Dear Ivy & Rose,

If you are reading this, I've died. Believe me, it's as shocking to me as I'm sure it is to you. Please know how much I love you.

There is no way for me to explain what I have done, or how I have behaved. I took advantage of both you.

I've always searched outside of me for a reason—to be here. To be a person of this world, a citizen, a man who lives outside of the internal workings of his mind. Your mother always thought I loved Colleen, Asher's mother, more than I loved her. That she was in competition with a ghost. Colleen died giving birth to Asher, and we had such a short marriage, I could never compare the two.

Love is a mystery, girls. When I met your mother she was a wild, progressive creature, ready for adventure…see, she took me away. I never had to look deep into myself until you girls were born. I'm ashamed to admit that every time I looked at the two of you, especially you, Rose, for reasons you either understand already or are soon to understand—you stirred feelings inside of me that reminded me of what I'd left behind. And your mother, she never wanted a sedate life at all. She would have kept traveling and having children at the same time. I was the one who insisted we settle down at my family's home. A place

I'd yearned to escape from myself, as a boy. I think I killed her spirit, only one of my many sins brought about by fear.

Here is what I know: I know that Asher went to war, and I know that upon his return, he was not well. I tried to see him. No...that's a lie. I wanted to see him. But I was afraid.

The truth is I couldn't face him. I left him the house as a consolation prize. I know that hurt you, Rose. But I also knew you couldn't live here forever, caught in some dream that would only wake you when you were old, and your life already gone. Trust me, I know because I recently woke up and it had happened to me.

I am enclosing his last known address, the name of his grandmother and his sister, Cat, who was five years older and never very fond of me, or so I thought.

I'll never forget when Colleen died and I carried Asher from our rooms to Nell's, and little Cat begged me to take her with me. She was so little, and she reached up her arms and cried out, "Papa! Don't go. Take me!"

How was I to leave my own infant behind and raise a child that wasn't even my own? There was no way. I thought, perhaps, when I met your mother that I'd gather them up, once we settled down somewhere, but I lost track of my desires once we stopped traveling.

So there you have it. Go find him, girls. Put the family back in its rightful order. Try and tell Nell that at least I understood her anger, even though I didn't care for her strict and shallow ways. And, girls, please tell Catherine that I should have taken her with me. Tell her I always remembered her, loved her and thought of her as my own.

And go to him, your brother. Remind him of who he is. I trust the two of you have learned enough of the world by now to do it the right way.

I also know that there were better, braver ways to tell you about my life before. But I'm not brave. I'm a coward.

If it is any solace at all, you, my darling little girls, have helped me to at least see, for a brief moment, the man, the father, I could have been to the other two I left behind.

Thank you,

Papa

Sometimes, when the earth is at the correct axis, we see things aligned perfectly. Our father had given us a gift with the letter he wrote, and Claudia had unwittingly given us the gift of keeping it from us, until the very moment we needed it.

We paced together and cried, then paced some more, clutching at each other and rereading it aloud in line and out of order.

"So that's that then," said Ivy. "Come, Claudia. Don't be upset. We wouldn't have known what to do with this letter if you'd remembered to give it to us. Let me braid your hair, won't you?" Ivy smoothed out the letter and folded it into a tidy square. She then placed it under her dress, in her brassiere close to her chest.

"Scandalous," I said.

She looked at me, and I watched her eyes go from worried that I'd been serious to realizing I was kidding. She broke into a terrible fit of giggles.

I started to laugh with her, and once we started, as inappropriate as it was, we couldn't stop.

I was losing my breath, and tears were streaming down both our faces.

"Can you even believe it? It's been in front of us this whole time!" she was saying.

"No, I cannot. How did we not know?" I said.

"Cat…Asher…Nell!" She laughed. Our stomachs were sore by the time we calmed down.

When the laughter subsided, we sat close together and paged through the photo album. Each one meant so much more to us because we finally knew that Nell, Asher and Cat were all connected to our father. And in a way, it was like looking at a family album.

Ivy was braiding Claudia's hair as we looked.

"Who's this little girl, though? She looks so familiar. Keep turning those pages, sister," said Ivy.

"It must be Daisy…they grew up together," I said.

At the very end of the album, there was a loose photo. One of Asher, looking handsome and carefree. Staring at a beautiful young woman with such love in his eyes. She had her head tossed back in laughter.

"Dear God, that's Natasha!" said Ivy. "She works at the Republic Theater."

"Natasha? No, that's Daisy! Ain't she pretty!" said Claudia.

"So now we know," she said. "What do we do next?"

"We go see Daisy," I said, and we left out the back fire escape. Just like real detectives, at last.

 CHAPTER 18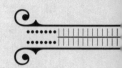

Ivy

WHEN ROSE AND I walked in, the denizens of the Republic Theater were busy preparing the space for a production and barely spared us a glance. Scruffy men in shirtsleeves moved chairs into haphazard rows, and a group of young girls clustered around Bertrand, the director. He nodded in our direction, jaunty beret tipping slightly on his head. I thought about him watching me take a dive the last time I stood on the stage, and my face grew hot.

"Do you see her?" Rose whispered, craning her neck to peer past the small crowd.

I didn't. The girls' faces were too jaded and lacked the serene quality of the woman I'd spoken with. I walked up to one of the fellas lugging chairs. "Is Natasha around?"

"Never heard of her," he said. "But I'm new, and people tend to come and go in this place."

"That's what I'm afraid of," Rose said.

"You're sure?" I pressed. "She's got blond hair, straight

and pulled back, not bobbed like mine. She wears a black dress sometimes, with lace at the collar?"

The man made a funny face, like he was the last person to notice a lady's attire. "There is a girl like that," he said after a moment. "Sometimes she cleans up around here, but she spends most of her time sewing costumes. Last I saw she was in the back, behind the stage."

I thanked him, my heart starting to race. Rose and I scurried backstage before anyone could tell us to beat it.

Backstage at the Republic was nothing to write home about. True to its Bohemian spirit, the actors' waiting area boasted a rickety spindle chair and a cracked mirror hanging on the wall. A number of closed doors lined a dank hallway, and some crumbling stairs led to a most likely rat-infested lower level. Not exactly the actors' quarters at the Winter Garden.

"Please let this not be a dead end," Rose said, her eyes closed as if in prayer. "Not now."

I thought about the girl with the sweetheart face, washing down the window with vinegar. "Rose, I'll look for a supply closet, you check the dressing rooms." She smiled at me, exhilarated by the task, and went searching.

I stepped carefully down to the lower level. The smell of ammonia masked more sour, earthier odors, and I fought the urge to cover my nose. I heard the scrape of metal against metal, but the basement was dark. "Natasha?" I called.

Not a sound. I felt someone behind me and froze, but when a hand softly touched my shoulder I knew it was Rose. "No luck," she whispered.

I silently gestured into the darkness. In the shadows I

caught a trace of movement, smoke against the night sky. "Daisy?"

"We don't mean to hurt you," Rose said quickly.

"But do you mean to hurt him?" Daisy stepped into the pool of light surrounding us. She held a bucket in one hand and a mop in the other.

"Of course not," I said, eyeing the mop warily. "Is there someplace we could to talk in private?"

Daisy looked at me, defiance twisting her pretty features. "He doesn't owe you anything."

"We're not here to collect anything," Rose said. "He's our brother, and we'd like to meet him. That's all."

Daisy tilted the mop against the wall and placed the bucket beside it. She walked up to Rose and boldly studied her face. "You do have his eyes," she said, her own welling up. "I can't deny that."

"He's my brother," Rose repeated.

Daisy nodded. "All right, I'll talk to you. But that's all I'm promising."

We followed her back upstairs to an empty dressing room. It was cramped, but clean and decently furnished. Rose and I sat on a low sofa with Daisy opposite us, perched on the makeup chair.

"I don't know what they told you," she began, "but you can't see him. They can't even see him."

"Nell and Cat?" I asked.

"And Sonny, Jimmy, the whole lot of them. Dr. Spence says it will set him back, and Asher..." It was the first time any of them had used his name in front of us and it felt like a door had opened deep and wide. "Well, Asher has suffered a great deal of setting back. I can't allow it."

"We're family," Rose said, but then flushed when she

realized her mistake. Nell and Cat were family, as well. That tactic had already failed.

Daisy was quiet for a moment. When she spoke, her voice was gentler, as though she'd decided that, at least to a point, we could be trusted. "I loved him before the war, when he was brash and impulsive. Have you been up to the roof at Empire House?"

"Rose has," I said, nudging my sister.

"Well, then you know how steep it is. Asher used to walk on his hands around the perimeter! I'd stand in the side garden and screech at him, but he never fell."

So like our father. Rose placed her hand over mine, and I knew she'd had the same thought.

"What has he been doing since the war?" I asked.

Daisy's hands found only each other, and she clenched them together. "I wish I could say recovering, but it hasn't been like that. Asher was exposed to mustard gas. It harmed his eyes and left scars in his lungs, but Asher's mind suffered the most serious wounds. It's more difficult to heal the inside and takes more time than you'd expect. Asher's been waging that battle for years, in and out of hospitals, disappearing and reappearing, with no explanation as to where he's been. He has episodes…Dr. Spence said it gets worse before it gets better." She trailed off, her eyes wet.

"It's been difficult for you," Rose soothed.

"I don't mind caring for him. I love him even more now," Daisy said fiercely. "What he did in that war…I don't think he would have done any different, even if he knew the outcome."

"He fought in the Argonne," I said, curiosity winning over good manners. "The Lost Battalion. Isn't that right?"

Daisy took a deep breath. "He enlisted with Sonny.

They were so proud that day, and we of them. They met Jimmy standing in line, and the three of them became fast friends. Ash wrote me letters, so many beautiful letters, but they stopped when their boots hit the ground in France.

"I didn't find out they were in the Argonne until later, when we got word he was in a French hospital. Sonny told me they'd spent most of the battle in a trench trying to stay alive. Asher was in charge of the company's gas masks. He must have miscounted or maybe there wasn't enough. He passed one to Sonny and one to Jimmy, and, covering his mouth with only a shirtsleeve, crouched down and hoped for the best when the Germans sent over their cloud of poison. No one realized at first that Asher hadn't any protection, and it was days before they left that damned forest. Jimmy and Sonny did the best they could."

Daisy straightened herself. "We've all done the best we could. When I found out Seacrest was closing, and they might ship the patients off to Ward's Island, I made the decision to take Asher quickly. His relationship with his family has always been problematic, and Dr. Spence says he must be kept calm at all times. It had to be me. So I got an apartment in the area and set him up."

"Why around here? Why not take him far away?" Rose asked.

"I didn't know what else to do. Bertrand, the director here, is an old friend. I thought I could hide in the shadows and sew. Greenwich Village is the only place I've ever known, and it's Asher's home. We grew up here and know its every nook and cranny. We know how to get lost, and we know how to be found if we want to."

Found. "Jimmy," I said, thinking back to how he subtly discouraged me from entering the theater. "He spotted you, didn't he?"

"He did," she said. "I was terrified he'd blab, but Jimmy was the only one who respected what I was doing. He understood. He feels…"

"Guilty," I finished for her. I wanted to think about that for a moment, to reassess my vision of someone I thought I had figured out. We were here for Asher, though, and I had to remember our purpose. "I'd still like to see my brother, Daisy. Can you let us see him for just a few minutes?"

Daisy shook her head. "He doesn't always recognize the people who visit him, and it's most upsetting. Sets him off for days."

"But he's never met us," I said, seized by the need to comfort this man, my brother. But was it a selfish impulse? I paused, but Rose took over.

"Do you intend to keep him locked away from everyone?" she said with a note of compassion in her voice. "That can't be healthy."

"It's working for now," Daisy said briskly. "He's as calm as he was at Seacrest."

"But is he happy?" I asked. I knew it wasn't appropriate, but the question was balancing at the tip of my tongue and slipped out.

"Are you questioning what I've done?" Daisy retorted, her face pink. "I've been caring for him for years, on and off. I know him better than anyone." She stood, and I thought she would leave us there to sit and stew in how abysmally we'd handled the situation. She glanced at the door, weighing something in her mind, and then sat down again. "I don't know if he is," she said softly. "We don't discuss it. We don't discuss much of anything. He rarely talks."

It was then I saw we'd put a crack in the wall Daisy had erected. I leaned forward, resisting the impulse to pull this sad girl into an embrace. "We don't want to hurt him…we just want him to know we're here. Our hearts are open to him, Daisy. We don't think so highly of ourselves that we consider our presence miracle-inducing, but why not take a chance that we could help him, even a little bit?"

Daisy was quiet for a very long time, but not still. She fidgeted with the sticks of greasepaint on the desk next to her and moved her knee up and down like a jackhammer. "Okay," she said, and I exhaled, not realizing I'd held my breath. "I'll think it over. This isn't a decision to be made lightly."

"Of course not," Rose soothed.

"Meet me tomorrow in Washington Square Park at the fountain," she said, her voice gaining strength. "Late afternoon, when it's not so hot." She stood again, and this time I knew she'd be leaving. "I'll tell you my decision then."

Grand Central Station in the early evening was lit like a Hollywood movie star. I walked through the crowded main concourse, my heels clacking on the marble floor. Earlier, after Rose and I returned from meeting with Daisy, I'd asked Maude if she had anything demure I could borrow, which sent her into such violent spasms of laughter I worried she'd pop an artery. I ransacked my closet again and again, finally settling on a rose-colored drop waist with a lemon-yellow grosgrain ribbon sash. The hemline wasn't overly short, but given the hoots and catcalls I'd collected on the walk from the subway, it was short enough.

Rose had insisted I go alone to pick up Mr. Lawrence, claiming she needed to spend time with Claudia. I knew what she was really thinking about Mr. Lawrence's arrival, and I sensed I felt the same, but still it had me worried. My expectations were as fragile as the thin slips of paper that built our relationship. Did he see me as a trusted friend, or something beyond that definition? Usually so good at reading other people, I was unable to read clearly between the lines in his letters. I did know I treasured them, and by extension, him. Mr. Lawrence's friendship mattered, and it wasn't until the past few weeks that I truly understood how valuable those relationships were.

The train from Albany was right on time. My stomach turned a couple of ragged cartwheels. Why was I so nervous?

"Disembarking," the conductor called. He blew into his whistle and the passengers began their tentative exit, stretching their travel-weary legs, blinking at the exploding chaos in temporary confusion.

A tall man in a crumpled linen suit helped an elderly lady navigate the steep exit stairs. It was John the Wonder being wonderful. After seeing the woman safely to the luggage retrieval, he took a leather valise from the porter, handed him a tip and came striding in my direction.

"So you noticed me," I said as he approached. "Thought I might have some stiff competition. I was waiting for you to shrug off your jacket and place it on the ground at her feet."

"That was Mrs. Greene, my companion during the entire ride from Albany," he said, smiling at the recent memory. "Did you know pineapple juice is capable of removing corns?"

"I did not."

"And that's only one of nature's fascinating remedies. You wouldn't believe how many others I was delighted to hear on the way down. I don't think I got a word in during the entire trip."

Grand Central was loud, but not loud enough to conceal the silence that descended like a curtain over the two of us. John looked older than he had in Forest Grove, the bustling train station highlighting the sharp intelligence in his eyes, his natural curiosity about the world around him. It was a very attractive trait.

"Are you hungry?" I said when it appeared we would stand there forever. "There's a lovely restaurant right in the station."

"I did give Mrs. Greene my liverwurst sandwich," he said sheepishly.

"Lucky girl."

"Ivy." John dropped his valise and took both of my hands in his. "While Mrs. Greene was discussing foot diseases, I was trying to come up with what I was going to say to you when I arrived. I had a pretty good monologue planned, as well scripted as any of my best closing arguments, but when I saw you standing there, all my witticisms flew right out of my head."

John smiled at me, a smile that warmed me from the inside out. "All I remember is this," he continued. "After I read your last letter, it occurred to me that you might need a friend, not a correspondent. I bought the train ticket and sent the telegram. I acted on impulse, taking my cue from one of your best attributes. Sometimes it's perfectly fine to act without suffering through endless internal debate."

I mentally weighed my most impulsive actions over the

previous month. Did I come out ahead or behind? I'd stolen Rose's journal, smoked a cigarette, stood on a stage and sung my heart out. "I think there is some wisdom in that," I mused, stepping forward to reach my hand around the back of his neck. Before he could say a word, I gently pulled him to me and kissed his surprised mouth.

"There," I said, pulling away before we crossed the line of decency. "Now we can go get something to eat without worrying about getting spinach in our teeth."

Too early for dinner, The Oyster Bar was nearly empty when we walked in. Though subterranean, the restaurant's ceiling, arched and cathedral-like, made diners feel as though they were slurping down oysters in the Taj Mahal. The waiter sat us in far reaches, and I tried not to think what Cat said about couples in corners.

I told John all about what we'd learned of Asher's whereabouts, and about my undignified departure from Empire House. He asked about Rose, and I was able to answer honestly. "I feel like we might have a new start," I explained. "And if that's what father left us, it means much more than a house, even to Rose. I don't think she will return to Forest Grove—this city is her home now."

"Is it yours?"

I thought for a moment. "I'd felt lost here, dreadfully so, but sometimes if one gets lost in the woods, the only way out is to find a new path. I've made such mistakes, John. I'd been so keen on coming to a city I'd constructed in my imagination I never allowed the reality of it to seep in." I smiled at him over my water glass. "So, I suppose the answer is, I don't know."

"That's a perfectly fine answer," he said. "It means there

is a great deal of thinking and conversing in your future, which is always something to look forward to."

Feeling as though I was monopolizing the conversation, I shifted course, asking him specifics about his life in Forest Grove, his interests, his family.

"My parents live outside Albany, and I see them often enough, and speak with them by telephone. I mentioned I was coming into the city, and they were falling over themselves with recommendations. They're secret city dwellers, and come to Manhattan as time allows." He cleared his throat. "My parents once dined at the Hotel Albert on Eleventh Street and said the waitstaff places the most exotic flowers on each table. I'd like to take you there, Ivy. Once you've settled things with Asher, I'll reserve a table. Do you have a dinner dress?"

"I can get one," I said, excitement zinging through me. "Are you trying to woo me, John-the-Wonder?"

"I've been trying to for ages," he said. "But this city certainly makes it easier."

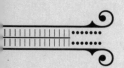 CHAPTER 19

Ivy & Rose
Ivy

NEW YORK WAS burning up with a hundred-and-two-degree fever. Sonny could fry his breakfast eggs on the sidewalk—my feet were blistering in my thin-soled shoes as Rose and I walked to Washington Square Park.

"If it was any farther, we might burst into flames before we get there," I said, uselessly fanning my hand in front of my face.

"It's two blocks," Rose said. "And complaining makes you hotter."

We stepped through the Arch and chose a bench in front of the fountain. A throng of children waded in the water, joyously splashing the cool water on their half-naked bodies. I envied them. "Do you think she's coming?" Rose said as the sun bore down on us.

"She's across the park," I said, watching Daisy approach. Outside of the dim theater, we were getting a look at Daisy in her full glory. She was taller than both of us, with an elegant neck and stick-straight posture that matched Rose's. They both wore cotton dresses that somehow stayed crisp. With my bobbed hair and crumpled chiffon short-waist, I'd look a sight sitting between the two of them.

She didn't sit down at all, which put a twist in my stomach. I'd thought for sure the answer would be yes.

"Part of me thinks what you're asking for is selfish," Daisy said, skipping any type of greeting. "You do realize that, right?"

Was it? I had been a selfish person; I knew that about myself now. I'd taken my father from my sister for so many years. I'd come to New York to benefit my own life, while letting my sister tag behind like a tin can bouncing from a newlywed's bumper. Was Daisy right? Was I putting my brother at risk to satisfy my own needs?

I looked into Daisy's fearful eyes. She wasn't a hard person inside, but had simply been placed in a situation where she decided what to do to help someone she loved. Did I have that strength inside me?

"On the day we buried my father," I said softly, "I found out I had this gift from him, the gift of an older brother. It was selfish of me, in a way, to assume that he would welcome me with the same fervor that I had in my heart from the moment I heard his name." I patted the bench next to me, and Daisy sat down. "I'll admit, we don't know Asher, not really, but we have learned that family is what keeps most of us going. When my father died it was the thought of Asher that kept me from throwing myself in the river. He did that for me. I'd like to do something for him in return."

I felt Rose's hand on my back, and I took a breath.

"The love of my sister healed me when I needed it," I continued. "Rose and I simply want the chance to tell Asher we're happy he's in the world, and if he wants any kind of a relationship with us—if he just wants us to sit with him for a while—we'd climb over a wall of fire for the honor to do it."

Daisy didn't say a word. She watched the spectacle of Washington Square Park parade by—the children playing tag, the man in the tweed suit strumming his guitar as though it was a cool fall day and not a scorcher, the painter adding the final touches to his masterpiece.

"I wish he was able to see this," Daisy said. "He loved this place before the war. Your brother has an artistic spirit."

Rose and I shared a look. *Like father,* her eyes seemed to say.

Daisy stood up again, stretched out her hand and pulled me up. "No longer than a few minutes," she said, her voice tremulous. "And I hope to God I won't regret it."

Rose

Daisy's apartment reminded me of her. It was pretty, very clean and soothing. I could tell she loved our brother very much, and that put me at ease immediately. No matter what happened with Asher, whether Ivy and I made the right decision or not, she'd take care of him, for better or worse.

"He's in the back bedroom. I scrounged a few extra bucks a month so I could have this flat in the back. Ash doesn't like loud noises, so it's worth the money. I swear

that bedroom faces almost all the back gardens in the village. You can't hear the street at all, even with the windows open."

"Daisy," I said, "thank you for letting us visit with him.
We really do appreciate it."

"Hell, you two didn't give me a choice, did you?" she
said, but she was smiling. It was a tired smile, one that
spoke volumes of the strain she'd been living under.

"It must be hard taking care of him all by yourself,"
said Ivy.

"It's an honor, not a job," she said.

The three of us stood at the beginning of a short hallway. There was a door, closed, at the very end.

"Is that his room?" I asked.

"Yep. At the back, like I already said. Let's get this over
with, shall we?" she asked.

The hall was covered in pictures, lovingly framed and
staggered from top to bottom, that depicted various stages
of Daisy's life with Asher before the war. As we walked
down the hall, Daisy first, Ivy and I trailed behind looking at them. Asher and Sonny as kids playing in Washington Square. Cat, Nell and Asher at Coney Island. Daisy
and Asher in all sorts of poses, first as kids, and then, as
their young romance blossomed, the pictures showed them
looking into each other's eyes.

"I could look at these photos forever," said Ivy.

"You don't have to," said Daisy, "you got the real thing
right here."

Daisy opened the door.

Asher's room was painted a soft, quiet blue. His bed was
made perfectly and covered with a white lace bedspread. I

recognized the lacework immediately. "Our mother made this," I said.

"Yes. Your father sent it as a gift in 1918, but Ash was already overseas. I kept it for him, though. He likes it, I think."

I was trying to look everywhere but at Asher, who was sitting in a chair by the open window. He hadn't turned to us when Daisy opened the door.

Ivy, on the other hand, had gone directly to him, and when I finally had the courage to peek beyond my periphery, saw that she had scooted another chair up next to his and had taken his hand.

Daisy sat down on his bed. "You might as well join her," she said. "There's another chair behind the door."

I brought the chair over to my sister and brother, lifting it so that it did not drag or clank across the floors.

I sat on the other side of him, taking his other hand. The three of us looked out his window together.

"We're here, Asher," said Ivy in a whisper. "Rose and I found you. Your friends are a tough crowd, but loyal... I got to hand it to them. You're lucky to have so many people watching out for you. We'd like to watch out for you, too, if you'd let us."

He stared straight ahead through the window. I didn't know what to say, so I followed his gaze.

Daisy was right—his view was a maze of rooftops and back gardens, an entirely different version of the Village. The interior version, more intimate than the crowded streets.

"Do you know us, Asher?" asked Ivy. "Do you know you have sisters?"

Asher didn't say anything, but his hands turned palm up, and his fingers closed around ours. Ivy and I looked at each other, smiling with excitement. Then we looked back at Daisy.

"He's holding our hands, Daisy! Do you see?" Ivy said, still whispering, but with sparkle.

"He does that sometimes," she said, but I could tell she was interested, at the same time as she didn't want to get her hopes up too high, because she came over to us and stood behind him.

"Rose and Ivy are here, Ash," she said, leaning down, placing her hands gently on his shoulders and speaking softly into his ear. "You should see them—they're a kick. Rose looks just like you, which is why Nell and Cat took to her even though they didn't want to. Me, too, I guess. But your sister Ivy. Oh, Ash, she's a beauty."

Ivy looked at Daisy with gratitude. I wanted more than anything for our brother to say those same words to her.

He didn't, not that day, but he did say something else.

"I've watched you," he said. His voice was scratchy and low from not speaking, but its tenor matched our father's, and when Ivy and I locked eyes, we both had tears forming. She nodded, because she'd heard it, too.

Daisy had taken a step back when Asher spoke, and her hand was over her mouth.

"Are you okay?" I asked.

"I need a glass of water. I'll be right back," she said, leaving. Though she closed the door behind her, we could hear her crying all the way down the hall.

"Don't worry, Asher. She's fine…those are tears of joy," said Ivy.

"I've watched you," he said again. "There." He pointed out the window.

Ivy stood up and leaned out to get a better view. "Rose, look! He's right. You can see into Sonny's garden! I'll be damned."

I looked, too. It wasn't a clear view, more sideways with certain parts hidden by trees and other buildings, but he'd been able to see us.

Ivy sat down and moved closer to Asher, placing her head against his shoulder. I was worried it was too much, too fast, and was about to urge her to move back, when he lifted his arm and wrapped it around her. Then he tilted his head so it leaned against hers. If I'd had a pen and paper, I couldn't, not in a million years, recreate the beauty of that moment, or the way my sister's face changed as I watched her exhale all her worries. How long had she been holding her breath?

I left them, then. Not because I didn't want Asher to wrap his other arm around me in the same fashion, but because I knew he would, someday. I left them there together, so they could heal.

I found Daisy sitting at her kitchen table smoking a cigarette. The ashtray was clean and sparkled in the morning sunshine. "Want one?" she asked.

"Sure," I said, taking one from her.

"So you were right," she said. "Seems he needed his family after all. I've been going out of my mind trying to get him to talk, and you birds walk in and he responds. Makes a girl feel a fool."

"Daisy," I said, reaching out over the kitchen table and covering her shaking hand with mine. "Don't you understand? You made him safe. If we'd come at any other time, before or after, he wouldn't have been able to see us. Trust me. We weren't ready. I'm surprised we didn't silence everyone we met the first two weeks we were here. We were a pair of unexploded bombs when we arrived. The City defused us."

"Really?" She laughed. "'Cause it usually just sets people off."

"Maybe that's the same thing," I said.

"You got a way with words, Rose. He does, too. I hope he comes around so you three can get to know each other."

"He will…I can feel it. And we're here now, me and Ivy. We have no plans to go anywhere. So we'll help, okay? You don't have to do this alone anymore."

"Thank you," she said.

Ivy stayed with Asher for an hour, and Daisy told me story after story about Asher growing up. What he was like as a boy and his friendship with Sonny. Ivy finally emerged, red eyed, but smiling.

"Hi-ya," she said, taking a cigarette from Daisy's case.

"Make yourself at home," said Daisy.

"I do believe I will," said Ivy as Daisy stood, and then playfully tugged on the ends of Ivy's hair that fell into her face as she lit her cigarette.

It was Daisy who told us about Colleen and our father. How Colleen had disgraced Nell by having Cat out of wedlock, and how when our father fell in love with her and married her anyway, Nell couldn't let go of her anger at her own daughter. And she told us that when Colleen had died in childbirth with Asher, that he'd left that night, never to return.

"Strangely, I do understand," Daisy said. "We all do. I mean, who would want to live with Nell if you didn't have to?"

"But he left them," said Ivy, visibly upset. "He left both of them behind."

"Seems to me, from what you've said and from what I've heard, your father wasn't really around even when he was. Get my drift?" said Daisy.

I looked apprehensively at Ivy, waiting for her to respond. She was always so protective of our father.

"Watch yourself, Daisy. I wouldn't want you to wake up one morning to a living room full of garbage straight from that Dumpster downstairs," she said. But she was teasing, and we all shared a smile.

"We'll get along just fine," I said.

And we did.

Walking away from Daisy and Asher that day, Ivy and I fairly glided across Washington Square Park. The heat didn't bother us half as much as it had on the walk over.

"Do you think that a secret, even if you don't know it exists, can still eat away at you?" I asked.

"Well, if it's eating away at the people raising you, you can't help but be affected, I guess."

"So that, along with everything else, is why we ended up the way we did. Because of a secret."

"If you mean, why we ended up stupid, yeah. I think you're right. Don't you feel it, Rose? The world opening up for us? Everything seems brand-new!"

I knew exactly how she felt.

She threw her arms around me and hugged me. "I love

you, Rose Adams," she declared, loud enough for people to turn and stare.

"And I love you, Ivy Adams."

"Daisy said we could go back tomorrow. Do you think he'll get better?"

"Yes, I think it will take time, but I'm sure he'll get better."

"I love him already," she said.

"So do I."

"I know, Rose. Thank you for that."

"For loving my brother?"

"For realizing you wanted to."

When we got back to the front stoop of Empire House, the girls were all sitting on the steps. Viv, Maude, Claudia and a few other faces I was beginning to put names to. Bessie, Claire, Ruth...

"What's goin' on here?" asked Ivy, waving her pocketbook and leaning against a car parked in front.

"Cat got tipped off about a raid, so she shut the whole place down for the day. Nothin' like getting the day off when all you want to do is go cool down in the ice room," said Viv.

"Ain't it always the way," said Claudia, sighing dramatically, making fun of her.

Viv got up to swat her, and Claudia ran into the house laughing.

"Want to go to Coney Island? Jimmy's comin' to get us," said Maude.

Ivy looked upset. "What's the matter, Ivy?" I asked. "Is it Jimmy?"

"No." She went to bite her nails and then put her hand down. "Cat said she had a dress for me, but if the store's closed, too, how am I supposed to pick it up?"

"Oh! That's right. I forgot to tell you. Cat's inside with Nell. Said to send you two gals inside when you got back from… Where'd you go, anyway?" said Viv.

Ivy and I pushed past them on the stoop in a rush to get inside. "We went to meet our future."

"There you are," said Cat, who was sitting on Nell's desk. We hadn't been in Nell's office since the first day. It was cool and dark inside. Cat was arranging fans over bowls of ice, and Nell was seated in a proper desk chair.

"Daisy called. Seems you two were good for our Asher after all," said Cat. *Their Asher?*

"Sit down, you two," said Nell, pointing to the two chairs across the desk from her.

"When you first arrived, you and that sister of yours, the Empire Girls here were twittering on about you, you know. They said you were both strange. As if you'd raised yourselves. Wild, with no real ideas about how to interact with people. That's when I began to understand that perhaps Everett had ruined the both of you, as well.

"So I took a harder look at you both, and to my dismay, I found you delightful."

"You sure hid it well," said Ivy.

"Thank you," I said.

"Gram, be nice. Asher is talking—didn't you hear Daisy? A lady can admit when she's been wrong," said Cat, who went and sat on the front window seat. She didn't seem half

her usual, elegant, frightening self. Now, with all the pre-
tense gone, she was a real person. We all were. Even Nell.

"Catherine, just because he's talking doesn't mean he'll
get well. I don't want you and Daisy getting all excited
again."

I cleared my throat. "Cat, before we go any further,
there's something I think you should read. Ivy, can you…?"

Ivy reached inside her dress and pulled out the two letters, damp with sweat. She unfolded them both to pick the
right one, then folded the other one and tucked it away
again. Cat, Nell and I watched her. "What?" said Ivy. "I
don't lose things when I put them there,"

She handed Father's note to Cat, who took it with two
fingers, smiling and making fun of Ivy. That is, until she
read the first few lines. "I think I'd like to read this alone,"
she said. "Do you mind if I leave you all for a moment?"

"Go right ahead," said Nell.

When the door was closed, Nell said, "What in the
hell was that? I haven't seen her so moved by anything in
a great while."

"It was a letter from our father, Nell," I said.

"A letter from your father, you say?" The way her voice
rose told me that she'd have stood up and chased us out
if she could.

"It isn't addressed to her, Nell. Calm down. It's addressed to us."

"Then why is she reading it?"

"Because he wanted to apologize to her, and we thought
she should read it herself," said Ivy.

I was reveling in the fact that we hadn't actually discussed it, she and I, but we had the same opinion anyway. *So this is what it feels like to have a sister,* I thought.

"What is he apologizing for? If anything, that letter should be addressed to me. And the apology directed to me, as well. Especially after what he did!"

"There's a message for you, too," I said. "He wanted you to know he understood your anger, and he felt he'd earned it."

Nell banged on the table with her fist. Her entire face was shaking.

"Don't have a stroke, Nell!" said Ivy. "Seems to me, everything is starting to work out, the only thing we would like to know...I think—" she looked at me, and I knew what she was going to ask, so I nodded "—is why? Why did you bring us here at all, if you wanted us to stay away? Then, when we were here, why did you continue to lie to us?"

"Haven't you girls ever heard the phrase 'keep your friends close, and your enemies closer'? Well, that should answer your first question."

"How could you have thought of us as enemies? We were two country girls from upstate," said Ivy.

"Two country girls from upstate with a father, who even from his grave, could ruin my life. I swear, that man. When we heard from the two of you, I didn't want to answer your inquiry. It was Cat, my smart Cat, who brought up the fact that perhaps the two of you could accomplish what we could not. Daisy, protecting Asher, had hidden him right here in front of us, and no matter how we tried, we couldn't find him.

"Can you imagine? Being separated from the person

you loved the most? Well, I suppose you can now. But we didn't know a thing about the two of you. So I decided to let you both come here and try to find him for us. Even though it was a terrible risk. Neither of you have any idea of the harm your father brought down on this family. And of the weak genes he delivered to our Asher, who has suffered from that particular weakness for his entire life."

"But Daisy told us that he married Colleen. One would think that you would have been pleased. I know he left you with two small children to raise, but now that we know you, I think you might have been more angry if he took them. So what did he really do?"

"He killed my daughter!" cried Nell. Her sorrow and rage filled up the whole room. "He came here, swept her off her feet, altered the course of her life, and she died delivering that weak little boy. I knew, if he came back, he'd do it again. Break something fragile that was not his to break!"

"Is that it?" asked Ivy, a look of dawning understanding on her face. "You thought he would come back and break Asher? Or were you worried we'd find him?"

"I don't know what you are getting at, Ivy," said Nell.

"I think what Ivy is trying to ask is *why*. Why did you hide your relationship to Asher from us? Why hide your relationship to Cat? Why coax this entire building to evade any mention of him? And now that we know many of the truths, they all seem connected to the final question. Why did Daisy keep you from Asher?"

"Well said, sister," said Ivy, patting my hand.

Cat reentered the office carrying a large dress box, in

the midst of the tension and just in time to hear the end of my litany of questions.

"Here's your dress, Ivy. It'll be grand for tonight. Don't open it up yet, because I'd like to hear my grandmother answer this question. Ladies, I've thought myself brave for my entire life. Brave and independent, I even gave myself the name LeGrand to make sure everyone knew it. But I have mustered up the moxie to ask her about Asher, and now that you have, I'm on pins and needles waiting to hear the answer." She said that without looking at us at all. She said it with her arms folded across her chest, staring straight at Nell.

"Well, he was weak! Sickly and scared his whole life. He worried me to tears, and I thought the war…I thought it would make a man of him."

"You were wrong," said Cat. "He was creative and thoughtful, and you pressuring him into enlisting was a mistake. He went to please you, and now he's lost to both of us."

Nell huffed and turned back to me and Ivy.

"He never ran around like Sonny—that boy had to fight for him in the streets. He couldn't stand up for himself, just like his father couldn't stay and raise him…or you for that matter, Cat LeGrand. A fake name for a fake girl. You run like the rest."

"That was a low blow, even for you, Grandmother."

"Ladies, please. If I may?" I asked.

The two women were standing now, facing each other with their arms crossed. The tension was thick and unbearable.

"Before this gets out of hand, and you both say or do

things you don't mean, Ivy and I would like to share something with you."

"Spill it," said Cat, still staring at Nell.

Ivy told Cat and Nell the story of Asher's heroic deed. And I told them of Daisy, and how wonderful she'd been taking care of him.

Our narratives did the trick, and soon both women were calm again. Ivy and I shared a knowing look…one that meant we knew all too well what kinds of things people who love one another can say in anger.

"We're glad he's safe and well cared for," said Cat, wiping a tear from her eye. "I've missed him so much. He was all I had for so long, and then he was gone."

"You had me," said Nell.

"You wanted me to be different than who I was. You wanted me to be my mother. And no one could ever take her place, Grandmother."

Nell started to defend herself, but then she did something that surprised all of us. She walked to Cat and enfolded her into a long embrace. The two of them cried together, and then sat close to one another on the window seat.

"I suppose I wanted Asher to be different, too. Is that it? Has this really come to pass? It took Everett Adams's other children to slap me with this information? How unbelievably odd."

"You know," I said, "one of the things I've learned this summer about myself, is that I can be obtuse to my own agenda."

"I'm not speaking about this anymore. All is well now, and we can get back to normal. Now that you'll be helping with Asher, I've decided to give you the nicer, full apartment on the second floor. You don't have to pay rent, but will have to contribute your earnings as any member of a family would."

I could tell my sister wanted more from Nell, and I knew that Nell had nothing more to give us. I'd learned that loving someone was both simple and complicated, and that there was no other answer than that she loved Asher and wanted to protect him. It was the only answer there was. So I was relieved when Cat broke the tension in the room.

"Let's go have a look at that dress, Ivy." She must have been used to giving up when it came to Nell.

Ivy and Cat went toward the door. "Ivy," said Nell, "you may like the fact that as a part of the family, you don't need to follow the rules as closely as you've had to in the past."

Ivy could not contain her laughter, and she and Cat almost fell through the door on their way out.

"Well, what are you waiting for? Go and be a giggling ninny along with the others. I have work to do," she said, pretending to blot invisible ink off a blank envelope.

"I like you, Miss Nell. I don't know why, but I do. So I want to tell you something."

"Go on," she said.

"I think you don't like it when people leave you. I think you made Asher weak in your own mind, so he would be tied to you forever. I think you wanted Ivy and I to come here, hoping we would want to stay. I think…you don't want to be alone."

"Nonsense," she said, as a tear fell onto the stationery below her.

"Nell, we won't be taking the apartment," I said. "But we aren't going anywhere anytime soon."

"Then why won't you take the apartment?" she asked.

"Why would we, when we already have the penthouse?" I replied.

All the girls from the stoop were now gathered in the penthouse watching Ivy get dressed. "What's this about The Albert?" I asked.

"Oh, not much. Mr. Lawrence wants to meet with me."

I looked at her, the dress, a silver beaded beauty over black silk with double-strung pearls pulling down the neckline to show off her perfect neck. She wore a silver band with a black feather around her head, and her hair was thick with the humid air.

"You look perfectly perfect," I said. "And I don't believe for one second that you are dressed for anything like a meeting. Ivy, I'm so pleased! I love Lawrence."

"Don't go jumping to conclusions, sister," she said. "Besides, I have to get by the doorman, and that's one ritzy part of town. I might be back sooner than you think."

We were all gathered together there. I'll admit, it wasn't a dinner table…it was better. I was sitting on my bed, and Claudia was behind me, braiding my hair.

Cat was adjusting more fans over bowls of ice, while Viv and Maude made sure Ivy's makeup was adjusted to every type of light we had in that attic.

"Don't worry about a thing, honey," said Cat. "You and your sister are part of this family now, and you don't need fancy names or fancy clothes, though they're fun to wear, or even friends in high places to get yourselves noticed in this world. Just walk straight into The Albert, and you know what that doorman will say? He'll say, "Move outta the way, folks. See that young lady over there—that's an Empire Girl, and Empire Girls, they make you drunk without even breaking the law. No gin required."

September 30, 1928
Dear Nell,
Well, we did it! We sailed across the ocean and are now safely ensconced in a villa outside of Paris. I really can't believe we're here. I wish you could have come with us! The ocean liner was more than comfortable; it was like sitting in the lap of luxury. At the beginning, Asher stayed on the deck. He even slept out there for a few nights. But Daisy, she stayed right next to him. You should see them, Nell. Ivy and I are constantly amazed by the playfulness between Santino, Lawrence and Asher. Asher has become quite fond of John—or John the Wonder as Ivy still calls him, even now that they're wed. They have long talks about politics and art. Cat is having the time of her life. As soon as we stepped off the boat, there wasn't one man in the whole of Europe who was safe. I must admit, we are a giddy crew. Ivy has just discovered she's expecting a child in April. We were relieved when the ship's doctor gave us the news, because we all thought she was suffering from a never-ending bout of seasickness.

Indeed, this news has given Santino ideas about starting a family of our own. Only you would understand, Nell, why I'm simply not ready to do that.

There are too many things to write, to discover, to feel! I was trapped, much like Asher, for so long. Ivy miraculously survived our childhood with her voice intact. And now? She's the voice for all of us. And what a lovely voice it is.

Though the journey across the sea was more delightful than expected, besides Ivy's initial sickness, of course, and our first few days traveling from England to France were ripe with laughter and true companionship—I don't want you to think it's all frivolity. Darling Nell, our itinerary and intention remains the same.

Ivy, Cat and I stayed up late last evening and sat on a veranda overlooking the French countryside. Santino, Asher, Daisy and Lawrence had already retired, but the three of us—your Empire Girls—sat together and talked about our brother. We'd been worried about bringing him back here, to the origin of his trauma. All of us, even Santino, were worried. Asher had finally been released from the prison of his mind. Forever changed, yes…with dark days every now and again, but each year brought more sunshine and less echoing of pain. Each one of us needed this trip, geared to help him face those days and perhaps bring even more light into his life. Daisy wants to have children. Santino needs a "brother in arms" to talk to about his own demons. It's a heavy burden to carry alone. Ivy and I needed to see a glimmer of the boy he used to be. And Cat? Cat needed him most of all. During our search for Asher, that wild and gin-soaked summer of 1925, we couldn't have known that

Asher had another sister who'd lost so much more than Ivy and I could have imagined. Part of our peace comes from bringing those two back together.

We know how difficult this was for you, Nell, but we're so grateful that you supported us. Hosted our weddings, finally began to forgive yourself, our father and even Asher for not living up to your expectations.

Know that we will take good care of him, and that we are all missing you. We are a family, and that, dear Nell, is what families do. We forgive, we love, we long for each other, and at the end of the day, if needed, we stand up for each other, straight and tall as the tallest skyscraper, to catch an errant star or two. Sending love,
Rosie

★ ★ ★ ★ ★

 ACKNOWLEDGMENTS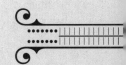

Suzanne

Writing this novel would not have been possible without the support, patience and incredible care that my coauthor, Loretta Nyhan, gave to me and to each word on the page. We are, in many ways, just like Ivy and Rose. This novel brought us on a very similar journey.

To my family: my husband, William (my very own Sonny). My daughters, Rosy, Tess and Grace, who show me each day what true sisters mean to one another. To the entire team at MIRA for their support. Especially our editors, Erika Imranyi and Leonore Waldrip. Both indefatigable, unflappable and extraordinarily open-minded with the many directions this book took before it found its way.

To my literary agent, Anne Bohner, who navigates the waters of the publishing industry when I would surely slip under the surface.

To my mother, Theresa Cooper, for fostering my love

of books. And to my Gram, Fay, for teaching me the value of pragmatism.

To New York City! Dreams *do* come true amid your multicolored chaos. And to the suffragettes who marched, fought and eventually won freedom for each generation that came after. The Empire Girls would have been very different young women without your generations of sacrifice.

Loretta

I heart New York.

For me, *Empire Girls* is a love letter to this most magical city. The vibrant, wonderful people who live in it nurtured my writing dreams when I was Ivy's age, and continue to do so. I'd like to single some out in particular.

My heartfelt thanks to Leonore Waldrip and Erika Imranyi, two sharp, savvy Empire Girls who tirelessly shaped this novel from their Harlequin MIRA offices overlooking Broadway in lower Manhattan.

Heading north to midtown, huge thanks to my agent and personal hero, Joanna Volpe, and her team at New Leaf Literary & Media—Kathleen Ortiz, Danielle Barthel, Pouya Shahbazian, Jaida Temperly and Suzie Townsend—for their gracious support. Also, to my all-girl Algonquin Round Table: Erica, Lisa, Laura, Joyce, Erin, Ann, Lori, Robin, Libby, Rachel, Jenny, Kelly, Tracey, Alexa and Jean.

Special thanks to William Richard "Dick" Haray of Flatbush, Brooklyn, and Astoria, Queens—he's gone on to play stickball outside of that Ebbets Field in the sky, but without Dick's not-so-subtle encouragement, writing a book would have remained a pipe dream. I still hear his Noo Yawk–accented voice in my head telling me to just get going. His wife, Maryann, daughter, Diane, grand-daughter, Jessica, and the rest of the Haray family deserve special recognition as well for their kindness today and all those years ago.

To my best boys, Tom, Dan and Jack, who are willing to climb the "mountains" of Central Park at my side— thank you for joining me on the adventure!

To the magical Suzy of New Haven, Connecticut (once of the Bronx)—when you stood on your porch, perched on tiptoes, you saw the lights of the city, didn't you? Thanks, doll, for your vision, friendship and perseverance.

And to my friends and family, especially my parents—I am ever grateful for your constant love and support.

EMPIRE GIRLS

SUZANNE HAYES & LORETTA NYHAN

Reader's Guide

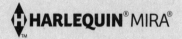

1. Ivy and Rose Adams, despite growing up together, have night and day outlooks on the world. Did you find yourself identifying more closely with free-spirited Ivy or serious Rose? How?

2. After the death of their father, Ivy and Rose are shocked to find that he has left their home to a brother they didn't know existed. What would you do in their situation—accept the terms, or try to fight them?

3. A theme of "lost and found" runs through this novel. Can you describe each character's journey from lost to found, or found to lost? How is this theme applicable to us as we make our way through life?

4. Relationships are forged, strengthened and broken over the course of Empire Girls. Would you say that the novel is a love story? What are the different kinds of emotions explored, and which did you feel were the most powerful?

5. The residents of Empire House and the Village provide a rich, dynamic backdrop to the story. Did you have any favorite secondary characters? Who?

6. The Adams sisters spend almost the entire novel looking for their elusive half brother after losing their family and home. Were you surprised by the new family and home they found? In what ways is it traditional or nontraditional?

As of the publication of your debut novel, *I'll Be Seeing You*, you had never met in person. What has your experience been like since, and what was it like to finally meet face-to-face?

Suzanne: This is such a hard question to answer. In many ways, when I met Loretta, it felt as if we'd known each other forever. Still, we only knew our best selves. The process of writing Empire Girls *was very different from writing* I'll Be Seeing You. *We had to be much more involved with each other's writing, lives and flaws. I'm fast and impetuous, prone to tantrums and quick recoveries. Loretta is the opposite (thank God!). Meeting her was the fulfillment of this dream that came true for both of us. It was surreal at the same time as it was the realest moment ever. If that makes any sense.*

Loretta: Our first meeting was magical—we cried (okay, truth be told—we sobbed!). And then, like old friends, we went out to lunch and talked each other's ears off. Since then, I think our relationship has evolved. We've always talked about all kinds of things, but after meeting in person, I've noticed we talk less about books and more about our personal lives.

What was your inspiration for Empire Girls? How, if at all, have your own personalities and backgrounds informed the characters of Ivy and Rose?

Suzanne: I think I was on the back lawn of the Rockport House when I called Loretta and said something like "Don't kill me, I have this idea... Two sisters in a tenement in New York." At first, we set it in 1918. But as the concept grew, the story moved itself to 1925. The interesting thing is that at the outset Loretta and I decided to write the character that was most opposite of our own personalities. I became practical Rose, and she became the devil-may-care Ivy. As we wrote, however, each of us discovered those parts of our personalities. That personal growth translated on the pages as Ivy and Rose discovered strengths and weaknesses in each other and themselves as the novel progresses.

Loretta: In order for Suzy and I to write historical fiction together, we needed to pick an era we both felt comfortable living in for a year. The 1920s appealed to us—who doesn't like flappers and speakeasies? As far as characters go, at the start I thought Ivy's personality was as far away from mine as it could be. I was so wrong. I began to see so much of myself in her—I don't think I did that on purpose, but after Suzy pointed it out to me, I began to understand. I moved to New York when I was twenty-two, and all the feelings I had—excitement, fear and even some disappointment—began to filter into Ivy to a degree.

You've created such a dynamic cast of characters—specifically Ivy and Rose—but the rest of the "Empire Girls," as well. When you started writing, did you have all of these players and their journeys planned out, or did they reveal themselves as you wrote? Did any of the characters surprise you or change along the way?

Suzanne: This novel had many different "lives," so to speak. Many of these characters arrived spontaneously, as others were taken and transformed from other versions. We wanted to create a community at Empire House, so that cast of characters, though peripheral, was vital to the novel. This is the portion where the coauthoring became essential. Loretta and I had to make sure we didn't overpopulate it, or underpopulate it, and that each of the characters lent something to the narrative. I have to say, I miss the world we created there already!

Loretta: Ivy and Rose had always been strongly defined characters, though they did end up quite different from what we'd initially planned! The other characters developed as a true joint effort. It was our hope that two opinions would add layers to our peripheral characters, ultimately enriching the narrative. In reality, two opinions sometimes meant two very opposing points of view, but Suzy and I had a way of working things out. We each stated our case and then ultimately decided together what was best for the story.

Empire Girls is, at the heart, a novel about the incredible bonds of sisterhood. Do either of you have sisters or friendships that influenced your· portrayal of Ivy and Rose's relationship?

Suzanne: I've learned more about sisterhood than I could ever imagine through my friendship with Loretta. I have a younger brother, and my three daughters who show me the bonds of sisterhood every day. My great-aunts were all so close, and they were the basis for my novel The Witch of Little Italy. Sisters fascinate me, and this novel helped me explore the complicated dynamics of DNA.

Loretta: I am lucky enough to have an incredible sister and sisters-in-law in my life. My sister, Joyce, is seven years younger than me, so I really didn't get to know her until we were both adults, which is reflective of Ivy and Rose. Though they're only a year apart, they lived separate lives until moving to New York. I also feel that women pick up sisters along the way as we form strong female friendships. Those relationships—though fraught with tension at times—are so valuable.

In Empire Girls, prohibition-era New York City is almost like a character in and of itself. What drew you to this setting and time period, and what kind of research did you do to bring this fascinating moment in history to life?

Suzanne: Loretta and I are huge history buffs. I'm a high school history teacher by day, and this era enchanted both of us. We wanted something that reflected women at a moment in history when social roles were changing. We'd had luck with that in I'll Be Seeing You, but wanted to move back in time a bit. I think, if you asked us both independently, we'd go back to 1920s New York City in a heartbeat. I mean, we're writers! Give us that, or Paris, and we're good to go! I think our love of the era shines bright in these pages. Research was primarily web-based for the time period, but the Village itself was part of my growing-up years. To this day there is an apartment on Carmine and Bleecker that still welcomes me back whenever I get to spend time in the city.

Loretta: New York has always been the place people go to follow their dreams, but Greenwich Village in the first half of the twentieth century was such a crazy, dynamic hot spot for painters, actors and writers, and for those simply looking for excitement. Following the brutality of WWI, people in the '20s wanted to let loose and have fun—there's an ebullience to the era Suzy and I both found irresistible.

Can you describe the process of writing a novel as a team? Do each of you write your own cast of characters (and if so, who wrote which characters)? Do you each take turns with the manuscript, passing it back and forth to each other? Or is one person the organizer (if so, who)?

Suzanne: I was Rose, and the characters closest to her. So Claudia and Santino were also created primarily in my chapters. But this book was so different, as Ivy and Rose interlap, that there were many characters we created together. Cat, Papa, Asher, Daisy—those were characters we ended up sharing. And even though each of us had specific characters, it was so important for us to fully explore, on our own, each player in this novel. We swapped the manuscript back and forth, and each took it one chapter at a time. This novel had several "lives" so to speak, and all that rewriting helped us overlap characters, arcs and plots. It was a wild and sometimes harrowing experience that left me wondering, more than once, if our lives weren't paralleling those of Ivy and Rose! Also, in terms of organizing...that would be Loretta!

Loretta: In I'll Be Seeing You we were in charge of our own separate worlds. In Empire Girls, we shared characters, which meant we had to come to agreement about physical characteristics, personality traits, story arcs, etc. It was definitely a difficult process at times, and our relationship grew as we both fought for certain things and made concessions. However, we were able to play with this a bit, as Ivy and Rose are two very different people and their impressions of others are colored by their disparate worldviews.